GINGER SNAPPED

This Large Print Book carries the
Seal of Approval of N.A.V.H.

A SPICE SHOP MYSTERY

GINGER SNAPPED

GAIL OUST

THORNDIKE PRESS
A part of Gale, a Cengage Company

GALE
A Cengage Company

Farmington Hills, Mich • San Francisco • New York • Waterville, Maine
Meriden, Conn • Mason, Ohio • Chicago

LIBRARY OF CONGRESS CIP DATA ON FILE.
CATALOGUING IN PUBLICATION FOR THIS BOOK
IS AVAILABLE FROM THE LIBRARY OF CONGRESS

ISBN-13: 978-1-4328-4824-8 (hardcover)

Published in 2018 by arrangement with Macmillan Publishing Group LLC/St. Martin's Press

Printed in Mexico
1 2 3 4 5 6 7 22 21 20 19 18

To my family, with love

ACKNOWLEDGMENTS

Friends are truly a blessing. I'd like to give a shout-out to a few of mine. First comes Deb Brys. I'm indebted to you for coming to my rescue when I was in dire need of a computer eight hundred miles from home. Stephany Klein is up next. I mentioned ginger and you promptly surrendered your precious research books into my care. Carol Mavity, my chef-on-demand, thanks for chopping, slicing, and dicing to perfect an imperfect recipe. Mary Ann Beyer, you gave me an invaluable gift — uninterrupted time to write — when you offered to pick up my prescriptions in Greenwood. Sandy Granger, you've been a trouper and remained a good friend even though I "killed" you off in *Curried Away.* Next on my list is my Red Hat group, the Purple Gang. Thanks for understanding my frequent absences as my deadline drew closer, then welcoming me back into the fold. The same goes for the

Sweet Tee's. You cheer me on after a lengthy absence regardless of how atrocious my golf game. Also a shout-out to my friend Patti Cornelius and her brother, Richard Vargyas, for sharing their treasured family recipe for Hungarian goulash. Bob, you've become the perfect househusband, and make my life simpler in ways too numerous to count. Jessica Faust, BookEnds Literary, having you as an agent is like winning the book-agent megalottery. My thanks wouldn't be complete without acknowledging the bloggers — Lori Caswell, Dru Ann Love, and Lisa K, only to name a few — who work tirelessly to promote the cozy genre. Last but by no means least, my sincere gratitude to readers who take time from their busy lives to let me know they enjoy my stories. Here's to you!

CHAPTER 1

"Like it or not, honeybun, Shirley and Wyatt make a strikin' couple."

Although my BFF's observation echoed my own, not even Chinese water torture could get me to admit this out loud. For the past seven minutes and thirty seconds, Reba Mae Johnson and I had watched an animated exchange between Shirley Randolph, Realtor and reigning diva, and Wyatt McBride, Brandywine Creek's hunky police chief, that was taking place on the sidewalk just outside my spice shop, Spice It Up!

I grimaced at hearing Shirley's peal of laughter. "Since when did McBride turn into a jokester?"

Casey, my mutt of many breeds, opened one eye at hearing the name of his favorite lawman. When there was no sign of him, however, Casey resumed napping under the counter.

Reba Mae shifted from her perch next to

my antique cash register to get a better view of the pair. "Could be Wyatt's harbored a secret ambition to be a stand-up comic and he's tryin' out his routine on Shirley."

"Hmph!" I grunted. "McBride's more the 'book 'em, Danno' type. The man's seriously lacking in the humor department."

"What's that old sayin'?" Reba Mae drawled. "Somethin' about opposites attractin'? Why, look at us."

"Point well taken." Outwardly the two of us were physically as different as could be. While Reba Mae tended toward the flamboyant and statuesque with hair color that changed with the seasons and soft-brown eyes, I had bright red hair, unruly curls, and eyes green as a tomcat's. Some people referred to me as short, but I preferred to think of myself as vertically challenged.

When Shirley placed a possessive hand on McBride's arm, I turned away and began rearranging spices I'd only have to unarrange later. "I don't see what those two could possibly have in common."

"Gee, let me think." Reba Mae struck a thoughtful pose. "You mean other than the fact that they're both drop-dead gorgeous?"

"Looks aren't everything." I lined up jars of sea salt according to grind: extra coarse, coarse, and fine. "Shirley doesn't seem his

10

type is all. She's a girlie-girl; he's more the hunting and fishing sort. She prefers shrimp and grits; he likes pulled pork. When it comes to Atlanta, she'd opt for a play at the Fox while McBride would rather see a play on the field at the Falcons' new football stadium."

"Piper Prescott!" Reba Mae's eyes held a teasing glint. "Since when did you become an authority on Wyatt McBride's likes and dislikes?"

"I couldn't care less what he does with his personal life. Makes no difference to me they've been seen having dinner a time or two." I could tell from my friend's amused expression that she wasn't buying my explanation. We'd been besties for years, and she could read me like a book. Granted, I felt a certain attraction to the man, but I didn't need to complicate my life falling for a bachelor with lady-killer looks. I had no claim on McBride, and he had none on me. Why, then, did I feel irritated each time I saw Shirley and him together?

"Don't let Shirley's appearance fool you," Reba Mae warned me with a shake of her head that set her gold hoop earrings swaying. "When it comes to business, she's a piranha on the hunt for Sunday dinner."

"And when did *you* become an expert on

Shirley Randolph?" From the corner of my eye, I watched Shirley conclude her conversation with McBride. To my surprise, instead of heading for her office at Creekside Realty, she strolled into Spice It Up!

"Hey, y'all."

"Hey, Shirley. How can I help you?" The woman would be easy to dislike. She was just too . . . too . . . darn perfect. Tall and slender, she possessed an exotic type of beauty with her dark, almost black, shoulder-length bob and almond-shaped eyes the color of espresso. I felt frumpy in comparison in my sunny yellow apron with its chili pepper logo over jeans and a T-shirt.

Reba Mae slid off the counter, straightened her flowered skirt with one hand, smoothed her hair with the other — hair that this spring happened to be dark auburn — and pointed at Shirley's feet. "Those are one snazzy pair of shoes."

I confess until now I hadn't noticed Shirley's footwear. My friend and Shirley shared an obsession with shoes. Pumps, sandals, or platforms, didn't matter. The exception being, Reba Mae purchased hers at discount stores and Shirley didn't. The pumps Shirley currently wore were a trendy suede leopard print with four-inch heels.

"Reba Mae, bless your heart, so kind of

you to notice my little ol' shoes," Shirley said in a voice sweet enough to induce a diabetic coma, then turned her attention to me. "Piper, I'm here to ask a great big favor."

My spate of arranging and rearranging over, I said, "Ask away."

"I was hoping you'd invite a prospective client of mine to Melly's bridal shower."

Never in a million years did I dream I'd be hosting a bridal shower for my former mother-in-law. But, as I've heard said, fact is stranger than fiction. Next Sunday afternoon, Melly Prescott was set to wed Judge Cottrell "Cot" Herman in a lovely outdoor ceremony in the gazebo at Felicity Driscoll's bed-and-breakfast. Melly's shower would take place tomorrow afternoon at Antonio's, Brandywine Creek's answer to fine dining.

"I realize my request sounds forward," Shirley continued, "but it's important Elaine Dixon experience some genuine Southern hospitality."

Reba Mae and I exchanged glances; then I shrugged. "What's one more person? I don't mind as long as Ms. Dixon doesn't feel uncomfortable surrounded by a roomful of strangers."

"Elaine is no shrinking violet," Shirley said. "She and her husband Kirby are interested in making an offer on Gray's Hardware. Kirby is enthusiastic, but his wife has . . . reservations . . . about life in a small town. I thought Melly's shower would help pave the way."

Reba Mae folded her arms over her impressive bosom. "What's this woman got against small towns? I've lived in one all my life, and it never bothered me none."

"The Dixons hail from New York. Syracuse," Shirley explained. "Elaine is used to the amenities a larger city offers. Apparently Syracuse boasts a symphony, museums, art galleries, and theaters."

Reba Mae didn't look ready to pack a bag and relocate. "I hope you gave her a tour of the opera house? Be sure to mention I played Truvy Jones in *Steel Magnolias* last Valentine's Day."

I fought the urge to roll my eyes. Reba Mae had been cast, fired, then rehired, for the role of Truvy but had taken literary license with names of the characters. Thankfully the rest of the cast adjusted to the changes. And to their credit, the audience had awarded the cast and crew with a standing ovation.

"Gotta run," Reba Mae said after a glance at her wristwatch. "Got one last haircut waitin' on me at the Klassy Kut."

Shirley gazed around my shop, taking in the heart pine floors, exposed brick, and open ductwork. "I confess I'm not into cooking. This marks my first time in your little store. It's cute."

"Cute" wasn't the word I'd had in mind when designing Spice It Up! I'd more aptly describe my shop in terms such as "charming," "unique," or "appealing." But then again, being the proprietor, I might be a trifle prejudiced.

"While I'm here, do you carry ginger?"

"Absolutely." I started toward the Hoosier cabinet where I kept most of my baking spices. "Powdered, crystallized, or rhizomes?"

Shirley trailed after me, a frown marring her smooth brow. "I didn't realize there was such a variety."

"If you explain how you plan to use it, it will make the decision easier."

"Recently I read an article claiming ginger is good for occasional indigestion. I ordered some from a health food store online, but, in the meantime, well, I thought I'd see what you'd recommend."

I plucked a jar of crystallized ginger from a shelf. "Ginger has been used for thousands of years to treat stomach upsets. As with any herbal medicine, however, you might want to check with your health care provider."

"My overall health is excellent!" she snapped. "An occasional tummy upset is all."

Replacing the jar, I took a knobby rhizome from a small basket nearby. "You could use this to brew yourself a nice cup of ginger tea."

"Surely you're not serious."

"Serious as a heart attack," I said, handing her the rhizome.

Shirley stared at the rhizome in disgust. "That ugly thing? Don't tell me it's edible?"

"It's the root of the ginger plant, commonly referred to as fresh ginger."

"What am I supposed to do with it?"

Sensing a sale, I walked back to the counter. "Well, there are numerous ways to prepare ginger tea. When I make it, I bring eight cups of water and one cup of thinly sliced, unpeeled ginger to a simmer until the liquid is reduced to about five cups. Once the tea's finished, I strain it, add honey as a sweetener, and dust with cinnamon. Ginger tea is also great served over ice."

"Thanks. I'll give it a try." She paid for the ginger and chatted while I bagged it. "I appreciate you extending a shower invitation to Elaine. Sale of the hardware store will be a huge relief for Mavis Gray; she's anxious to move closer to her sister in Tampa."

I wanted to add that the sale of Gray's Hardware would be huge for Shirley, too, in the form of a commission. As I closed up afterwards, I wondered uncharitably if the meals she'd purportedly shared with Mc-Bride were the cause of her indigestion. The thought of them with their heads together gave me indigestion as well.

Guests were due to arrive any minute for Melly's bridal shower. I stood in the center of the restaurant and gazed around. Starched white tablecloths with red or green napkins. Check. Small cellophane bags filled with Italian wedding cookies at each place setting. Check. Carnation centerpieces flying tiny Italian flags. Check. Mock passports and boarding passes along with travel brochures were scattered on each table. Colorful posters of iconic Italian destinations — The Colosseum, Vatican City, Venice, Lake Como — hung on the walls. Yes, I could tick all the boxes.

"Mom, where do you want this?" Lindsey, my blond-haired, blue-eyed, teenage daughter, a high school senior, held a floral arrangement of white carnations, lots of greenery, and a large red bow.

"Set it on top of the vintage suitcase on the gift table."

Amber Leigh Ames-Prescott was next to arrive. In my more generous moments, I refer to the leggy brunette as Miss Peach Pit. The former runner-up in a Miss Georgia beauty pageant had snagged my former husband while he was taking a respite from married life. Instead of finding his "space," he found Amber Leigh. The rest, as they say, is history.

Amber eyed my emerald green print dress with distaste. "Honestly, Piper, with your red hair and green eyes, you could be mistaken for a leprechaun. And what's with all the red, white, and green? This place looks ready for Christmas, not a bridal shower. I knew I shouldn't have left you in charge of details."

I felt the urge to slap her silly but restrained myself. What in Amber's opinion constituted a fair division of labor ended up being me doing all work and her writing a check. "If you recall," I said, "we agreed on a travel theme. Red, white, and green happen to be the colors of the Italian flag. Since Cot and Melly are honeymooning in Tuscany, I thought the colors appropriate."

Amber dropped her bulky Michael Kors bag on a nearby chair. "I swear the only reason Melly's hell-bent on goin' to Italy is because CJ and I are plannin' a trip there this summer. She wants braggin' rights. I can hear her now: 'We did this; we did that. Blah, blah, blah.'"

"For your information, Italy was Cot's idea, not Melly's."

"Whatever," she said, and stalked off to join Lindsey.

Gina Deltorro emerged from the kitchen wearing an apron around her plump figure with the words I DON'T NEED A RECIPE, I'M ITALIAN emblazoned across the front. The mouthwatering fragrance of garlic wafted into the dining area. "How does everything look?" she asked.

"You and Tony did a fabulous job, Gina. The place fairly screams 'take me to Italy!'"

Gina's chocolate brown eyes glowed at the compliment. "Judge Cottrell is one of Antonio's best customers. We wanted to do right by him."

If it weren't for the judge, Tony would have turned down my request to hold Melly's shower here. Tony, being Sicilian, still harbored a grudge against me for naming him as a possible suspect in the murder of Mario Barrone, the restaurant's ambitious previous owner. A simple mistake. It was time he move on.

Reba Mae sailed through the door of the restaurant followed by a bevy of women, Melly included, who all seemed to be talking at once. "Showtime," Reba Mae said, giving me a wink as she passed by to deposit a gaily wrapped package on the rapidly filling gift table.

Gina hurried off to pour wine — both red and white — into glasses sitting on the bar next to pitchers of sweet tea. I noticed Melly Prescott working the room with the ease of a seasoned politician. When she caught my eye, she gave me a thumbs-up and mouthed, *Thank you.*

Love had transformed my ex-mother-in-law into a softer, prettier woman. Although Melly still wore her silver hair in a neat pageboy and was rarely seen without her pearls, these days she smiled more and criticized less.

Among the last to make an appearance was Shirley Randolph. She was accompanied by an unsmiling woman with pale blond hair and a slender figure bordering on anorexic who I assumed was Elaine Dixon. I stepped forward and held out my hand. "I'm Piper Prescott. So happy you were able to join us."

20

"Shirley insisted I come," she said by way of a greeting. "She simply wouldn't take no for an answer."

"I've won a reputation as being persistent." Shirley's smile seemed forced. "Piper owns Spice It Up! just a few doors down from Gray's Hardware."

Vicki Lamont, rookie real estate agent, strode toward us, flicking her long dark hair over her shoulder as she walked. "We need to talk," she said to Shirley without preamble. Taking her by the elbow before she could protest, Vicki led her out of earshot.

Elaine raised a perfectly arched brow. "What was that all about?"

Judging from the angry hand gestures, the conversation between Shirley and Vicki didn't appear amicable. Some introduction this was to Southern hospitality. "Probably a minor difference of opinion," I said, trying to downplay the incident. "Shirley has been helping Vicki prepare for her real estate exam."

I was grateful when Gina appeared with a tray of wineglasses. Elaine and I each took a glass of white wine. Gina smiled and moved on. A diamond the size of a lima bean twinkled on Elaine's ring finger as she took a sip. More diamonds, I noticed, sparkled in her earlobes.

"I usually do aerobics five times a week," Elaine said. "I don't suppose this town has a fitness center?"

"Er, no, we don't. But if you like to jog, Brandywine Creek does have a variety of routes."

"I prefer to exercise in places that have air-conditioning, changing rooms, and a juice bar."

Out of the corner of my eye, I glimpsed Reba Mae worming her way through the crowd. "Hey, y'all," she said when she reached us. "You must be Elaine Dixon. I'm Reba Mae Johnson, owner of the Klassy Kut, best little ol' beauty shop in Brandywine County. Pleased to meet you."

I welcomed the interruption. Reba Mae was a ray of sunshine after a downpour — the downpour being Elaine. "Elaine and I were just getting acquainted."

"Shirley said you and your hubby are thinkin' of buyin' Gray's Hardware and movin' here. How do you like Brandywine Creek so far?"

The look Elaine gave Reba Mae could have withered tomatoes ripe on the vine. "So far, I hate everything about this town. In fact, I could shoot Kirby for coming up with this harebrained notion. As for Shirley, she's also in my sights for encouraging him.

22

This isn't how I planned to spend retirement. Now if you ladies will excuse me" — she set down her wineglass — "I'm off to find a bartender who can make a decent martini."

Reba Mae leaned closer and lowered her voice. "Did that woman really threaten to shoot her husband?"

I took a sip of my wine before answering. "An innocent remark. I'm sure she didn't mean it."

"Let's hope Kirby doesn't end up with a bullet hole in the middle of his forehead."

I surveyed the crowd. Vicki and Shirley were off in a corner and, from their grim expressions, were still exchanging heated words. Elaine Dixon accosted poor Gina Deltorro and was demanding a martini. Tony Deltorro poked his head out of the kitchen long enough to glare at me, then ducked out of sight. Was this the bridal shower that would live in infamy?

As though attuned to my glum thoughts, Reba Mae looped her arm through mine. "C'mon, honeybun. Let's have us some fun before someone gets killed. Wait till Melly sees the undies I bought her at Victoria's Secret."

I chuckled in spite of myself. "Embarrass

Melly in front of her friends and you'll wind up the murder victim."

CHAPTER 2

It was a perfect day for a wedding.

The Turner-Driscoll House provided the ideal venue for April nuptials. The lawn looked as lush as cut green velvet. Masses of pink and white azaleas flanked the flagstone patio while a trellis groaned under a profusion of dainty yellow Lady Banks roses. Deep purple wisteria fairly dripped from the eaves of the gazebo where the ceremony would take place. Women in pretty summery dresses and men sporting suits and ties congregated in small groups while others had already taken their seats. It looked like a scene straight from the pages of *Southern Living*.

Reba Mae tugged my arm and prodded me toward the rows of white folding chairs that had been positioned on either side of a crushed-shell path leading to the gazebo. "Let's sit where we can take a gander at who's who."

We slipped into chairs in one of the back rows. I motioned toward the people in the front row. "That must be Cot's daughter and her family from Atlanta."

"Too bad Chad couldn't get away for his meemaw's weddin'. Sure would have been nice, him seein' Melly marry her Prince Charmin'."

I sighed. "I wish he could be here, too."

My son's studies as a pre-med student at the University of North Carolina at Chapel Hill, took precedence over everything else. As one of a group of elite students, Chad had been selected to attend a seminar in Boston this weekend where one of his professors was a guest speaker. Chad had been torn with indecision, but, in the end, Melly had made the choice easier by reminding him of the bright future awaiting him. They agreed to share quality time together during his summer break.

Mavis Gray, a sour-faced woman in her mid-to-late sixties and one of Melly's bridge buddies, paused next to us. "Has either of you seen Shirley? She said she was bringing the Dixons with her."

I twisted in my seat and scanned the crowd. "No. Sorry, I haven't seen her or the Dixons."

Mavis clucked her tongue. "Shirley promised to do everything in her power to make a favorable impression on the couple. She knows how desperate I am to sell."

After Mavis moved on to a vacant seat next to Mayor Hemmings and his wife, Dottie, Reba Mae leaned closer and said, "I thought for sure Shirley would be here, dressed to the nines, and bring Wyatt as her date."

I shot Reba Mae a look designed to let her know I didn't want to hear about McBride and his love life. "Great turnout," I said, refusing to rise to the bait. "This was originally supposed to be a small, intimate affair, but the guest list kept growing and growing."

"Why do you suppose Melly invited that Dixon couple to her weddin'? She only met Elaine last week at the shower."

"Shirley asked that they be included. It turns out, Cot is acquainted with Kirby's uncle who is also a judge. Years ago, they were on the same panel at a symposium in upstate New York. Small world, isn't it?"

Reba Mae nodded, sending her chandelier earrings dancing. "The Kevin Bacon principle strikes again."

"What *are* you talking about?"

"You know," she said. "Six degrees of separation." At my blank look, she went on to elaborate. "It's based on the theory that no one is more than six relationships away from any other person in the world. Apparently it started as a parlor game, Six Degrees of Kevin Bacon, where players linked celebrities to Bacon by movies they had in common."

McBride, I knew, was a movie buff just as I was. I wondered how he'd score playing the game. It might be fun to find out — provided he wasn't spending all his free time with a certain real estate agent.

All conversation ceased at the first notes of a processional from a string quartet who were stationed a discreet distance from the gazebo. That was the cue for Cot and a man with a clerical collar whom I recognized as the priest from St. Mark's Episcopal Church to proceed down the path to the gazebo.

Melly would be proud as punch of her bridegroom. For someone who managed to be rumpled even in permanent press, Cot appeared uncharacteristically dapper and wrinkle-free in a three-piece navy suit. For his special day, he'd even trimmed his mustache and tamed his mop of gray hair into submission.

As Cot and the clergyman climbed the steps of the gazebo and took their places, all heads turned toward the house. French doors of the Turner-Driscoll House opened, and a little five-year-old girl stepped onto the flagstones. Melly had informed me that Cot's pride and joy, his great-granddaughter, Emma Grace, was to be part of the ceremony. Emma Grace, all bouncing curls, ruffles and ribbons, smiled shyly, then, at a nod of encouragement from Great-Granddad, started forward sprinkling rose petals along the way from a small basket.

Lindsey, who was acting as her grandmother's maid of honor, appeared next. My heart swelled with maternal pride at the sight of my girl, pretty as a picture, all grown-up, yet still my baby. The silk of her pale blue dress rustled as she slowly walked down the crushed-shell pathway holding a single white calla lily.

Behind her, Melly, positively radiant in a dupioni silk suit that was the same blue gray as her eyes, advanced down the path on the arm of her son. CJ cut a fine figure, his blond hair gleaming in the late-afternoon sunlight. My heart gave an unexpected lurch at the sight of him, then settled back into place. It wasn't that I still harbored feelings for my ex, yet for a fleeting second my mind flashed back to another time, another life. Under a veneer of sophistication, he still

29

bore traces of the sunburned youth I'd fallen head over heels in love with light-years ago.

Melly mounted the steps of the gazebo and stood beside Cot facing their wedding guests. After giving his mother a kiss on the cheek, CJ took his place alongside Amber, who occupied a prominent seat in the front row across from Cot's family.

The priest opened the *Book of Common Prayer.* "We are gathered here today in the presence of family and friends to unite . . ."

"Sorry, sorry." An out-of-breath Vicki Lamont squeezed past Reba Mae and me to take the single remaining seat. "I know, I know, I'm late, I'm late."

I didn't know whether to be annoyed at her tardiness or amused by her rendition of the White Rabbit. Poor Vicki, the woman really did seem harried. She hadn't even taken time with her hair or makeup, which was totally out of character for the divorcée. I decided to cut her some slack and returned my attention to the wedding in progress.

"For richer, for poorer . . ."

Off to my left, I heard the heart-thumping, full-of-foreboding, iconic theme song from the movie *Jaws.* I craned my neck to find the source and saw Beau Tucker, sergeant in the Brandywine Creek Police Department, frantically digging through the pockets of his too-tight sports coat while his wife, Jolene, gave him the stink eye.

"In sickness and in health . . ."

I noticed that Beau finally managed to silence his phone but after listening to the caller scrambled from his seat and hurried off.

"To love and to cherish from this day forward," the priest continued, unfazed. "To share the good times and the bad. Till death do us part."

As if conjured by the word "death," the unmistakable chalk-on-a-blackboard screech from Alfred Hitchcock's *Psycho* shrilled loudly. It was as though an invisible hand pulled a switch. Everyone did a freeze-frame. Even the musicians ceased playing. In front of me, John Strickland, mortician and country coroner, rose and, cell phone in hand, eased out of his seat. " 'Scuse me," he muttered as he hastily made his exit.

The priest cleared his throat, and everyone seemed to snap out of the strange spell. "Cottrell Herman and Melly Prescott, I now pronounce you man and wife. Cot, you may kiss your bride."

I couldn't tell who looked happier, Cot or Melly. A spontaneous burst of applause greeted the couple's first kiss as man and wife.

Suddenly the toe-tapping strains of Garth Brooks crooning "Friends in Low Places" blared out. I couldn't believe my ears at the timing. A glance at the musicians' startled and confused faces showed they were equally perplexed.

"Is this turnin' into a karaoke weddin'?" Reba Mae asked in a low voice.

Up front and to the right, I saw Bob Sawyer, reporter and photographer for *The Statesman,* Brandywine Creek's weekly newspaper, stare at the screen of his cell phone. He mumbled excuses to his wife of thirty-some years and left the wedding with a bounce in his step that signaled breaking news.

To their credit, Cot and Melly ignored the rash of phone calls and odd ringtones and proceeded back down the aisle as though nothing out of the ordinary had transpired.

"Well," I said to no one in particular. "That was certainly interesting. What do you suppose is going on?"

"Don't have a clue, hon, but I'm ready for a snack or two washed down by a nice glass of champagne."

Beside us, Vicki scooped her hair into a ponytail and fastened it with a scrunchie.

"Lead the way."

After passing through a receiving line exchanging hugs and kisses, Vicki, Reba Mae, and I made a beeline toward a long linen-draped table laden with a wide assortment of finger foods. A three-tiered wedding cake anchored one end. We heaped our plates with dainty sandwiches, mini crab cakes, and the ubiquitous deviled eggs and cheese straws.

While Vicki and Reba Mae discussed the pros and cons of outdoor weddings, my eyes scanned the crowd. Beau Tucker was nowhere to be seen. His wife seemed bent on making the best of her husband's absence by sticking close to her friends Gerilee and Pete Barker. I looked but didn't see any sign of either the coroner or reporter. All three men had simply vanished. *Curiouser and curiouser.*

"Am I the only one who thinks it strange the county coroner left before the final 'I dos'?" I asked, nibbling a tea sandwich — dried tomato and basil on a triangle of dark pumpernickel spread with cream cheese. "You don't suppose . . . ?"

"Nah" — Reba Mae sampled chicken salad nestled in a lettuce cup — "we haven't had a murder in Brandywine Creek for what? Five or six months?"

I shuddered at the grim statistic. Our postcard-pretty town where nothing ever happened had experienced a crime wave, but, much to the relief of the mayor and town council, things had settled down. Mayor Harvey Hemmings had threatened to hand in his resignation and move to Florida the next time a body was found dead under mysterious circumstances.

"Maybe old man Abernathy finally kicked the bucket," Vicki suggested. "Brig must be old as Methuselah."

Reba Mae nodded sagely. "The old geezer is gettin' on in years. He must be close to ninety."

"Shirley says Brig's still sharp as a tack. She claims he even uses a computer." Vicki added one of the lettuce cups to her plate. "According to her, he keeps a firm hand on the reins of the businesses he owns."

"Or all the fuss might could be an old lady over at the nursin' home." Reba Mae made room on her plate for a strawberry tart. "Probably protocol to call out the troops whenever one of their patients passes on to their heavenly reward."

"I suppose. . . ."

Reba Mae pointed her fork at her plate. "You oughta try one of these, sugar. This curried chicken salad is so good it will make you drool."

"No, thanks. I'm saving room for cake." My mind wandered from food back to the guest list. Other than Shirley and the Dixons, her perspective clients, certain people were conspicuously absent. Wanda Needmore, CJ's paralegal, and Dale Simons, her beau, either hadn't received an invite or had opted out of attending a garden wedding. I also realized belatedly that neither Mary Beth nor Matt Wainwright was present, which I found rather odd. Melly knew the couple well since Matt and CJ were law partners and had been for years. Surely Matt and Mary Beth would have been invited to the festivities.

When Vicki ambled over to talk to CJ and Amber, I dragged Reba Mae away from the refreshment table. Partially hidden behind the Lady Banks roses, we were close enough to eavesdrop on the conversation Jolene Tucker was having on her cell phone. From what I could gauge from Jolene's voice, she didn't sound happy.

"What do you mean you're not coming back?" Jolene snapped.

Reba Mae started to speak, but I held a finger to my lips to shush her.

"How do you expect me to get home?" Jolene asked. "Walk?"

A silence ensued as the party on the other end gave a lengthy explanation for his absence. Assuming she was talking to her husband, Beau, who had left midway through the ceremony, I inched closer.

"Fine," Jolene sighed in resignation. "Of course you can't leave a crime scene. I'll have Pete and Gerilee give me a lift."

Crime scene? Reba Mae's eyes widened at hearing this. Mine probably did the same. Had a perfect day for a wedding turned into a perfect day for a murder?

CHAPTER 3

Felicity stood on the flagstone patio and clapped her hands for attention. "Ladies and gentlemen. It's time for the bride and groom to cut the wedding cake."

" 'Scuse me." Lindsey skirted around us. A Nikon camera, an early high school graduation present from her father, hung from a strap around her neck. She was the self-appointed unofficial photographer for the day. Guests gathered in a loose semi-circle to watch the traditional cake cutting while Lindsey snapped photos to capture the occasion.

I didn't need cake; I needed information. My mind was still reeling from hearing the words "crime scene." I drifted over to where a makeshift bar had been set up at the base of a huge pecan tree. I found Ned Feeney, gofer and jack-of-all-trades, wrestling with a bottle of champagne. The champagne appeared to be winning the battle.

"Hey, Ned," I said. "I see you've been pressed into service."

"Yes, ma'am," he said, giving me a loopy grin. The handyman never failed to remind me of the character Gomer Pyle, ably played by Jim Nabors, on *The Andy Griffith Show*. "Beside tendin' bar, Miz Driscoll hired me to help with settin' up and takin' down."

A glance over my shoulder showed people still hovered around the wedding cake. "Um, Ned, I know you also help Mr. Strickland over at the Eternal Rest. He was here earlier, but he had a phone call and disappeared. I wondered if you knew why."

"Gosh, no! Better check my phone." Ned plunked the champagne bottle on the bar and extracted a flip phone from the pocket of baggy black slacks that looked stiff and new. "Uh-oh. I'm in trouble now. Guess I forget to turn my phone back on after the ceremony."

I watched his panic escalate as he listened to a voice mail.

"What is it?" I asked.

Ned whipped off his bartender apron and flung it aside. "Mr. Strickland wants me to drive the coroner's van out to Chief McBride's place. He sounded real upset."

"The coroner's van?" I echoed.

"He said a weddin' was no place for the

van so he drove his Buick instead. He always keeps extra supplies in the trunk — in case of emergencies — but needs the van to transport the body."

I grabbed Ned's sleeve before he could run off. "What body? Who died?"

"Didn't say." Ned's prominent Adam's apple bobbed up and down. "Gotta run. Tell Miz Driscoll I'm on an important mission."

A dead body at McBride's? McBride . . . ?

I shivered, suddenly chilled to the marrow of my bones. Blood hammered so fiercely through my veins I was finding it hard to think.

"Hey, honeybun." Reba Mae appeared at my side with a plate of wedding cake. "I wondered where you ran off to. You need to taste this. It's amazin'."

I snatched the plate out of her hand and set it on the bar. "Let's go."

"Go . . . ? Go where?"

Practically at a run, I headed for the front of the house where I'd left my VW at the curb.

"Hey, girlfriend, slow down," Reba Mae protested, trying to keep up with my brisk pace. "Show some mercy. I'm wearin' brand-new four-inch heels."

Thankful my Beetle wasn't hemmed in by

all the vehicles clogging Felicity's circular drive, I jumped in and started the engine. Reba Mae barely had time to slam the passenger door shut before I peeled off down the street.

"What's so all-fired important that we couldn't enjoy a nice piece of cake?"

"A body was found out at McBride's place."

"Aw, c'mon. You don't think anythin's happened to Wyatt, do you?"

I impatiently waited for the stoplight to change from red to green. "I don't know what to think, but I can't just sit around not knowing."

"The Wyatt McBride I know has the constitution of a rhinoceros. He probably eats Wheaties for breakfast and chews nails for a snack."

The instant the light changed, I pressed hard on the gas pedal. There was almost no traffic to speak of on a Sunday afternoon as I left Brandywine Creek behind me. I stared straight ahead out the windshield. "Accidents happen all the time. People, seemingly healthy people, have heart attacks, strokes. Aneurysms."

The remainder of the ride was done in silence.

McBride's fixer-upper was located off

Route 78, a two-lane county road about five miles out of town. I braked and turned down a gravel drive marked by a shiny black mailbox with MCBRIDE neatly stenciled on the side. I navigated my Beetle through a maze of emergency vehicles parked haphazardly, half on, half off the grass. EMTs congregated next to their orange and white ambulance gossiping with a group of firefighters. I counted six police cruisers of various vintage. Depending on the city's budget, they ran the gamut from the old standby Ford Crown Vic to several late-model Ford Tauruses. I wedged my VW into a gap between John Strickland's sensible Buick and a spit-polished Harley-Davidson.

"Hey, hon, wait up!" Reba Mae called as I hopped out and rushed toward a group of first responders gathered by the tree line behind McBride's house.

I didn't pause to answer her. Ned Feeney, leaning against the bumper of the coroner's van, gave me a halfhearted wave as I flew past. McBride's black Ford F-150 pickup, I noted, was parked in its usual spot. Was that a good sign or not? I couldn't escape the heavy sense of dread that threatened to overwhelm me. The coroner hadn't been called away in the middle of a wedding for a trip and fall. No, something bad happened. Something really bad.

Reba Mae caught up with me. "What do you s'pose is goin' on?"

"Wish I knew." I felt as though I'd run for miles, so I slowed my pace to catch my breath.

"Just wait, hon; you'll see." Reba Mae put her arm around my shoulders and squeezed. "Wyatt's gonna be right as rain."

But what if he wasn't? a little voice inside my head whispered. I was a grown woman, no longer naïve. I'd learned that bad things happen to good people all the time.

And for no apparent rhyme or reason.

"Hey, look! There's my boy." Reba Mae singled out a strapping six-footer with dark hair wearing a uniform with an arm patch declaring him AUXILIARY POLICE. "Clay will tell us what's goin' on."

Hope surged through me at the thought of having some questions answered.

"Yoo-hoo, Clay!" Reba Mae waved her arm wildly. "Over here."

Not only Clay but the entire gathering turned to stare at the two women, dressed in wedding finery, who pranced toward them while trying not to snag their high heels in the tall grass or Georgia red clay.

As we drew nearer, I noticed yellow crime scene tape cordoned off the stretch of woods behind McBride's house. My heart slammed against my rib cage. "Clay, what's going on? What happened?"

"Sorry, Miz Prescott." Clay shifted his weight from one foot to the other. His hazel eyes, so like his daddy's had been, looked troubled. "I've been assigned crowd control. Got strict orders to keep my mouth shut and folks out."

"Surely that doesn't apply to your momma," Reba Mae protested, outraged at the notion. "Son, you been confidin' in me since you were knee-high."

Clay's face reddened, as he knew everyone was watching the exchange between him and his mother. "Sorry, Momma, but my lips are sealed. You don't want me to lose my new job now, do you?"

Reba Mae huffed out a breath but didn't press her son for information. Frustrated by Clay's lack of cooperation, I scanned the crowd in search of a friendly face. I considered approaching Bob Sawyer, but the reporter was involved in an intense conversation with a dark-skinned man who appeared to be a fisherman, while feverishly writing in a small notebook. My gaze happened next on a bearded man somewhere in his late fifties or early sixties who was the leader of a local motorcycle club that boasted an unlikely assortment of members. Hoyt and I first met last November when he'd caught me trespassing on his property. After lowering his shotgun, he introduced himself. Since then he'd become a regular customer of mine at Spice It Up!

Summoning a smile, I beckoned to him. "Hoyt, I'm surprised to find you here."

"Hey there, how's my favorite redhead?" he asked, separating himself from the group. "I bought myself one of those police scanner thingamajigs so thought I'd ride over, see for myself what was going on."

Determined not to be ignored, Reba Mae stuck out her hand. "Don't believe I've had the pleasure of your acquaintance. I'm Reba Mae Johnson. That handsome young police officer — who refuses to give his momma the time of day — happens to be Clay Johnson, one of my twins."

"Friends call me Hoyt."

"Hoyt?" Reba Mae arched a brow. "That a first or last name?"

"S. W. Hoyt at your service, ma'am. Mostly I answer to just plain Hoyt."

I gave Reba Mae a sharp jab in the ribs. My BFF had picked a fine time for a flirtation when there were more important matters at sake. "Hoyt, what have you been able to find out so far?"

44

He folded his arms across his burly chest and shook his head. "Not much. All I know is folks claim a body was found floating facedown in McBride's favorite fishing hole."

My stomach lurched at hearing this. The little bit I'd eaten at the wedding reception threatened to return for an encore. "Do you have any idea who the body belongs to?" I asked; my voice was barely above a whisper.

"Nope," Hoyt said with a shake of his head. "Don't have a clue."

"Where's Chief McBride?" a male voice bellowed. "I demand he tell me what the Sam Hill's goin' on!"

Everyone turned to see Mayor Harvey Hemmings, trailed by his wife, Dottie, make his way toward the cordoned-off area. Impatient with the lack of parking, the man had driven his Chevy Impala as close as he could before getting out, even though it meant leaving ruts in McBride's lawn. The mayor's round-as-a-dinner-plate face was flushed an unhealthy shade of red. Sweat dripped from his brow. Dottie, stiffly corseted in a pink-flowered dress, hurried to catch up with her husband.

"Isn't that just like hizzoner?" Reba Mae muttered. "Reelection's comin' up right quick. Hope next time around the mayor's finds some tough competition."

" 'Bout time," Hoyt agreed.

Reba Mae's son Clay observed Hemmings heading straight toward the roped-off area and stepped forward to intercept him.

"Out of my way, sonny!" the mayor growled, and made to brush Clay aside.

Clay held firm. "Sorry, sir, but with all due respect, no one is allowed beyond this point. It's a crime scene."

"Crime scene!" the mayor hollered. "I told McBride, in no uncertain terms, no more crime scenes."

"Harvey, dear" — Dottie patted her husband's arm — "remember what the doctor said about your blood pressure."

"This town — my town — is getting a bad reputation." He poked a pudgy finger in Clay's chest. "I'm warnin' you, son, let me pass, or you'll be out on your ear. I've got clout around this town, so don't test me."

As though by magic, McBride emerged from the woods. "Lay another finger on my officer, Mayor, and I'll bring you up on charges of assault and battery."

Hemmings dropped his hand as though burned.

A profound sense of relief washed over me at McBride's sudden appearance. I stared at him. I simply couldn't drag my

46

eyes away. He wasn't dead but hale and hearty and as handsome as ever. Instead of a uniform, he wore faded jeans, ripped at the knee, and a gray T-shirt bearing the logo of the Miami-Dade Police Department, where he'd worked as a detective before returning to his hometown. His dark hair was mussed as though he'd plowed his fingers through it countless times. But he was alive. Alive and unharmed.

"You threatening me, Chief?" Hemmings demanded. Sucking in his rotund belly, he drew himself up to his full five foot six, which still left him more than six inches shy of McBride's height.

"More than a threat, Mayor." McBride didn't raise his voice. He didn't have to. A look at his glacier-blue eyes told everyone that he meant business.

Reba Mae nudged me. "See what Wyatt's holdin'?" she whispered.

It was then that I noticed the plastic evidence bag he carried. I moved forward a fraction for a better look and made out the shape of a shoe. A woman's shoe.

The crowd, me included, drew closer, propelled by an invisible force field called a need to know. Which, in my case, translated into just plain nosiness.

Bob Sawyer wasn't easily intimidated. An

attribute that made him excel at his job as a reporter. "Chief, were you able to identify the victim?"

His jaw set, McBride started up the lawn toward where the emergency vehicles were parked. "No comment."

"What happens next?" Bob persisted, following McBride like a bloodhound on the heels of breaking news.

"The body will be sent to the GBI crime lab in Atlanta for an autopsy to determine cause of death."

"Can you at least tell us if the victim was male or female?"

"Female!" Reba Mae called out. "I'd know that suede leopard print pump anywhere. It's Shirley Randolph's."

"Shirley's?" I gasped.

The mayor scratched his head. "Why in tarnation would Shirley's shoe be floatin' in a fishin' hole?"

"Are you positive the shoe was hers?" Bob Sawyer asked Reba Mae, his notebook out, his pen poised.

"Of course I'm positive." Reba Mae turned to me for support. "Do I know shoes, or don't I?"

I nodded. "Reba Mae is my go-to person whenever it comes to footwear."

"I suffered a severe case of shoe envy the

first time I saw Shirley in them shoes," Reba Mae proclaimed for everyone to hear. "They must've cost a pretty penny."

"What do you suppose Shirley was doing way out here?" Dottie Hemmings asked, sounding innocent as a lamb.

Harvey took out a snowy linen handkerchief and mopped his brow. "How am I supposed to know what goes on in a woman's head?"

"Were Shirley Randolph and the chief . . . sweet on each other?" Hoyt stuffed his hands into the pockets of his jeans and rocked back on his heels.

"Rumor has it that Shirley and McBride were an item," Dottie informed him, looking smug. "Maybe they had a lovers' quarrel?"

"Really?" I'd heard enough. There were few things in life Dottie loved more than gossip. If gossip wasn't readily available, she'd create some. "Dottie, are you implying Shirley drowned herself because she and McBride argued?"

Dottie patted her blond beehive that was lacquered harder than a linebacker's helmet. "Women in love, dearie, have been known to behave foolishly."

Bob Sawyer cocked his head to one side. "So, Dottie, you're telling me you believe

Shirley and McBride were lovers? You think McBride might've wanted to break it off and, as a result, Shirley committed suicide? Can I quote you on that?"

"No comment. Come, Dottie." Mayor Hemmings took his wife by the arm and dragged her away.

From the look on Dottie Hemming's face, I could tell she wasn't happy at leaving. If she'd had her way, they would've stayed until the last juicy morsel had been squeezed dry. *Why would anyone think Shirley killed herself?* I wondered. Shirley seemed to have it all: beauty, brains, money, career. And why chose to do the deed on McBride's property? I know she and McBride had a friendship of sorts — was friendship another name for relationship? — because I'd seen them dining together a time or two. Had that progressed into something more than sharing a plate of chili cheese fries?

Bob Sawyer turned his attention on me. "What about you, Piper? You've earned a reputation as an amateur sleuth. Surely you must have a theory or two you'd like to share with our readers."

Before I could frame an appropriate reply, a trio of men, led by the coroner, John Strickland, broke through the woods bearing a body bag on a stretcher. The coroner

50

held a second evidence bag, this one containing what appeared to be women's clothing. Silence greeted the men's appearance. Slowly, wordlessly, the entourage made its way across McBride's yard to the van waiting to transport Shirley's body to the state's crime lab.

I frowned. The women's clothing didn't make sense. It was too early in the season — even for kids — to go skinny-dipping. I couldn't imagine Shirley undressing, jumping into a spring-fed pond, then dying. In my humble opinion, it almost seemed the clothes had been planted at the site as an afterthought.

But if not suicide, then what? Homicide . . . ?

CHAPTER 4

Monday, Monday, can't trust that day . . .

The lyrics of the Mamas & the Papas classic played through my head as I scooped coffee beans — Colombian — into the grinder in my kitchenette at the back of my shop and turned on the switch. I'd spent a restless night trying to piece together the puzzle of Shirley Randolph's death. Reba Mae and I had hung around till the last of the emergency vehicles rolled out. Next, Hoyt roared off on his Harley. As best as I could calculate from comments I'd overheard, the vote was split fifty-fifty between homicide and suicide with a few holdouts in favor of accidental drowning. Personally, I wasn't ready to cast my ballot.

"So, do you think McBride's responsible for what happened to Shirley?" Dottie asked as she breezed through the door resplendent in purple polyester.

I turned off the coffee grinder and

dumped the ground beans into the filter basket of the coffeemaker. I'd already had my first cup of java upstairs in my apartment, but this promised to be an entire-pot kind of day. "Isn't it a little early to be jumping to conclusions?"

"It doesn't take me long to make up my mind. I have a sixth sense about certain things."

"Well, I'm glad there are medical examiners who rely on science rather than ESP."

Dottie plunked her purse on the counter, a surefire sign she planned to stay awhile. "McBride and Shirley were seeing each other. I watched him go in and out of Creekside Realty numerous times. And once I saw them having dinner at North of the Border. They were sharing a basket of tortilla chips."

"That isn't exactly the same as picking out a china pattern." I filled the reservoir of the coffeemaker, then hit the ON button.

"Everyone agrees McBride is not one to be tied down. But, then, he probably never encountered a more persistent woman than Shirley. No challenge too big, no challenge too small. Once she set her sights on McBride, he didn't have a snowball's chance in hell. She wasn't one to give up easily."

Not many people were aware McBride

was a widower, not a bachelor. He'd confided once in a rare moment that he'd been married briefly in his early twenties while serving in the army and stationed at Fort Huachuca, Arizona. The marriage had ended tragically when his young wife had been killed in a car crash. He'd never remarried.

Using a microfiber cloth, I wiped water droplets off the counter. "So you're convinced that when things didn't work out with McBride Shirley drowned herself?"

Dottie pursed her lips, but before she could frame a response Gerilee Barker, a sturdy no-nonsense woman with permed hair dyed a determined brown, arrived. Gerilee's husband, Pete, owned and operated Meat on Main, the butcher shop across the square. "Morning!" Gerilee called. "Shame about Shirley, isn't it? Can't believe our town might have another murder on its hands."

"Murder . . . ?" Dottie's hand fluttered to the neck of her ruffled blouse. "Lord have mercy, give me strength. If that's the case, Harvey swears he's leaving town. He's worried about his legacy as mayor. Doesn't want Brandywine Creek during his tenure being remembered as the murder capital of the county."

"That's ridiculous!" I protested. "Violent crimes aren't restricted to big cities. Brandywine Creek is simply undergoing a . . . a . . ."

". . . epidemic?" Gerilee suggested helpfully.

"I prefer to think of it as an unfortunate series of events." Draping my cloth over the faucet, I pulled mugs from a cupboard. "Coffee, anyone?"

"No thank you, dear," Dottie said. "I have a sensitivity to caffeine. Drink even one cup and I talk nonstop."

To keep from making a smart-aleck remark — such as *How do you tell the difference?* — I concentrated on pouring coffee for Gerilee and myself. "Why would Shirley kill herself?"

"Good question." Gerilee took a sip and gave a nod of approval. "The woman had everything going for her. Beauty. Successful career. And — judging from the car she drove and the home she just purchased — an enviable income."

"Maybe her death was an accident," Dottie suggested. "Ned Feeney told me the body was found naked. What if Shirley decided to go skinny-dipping and ended up with that thing people get when they freeze to death?"

"Hypothermia?" I suggested.

"That's the word. Water's spring fed, won't warm up till the Fourth of July."

"Or could be she died of natural causes," Dottie said, her supply of theories seemingly bottomless. "Am I the only one who noticed Shirley hasn't seemed her usual self lately? I thought she looked a mite peaked at Melly's shower."

"Well, regardless of what happened, dead is dead," Gerilee said with finality. "I almost forgot the reason that brought me here. Piper, I need the biggest jar of cloves you carry."

Coffee mug in hand, I moved toward the Hoosier cabinet. "Ground or whole?"

"Whole."

"Here you go." I handed the cloves to Gerilee.

"Plan on making cookies?" Dottie asked her.

"I had Pete set aside a smoked ham. I thought I'd bake it up to serve at the reception after Shirley's funeral."

Dottie's eyes gleamed at the prospect of a funeral. "Do you know when it will be?"

"Not yet." Gerilee finished what coffee was left in her cup. "I need to check with Chief McBride to find out when he thinks the body will be released. Afterwards, I'll visit the rectory at St. Mark's Episcopal and talk to the priest."

Dottie patted her hair. "Shirley deserves a real nice send-off. The women's guild at St. Mark's always puts on the loveliest funeral luncheons. Harvey swears the Methodist ladies make the best desserts, but when it comes to fancy, the Episcopal women can't be beat."

"Anything else?" I asked Gerilee, hoping to sidetrack Dottie before she delved into doom and gloom.

Gerilee must have been operating on the same wavelength, because she quickly followed my lead. "While you're at it, I'll take a small jar of powdered mustard. I used up the last of mine, and I like to add it to my glaze."

"Does Shirley have family close by?" Dottie asked. "I don't recall her mentioning anyone."

"I believe she has a brother in Macon, or maybe Albany."

I had returned to the counter with the powdered mustard and started to ring up the sale when Mary Beth Wainwright walked into Spice It Up! Mary Beth was the wife of CJ's longtime law partner, Matt Wainwright. Only five foot four with a muscular build, Mary Beth wore her streaked hair short in an easy-to-care-for style. She kept busy volunteering at the high school where she had worked as PE teacher. Once upon a time we had been friends of sorts, but our friendship had waned since my divorce.

"Hey, Mary Beth," I said with a smile. "I'll be with you soon as I finish helping Gerilee."

Mary Beth didn't return the smile. "Take your time."

"I was surprised you and Matt weren't at the wedding," Dottie commented. "Did you and Melly have a falling-out?"

"No, of course not," Mary Beth replied, her tone curt. "Something came up, so we sent our regrets along with a generous gift."

Gerilee handed me a twenty. "Terrible about Shirley, isn't it?"

"Yes, it's all everyone is talking about."

I glanced up from making change. "Did you know her well, Mary Beth?"

"Not very, but Matt was her attorney. Not long ago Shirley had him draw up her will. He didn't think a thing of it at that time, but in retrospect . . ." She shrugged.

Dottie's bleached bubble of hair bobbed up and down in agreement. "A will is the only sensible thing for a single person to do. My advice is don't die without one."

"Dottie's right, you know," Gerilee said.

"Pete's cousin Judy died without a will and it took him more than two years as executor to settle her estate."

"What about you, Piper?" Dottie asked. "Do you have a will?"

"Um, no, I don't."

"Shame on you." Dottie wagged her finger at me. "Now that you and CJ are divorced, you need to step up. Face your responsibilities. Surely you don't want your poor children to be saddled with tough decisions. Besides a will there are dozens of details to address. You need to let your loved ones know what you want to wear at your viewing. And don't forget to divide up your good jewelry. Last thing you'll want is for Lindsey and Chad to squabble over who gets your engagement ring and who gets your pearls."

Gerilee rolled her eyes, then took the bag of spices I handed her. "Thanks for the coffee, Piper. Sorry, but I've got errands to run."

Mary Beth looked as though she'd like to race her to the door. "I can't stay either, Piper. I only stopped by to ask if you'd be willing to serve on the Parents Prom Committee. As you know, senior prom is almost here, and there are still some vacancies to fill."

"Sure," I said. "Sign me up. I'll be glad to

59

help wherever I can."

"Great! I'll get back to you." With that, she turned and departed.

Dottie stared after her. "That's odd. Mary Beth seemed more concerned about the prom committee than she did about Shirley."

"You know Mary Beth is involved in most of the school activities. She probably has a lot on her mind. Plus, it wasn't as if she and Shirley were buddies."

"I suppose, but don't you'd think she'd at least show some emotion?"

Wishing Dottie would leave, too, I'd just taken another sip of coffee and discovered it had grown cold when a stranger wandered through the door. A man, who appeared to be in his late twenties, stood in the center of the shop and gazed around looking perplexed. Dottie stared at him as though he were an alien from another planet.

The stranger could have been the poster child for Mr. Average American. Average in height, weight, and build, with medium-brown hair cut short and neatly parted, he wore tortoiseshell eyeglasses that lent him a professorial air. His shirt and jeans were as crisp as a newly minted dollar bill. He was the type to easily blend into a crowd and instantly become invisible.

"Can I help you?" I asked, reverting to my role as friendly shopkeeper.

He gave me a tentative smile. "I noticed women coming in and out of here so I decided to find out what the attraction was. Is this a cooking store of some sort?"

"To be more exact, this is a spice shop. Every spice a cook might possibly need from *A* to *Z*, anise to za'atar." I had yet to make my first sale of za'atar, a Middle Eastern table condiment blended from a multitude of spices, but I liked to boast that I literally stocked everything from *A* to *Z*. "Feel free to browse. I'll be happy to answer any questions you might have."

Not waiting for an introduction, Dottie stuck out a pudgy hand. "I'm Dottie Hemmings. My husband's the mayor of Brandywine Creek. I don't recall seeing you before. You must be either new in town or a visitor."

"How do you do?" he said, shaking Dottie's hand. "I'm Colin Flynn. This is my first visit to Brandywine Creek. I'm thinking of buying a place here and settling down."

I folded my arms across my chest and studied the earnest young man. "Why choose Brandywine Creek?"

He shrugged. "I was looking for a place off the beaten path. Somewhere peaceful

61

and quiet."

If he were familiar with the town's recent history, Colin Flynn might have decided to hightail it out of here as fast as he could. "If there's any way we can be of help . . ."

"Actually, there is." He tugged his earlobe. "I planned to check out some real estate. I had a meeting scheduled for this morning with a Realtor, but there must've been a miscommunication. Creekside Realty has crime scene tape strung across the entrance."

Dottie and I looked at each other, neither one of us eager to break the news about Shirley.

"I don't suppose," Colin continued, "you know where I might find Ms. Randolph. We've corresponded a number of times via email. She promised to have a few properties lined up to show me. I've been calling and texting her, but no response."

I tucked a wayward strand of hair behind my ear. "I, ah, hate to be the bearer of bad news, but Shirley Randolph's dead."

"Dead . . . ?" His jaw dropped and his eyes widened in shock. "How? What happened?"

"Do you want a glass of water?" I don't exactly know what miracle water is supposed to perform, but it seemed to be the standard remedy in times of stress.

"Thanks, no," he said with a slight shake of his head. "Do you know what happened?"

"It's too soon for anyone to know the details, but her body was found yesterday afternoon," I explained.

"She drowned," Dottie volunteered. "It might've been the result of a lovers' quarrel."

"This is all quite a surprise," he murmured. "I don't want to sound callous, but will someone be taking over for her at the real estate agency?"

I hadn't given the matter much thought, but his question was valid. "I'm not sure," I said slowly.

Dottie snapped her fingers. "Vicki Lamont. She's the person you need to contact. She's relatively new to the business, but I'm sure she'll be more than happy to help you. Her name's in the phone book. *L-a-m-o-n-t.*"

"Thanks, I'll look her up. Appreciate your help, ladies."

As he turned to leave, I noticed the price tag still attached to the back pocket of his jeans.

Dottie's brow puckered in a frown. "Can't

quite put my finger on it, but there's something fishy about that young man."

64

CHAPTER 5

Later that afternoon Reba Mae swung into Spice It Up! holding a take-and-go container. "Hey, honeybun, I brought you leftovers."

I took the container from her and peeked inside. "Mmm, yum, your grandmother's goulash. What's the occasion?"

"Nothin' special." Reba Mae stooped to pat Casey on the head, then waltzed over to the coffeemaker and filled a mug with coffee. "Couldn't settle after gettin' home yesterday, so I did some kitchen therapy. Made enough to feed a small army."

"Well, your leftovers found a good home." I placed the container in the fridge, then, even though I'd already met my daily quota of caffeine, poured myself another cup.

"Cook up some noodles, reheat the goulash, and you'll have a nice meal for you and Lindsey."

Cradling my mug in both hands, I leaned

next to Reba Mae at the counter and savored the peace and quiet after a nonstop morning. Somehow my little shop had become a hub when it came to exchanging of information — I prefer the term "information" rather than "gossip." Today all the women were eager to learn and rehash details surrounding Shirley's death. At last count, the pendulum of popular opinion was swinging toward suicide. No one wanted to consider the alternative. Yet the notion of a homicide lingered in the air like the smell of a cheap cigar. I couldn't help wish the cause of death had been determined. If so, it would put an end to much of the speculation running rampant.

"The first anniversary of Spice It Up! is coming up soon," I said to Reba Mae as a diversion. "I want to do something special to mark the occasion. I'm thinking along the lines of a cooking demonstration and giveaway. Would you be willing to show everyone how you make your Hungarian goulash?" I held up my hand to forestall the objections I saw brewing. "I know you don't have a bashful bone in your body, so don't try to tell me you get nervous talking in front of people."

"I'm not sure folks would be all that interested. What if no one shows? You know how easily my feelin's get hurt."

"You don't have to give me your answer this minute. All I'm asking is for you to sleep on it. You've been making that recipe for years and could probably fix it in your sleep."

Reba Mae narrowed her eyes and shot me a calculating look. "What's in it for me?"

"How about next time we go to North of the Border it's my treat?"

Reba Mae pretended to ponder my offer, then grinned. "Sure, why not? Guess I can be bought for the price of margarita and a beef burrito."

"Fantastic. I'll set the wheels in motion." We clinked coffee mugs to seal the deal. "A stranger wandered into the shop earlier," I continued in a different vein. "He claimed he had an appointment with Shirley to view some properties but hadn't been able to reach her. Dottie and I had to break the news that Shirley was dead. Don't suppose any of your clients might've mentioned if, or when, Creekside Realty might reopen?"

"Mary Lou Lambert was in the Klassy Kut early this mornin' for a touch-up. Accordin' to her, Vicki Lamont's the one who'll most likely be takin' over. Also accordin' to Mary Lou, Vicki was madder than a wet hen at Shirley. Said she won't be sheddin' any tears at her memorial service."

How mad could a "wet hen" get? I wondered. "I thought Vicki and Shirley were good friends. Especially since Shirley helped Vicki break into the real estate business when she desperately needed a job after her divorce from Kenny."

Reba Mae nodded. "It was either that or take a job at the water department."

"What happened to cause a rift?"

"From what I heard, Vicki considered them good friends, too, until Shirley showed her true colors."

"I want details, nice, juicy details." I crossed one ankle over the other and sipped my coffee.

Reba Mae copied my casual pose. "Shirley stole a potentially hefty commission right from under Vicki's nose, that's what happened."

"No way."

"Way." Reba Mae bobbed her head for emphasis. "Mary Lou said Vicki told her that she was the one who first mentioned showin' the Granger house to the Dixons. You know it's stood empty since Craig moved back to Michigan. Next thing Vicki knew, Shirley was showin' the Dixons around, actin' like it was all her idea. Vicki called it a double dip. Both listin' and sellin' the place would bring in a sizeable sum." She rubbed her thumb and fingers together to simulate *show me the money.*

"That must've gotten Vicki's goat."

"Not just her goat, hon, the whole freakin' farm. Vicki was livid. Absolutely livid. Ask Mary Lou her opinion, she'll tell you Shirley needed to buy herself a Kevlar vest."

"Interesting," I said. "Vicki's been struggling with finances ever since her divorce. She counted on Kenny setting her up with the lifestyle to which she'd grown accustomed."

"Instead, Kenny declared bankruptcy." Reba Mae gestured with her coffee mug. "Talk has it, he's tendin' bar at some sleazy dive in Key West. Vicki's convinced he's hidin' his money in the Caymans, but can't prove it. She complained she'd been outlawyered."

"Who was her lawyer?"

"None other than your ex."

I finished my coffee. "CJ found his niche with trip and falls. He shouldn't venture out of his comfort zone."

"Uh-huh," Reba Mae agreed. "Vicki's makin' noise about suin' CJ for incompetence but can't afford to."

I glimpsed a familiar figure clad in a navy blue uniform outside the front entrance.

69

"Looks like we're about to have a visitor."

Reba Mae and I straightened automatically as Wyatt McBride strode through the door. His face with its sculpted cheekbones and strong jaw, generous gifts of DNA, wore a set expression. His mouth was a grim line and shadows underlined his cool blue eyes.

"Hey, Wyatt," Reba Mae chirped. "You don't look too good."

I'd debate that point with my friend later. McBride *always* looked good. It wasn't just me either; I'd bet a jar of pricey saffron most of the ladies in town would agree with my assessment of movie-star handsome. It would take more than dark circles to detract from his blatant sex appeal.

"Thanks for pointing that out, Reba Mae," he said.

"Cheer up. Nothin' a good night's sleep won't fix."

"Sleep's not high on my priority list right now. Not after finding a body at my fishing hole."

"It's a shame about Shirley," I said, smoothing an apron that didn't need smoothing. "Everyone's saying you were close."

Casey scampered out of the storeroom, his tail wagging furiously, and practically begged McBride to scratch the sweet spot behind his ears. McBride obliged, then straightened. "I'd hardly call us 'close.' She was my Realtor. We had dinner together on a couple occasions to discuss business."

So . . . they weren't an item? I felt my mood traitorously lift at hearing this.

"Hey, Wyatt, just so you know up front, Piper and me aren't buyin' the gossip goin' around about you and Shirley havin' a lovers' spat."

"Good to hear, Reba Mae. I'll rest easier knowing you don't think I'm responsible for Shirley dying."

"Has the medical examiner come back with a report on cause of death?" I asked.

"I'm waiting on it. Until then, my department treats every suspicious death as a possible homicide." He pulled a small notepad and pen from his shirt pocket. "I'm making the rounds on all the merchants along Main Street who might've seen or talked to Shirley in the last week or two. Piper, do you recall when you last saw her?"

"Let me think." Picking up a cloth, I rubbed an imaginary spot off the counter. "With Creekside Realty down the block, I've seen her come and go a few times. She always carries . . . carried . . . her computer whenever she left the office."

McBride jotted this in his little black

71

book. "When did you last to talk to her?"

"We exchanged a few words the day of Melly's bridal shower."

"And what about the day before?" Reba Mae piped. "Remember, Shirley comin' and askin' you to invite Elaine Dixon, the wife of a potential buyer she had on the hook for Gray's Hardware? Shirley wanted her client to experience a dose of real Southern hospitality."

I abandoned my housekeeping chores. "Oh, that's right. I'd nearly forgotten. She dropped in shortly after we watched you and Shirley on the sidewalk laughing it up."

He raised a brow. "I didn't realize our conversation made headline news."

I shrugged. "Didn't matter to me one smidgen."

Reba gave me a look as if to say, *Liar-liar-pants-on-fire.*

"The last conversation I had with Shirley was about ginger," I offered.

"Hmm." Reba Mae gave McBride an arch look. "Shirley plannin' on doin' some cookin'? Maybe havin' a certain somebody over for a cozy dinner for two?"

A muscle ticked in McBride's jaw, a telltale clue he was irritated, but otherwise he didn't react. "Did you think her buying ginger was significant?" he asked.

"Shirley didn't cook."

"If she didn't cook, why did she need ginger?"

I tucked an unruly red curl behind one ear. "She said she'd read in a magazine that ginger relieved occasional indigestion. I suggested she try making ginger tea."

Ginger tea and indigestion didn't seem to merit a notation in McBride's book. "Was Shirley acting strangely? Seem depressed? Worried?"

"Seemed on top of the world," Reba Mae volunteered. "She appeared happy as a clam at the prospect of sellin' Gray's Hardware."

"What do you suppose happened?" I watched McBride close his notebook and slip it into his pocket. "How did Shirley end up on your property?"

"Think it's a suicide?" Reba Mae asked before he had a chance to answer.

"Haven't figured it all out yet."

"Did Shirley leave a note?" I asked

"If she did, we haven't found it."

I trailed after him as he started toward the door. "No suicide note? Isn't that unusual?"

"Not really." He shook his head. "Sadly, only a small percentage of suicide victims leave a note."

I followed so closely I nipped at his heels. "The ME will be able to rule out natural causes, won't he? Except for mild indigestion, Shirley insisted she was in excellent health, unless . . ."

McBride stopped and turned so abruptly we nearly collided. "Unless what?"

I'd seen that icy glare before and refused to be intimidated by it. "Unless it was homicide. Just sayin', is all."

"And who do you think might've wanted her dead?"

"Who knows?" Reba Mae trailed after us. "Could be most anyone."

I pointed an accusatory finger at my BFF. "I once heard you say you'd kill for shoes like Shirley's."

"Stop tryin' to get me in a mess of trouble. You know that was just a figure of speech. An innocent remark like that already got me into one jam," Reba Mae reminded me, referring to an incident a few months back when she had narrowly escaped being measured for a prison jumpsuit.

"Sorry," I said. "Listen, McBride, if it were up to me to put together a list of suspects, I'd make sure Vicki Lamont's name was on it. I noticed the women arguing at Melly's bridal shower. From the conversation Reba Mae had with Mary Lou Lambert this morning, Vicki was one unhappy camper."

"Haven't I warned you about making a persons of interest list? You've alienated half the people in town as it is."

"It's how I whittle down the number of people on my Christmas card list," I fired back. "Off the record, McBride, what's your theory?"

He pinched the bridge of his nose between thumb and forefinger. "Still working on one."

"Surely there must be at least one small detail you can part with," I wheedled. Subtle has never been my strong suit.

He sighed in resignation. "Since it'll be public knowledge soon enough, I don't suppose it will do any harm. My men found Shirley's Cadillac hidden in the brush not far from where the body was found. I had Officer Moyer dust the car for prints. Never know what that might turn up."

"Any idea what time she died?"

"Still too early to draw any conclusions. I'll know more when I get the preliminary report from the medical examiner in Atlanta. From the condition of the body, I don't think she'd been in the water long. Probably less than twenty-four hours."

Reba Mae and I watched him leave.

Less than twenty-four hours?

"That would put the time of death late

Saturday night or early Sunday morning," I said aloud. "And it sounds to me like someone went to a great deal of trouble to hide her car."

"You're not thinkin' what I think you're thinkin, are you?"

"Uh-huh." I nodded. "If a person was planning on killing themselves, why bother to hide their vehicle? That doesn't make sense. Can't help but wonder if Shirley was murdered and whoever did it wanted to point the blame at McBride."

Reba Mae rolled her eyes heavenward. "Boy howdy! Now that's a real dog's dinner."

CHAPTER 6

Leftovers are a boon to a working mom's busy schedule, and I was no exception. After being on my feet all day, I'd looked forward to coming upstairs to my apartment, kicking off my shoes, and doing nothing more strenuous than reheating goulash. Lindsey quickly put an end to my pipe dream. "I thought you loved Reba Mae's goulash," I protested when she nixed my meal plan.

"I do, but" — Lindsey patted her trim tummy — "way too many calories. Prom's less than two weeks away. I'm watching my weight so I look good in my dress."

"Linds, you'll look amazing with or without a plate of goulash."

"Sorry, Mom, can't take the chance. Until prom, I'm sticking to only salads for dinner."

I'd decide later whether to freeze Reba Mae's specialty or binge and eat it all myself. For the time being, however, I'd join my daughter on the rabbit food diet. Reluctantly, I slid the container of goulash into the fridge and pulled out an assortment of veggies.

While I concocted a salad, Lindsey set the table. "Amber told me that during beauty pageants contestants practically starve themselves before the bathing-suit competition."

I gritted my teeth and wished — not for the first time — that satin sashes and rhinestone tiaras came with expiration dates. I vented my frustration slicing and dicing a hapless tomato and cucumber. "I hardly think you'll be wearing a bathing suit to prom."

"Seriously, Mom. Amber says it's never too early for a woman to cultivate good eating habits. She said it's imperative to create a positive self-image and to never underestimate the importance of an attractive appearance."

For protein, I added a hard-boiled egg, cubed some cheddar, and diced two lone slices of turkey breast from Piggly Wiggly's deli. "I've read it's unhealthy for young women to become obsessed with body image. It leads to eating disorders such as anorexia and bulimia."

Salad completed, Lindsey sat opposite me

at the kitchen table. "Don't worry. I like ice cream too much to ever become anorexic."

"Thanks for putting my mind at ease." I speared a forkful of salad.

Lindsey splashed a miserly amount of my homemade oil and vinegar dressing on her salad. "Amber is buying a whole new wardrobe for her trip abroad with Daddy this summer. But she's waiting until Italy to buy shoes. She swears Italian leather is the best."

If it was possible to be vaccinated against certain virulent diseases, why couldn't someone do humanity a favor and discover a vaccine against toxic people? Amber Leigh Ames-Prescott acted on me like an appetite suppressant. I shoved my salad aside, no longer hungry.

Apparently Amber didn't have the same effect on my daughter, because Lindsey devoured every last morsel of romaine on her plate. "Mind if I go to Taylor's after dinner? We're reviewing a list of college courses one more time before making our final decision."

"Sure, go ahead. I'll clean up." Though Lindsey would be barely eighteen, my baby girl would enroll in college this fall. I was delighted her ACT/SAT scores were high enough to gain her admission to various universities. A fact that flummoxed her brother, Chad, who had always been considered the student in the family. Already I was starting to feel the empty-nest syndrome creep closer.

"At least you won't desert me, will you, boy?" I said to Casey, my furry friend, after Lindsey had left for Taylor's.

Casey thumped his tail against the floor in a show of solidarity.

Although I was loathe to admit it, Amber's advice to Lindsey carried a ring of truth. Now that I was a woman of a "certain age" — translated to mean a woman over forty — I'd discovered it took more effort to maintain my girlish figure than it had in my youth. While reluctant to resort to drastic measures such as giving up pepperoni and mushroom pizza, I jogged on a semi-regular basis. Not only did an occasional run help control my weight, but it also helped relieve stress and clear the cobwebs from my head.

Ten minutes later, I'd changed into a sleek pair of black running capris and snug lime green half-zip hoodie. I'd decided to class up my act — my jogging act, that is — by cashing in gift cards I'd received for my birthday. I'd traded in my disreputable sweat pants, baggie T-shirts, and shapeless hoodies for more fashionable ensembles and morphed into a spiffier new me. After I tucked a spare house key into the zippered sleeve of my shirt and snapped on Casey's leash, my pet and I set off at a nice, leisurely pace. Thanks to daylight savings time, it would be light for another hour or so.

It didn't take long to find my rhythm. Soon I turned off Main Street and onto Lincoln. As I ran past the Brandywine Creek Police Department, I wasn't surprised at the sight of McBride's pickup in the adjacent lot. If I knew the man at all, he'd be putting in extra hours until the mystery surrounding Shirley Randolph's death was solved. His connection to Shirley had become a hot topic of conversation. Long before the advent of the internet, the citizens of Brandywine Creek had perfected their own form of social media. A form that didn't require fiber optics to get news out with lightning speed. Though McBride insisted his dinners with Shirley were strictly a matter of convenience for both parties, people preferred their own romanticized versions.

I veered away from Lincoln Street and onto Jefferson. A block later, I jogged in place while Casey watered a sycamore two doors from Melly's home. Her house was locked and the living room drapes drawn, giving the place an unlived-in appearance.

Cot, I knew, was trying to convince his bride that the time had come to move into a condo, which meant less maintenance. I had to hand it to my ex-mother-in-law. When it came to making changes, Melly excelled. In the blink of an eye she'd blossomed from wife, mother, grandmother, and a widow in small-town USA to newlywed and world traveler.

"C'mon, boy," I urged Casey. "Let's get a move on."

We circled back through the residential streets to Main Street. As I neared Spice It Up! I noticed a silver gray Mercedes-Benz with New York plates parked outside Gray's Hardware. I slowed to a stop, bent over, and rested my hands on my knees to regulate my breathing. Who else could the car belong to other than the Dixons? I'd met Elaine briefly at Melly's bridal shower but had yet to meet her husband. No time like the present to be neighborly, I thought, straightening.

"Hello!" I called, slightly out of breath, through the store's partially open door. Although it still wasn't dark, fluorescent lights blazed inside. Yet there were no signs of occupants.

When there was no response, I stepped inside with Casey right on my heels, his bright eyes alert for signs of trouble. "Hello!" I called again, louder this time.

I expected to find Mavis, but instead a man emerged from a room at the rear of the store that I assumed was an office. He immediately put me in mind of a bulldog with his stocky build, pugnacious jaw, and intelligent dark eyes. A full head of hair, more salt than pepper, was swept back from a wide brow. Although he seemed puzzled at finding me, he quickly recovered and approached with a confident stride.

"Kirby Dixon," he said, extending his hand.

"Piper Prescott," I replied, returning the handshake. "I own Spice It Up! just down the block. I saw a car outside that I assume from the license plate must be yours and thought I'd drop in and welcome you to Brandywine Creek."

"Nice to meet you." He smiled, a brilliant flash of white in a tanned face. "I love the friendliness of everyone in your charming little town. It's one of the reasons I'm considering buying property and relocating."

"Kirby," Elaine called from the rear, "who is it? Did your Realtor finally decide to make an appearance?"

"Elaine, honey, we have a visitor. Come

out and say hello."

I could be wrong — after all, I'd just met the man — but this was less request, more demand. Kirby Dixon struck me as the type who liked to be in control and have his orders obeyed without question. It was telegraphed by his casual, yet purposeful, bearing. A matter of attitude, attitude, attitude.

Casey perched at my feet, watchful and wary.

Elaine brushed dust from her hands as she came out of the office. Recognizing me, she smiled, but it lacked her husband's warmth. "Hello, Piper. We've been out of town. Shirley gave us a key before we left, so Kirby insisted we take another walk-through before checking into the bed-and-breakfast where we'll be staying."

"We expected to find Shirley waiting for us," Kirby said. "I've tried calling numerous times, but her phone goes straight to voice mail."

"Doesn't seem like the woman's very interested in selling real estate if this is any indication of how she treats her clients." Elaine stared hard at Casey, who stared back. "What type of dog is that anyway? He doesn't look like any breed I'm familiar with."

84

I felt compelled to defend my mutt from the woman's obvious disdain. "When it comes to breeds, Casey is one of a kind."

"Hmph!" Elaine sniffed. "A mutt."

Stooping down, I scooped Casey into my arms and addressed my remarks to Kirby. "You might try contacting Vicki Lamont with any questions or concerns you might have about purchasing Gray's Hardware. She'll be handling all Shirley's accounts from now on."

Kirby frowned. "It's my understanding that Vicki's relatively new to the real estate game. I'd prefer entrusting the details to someone more experienced, such as Shirley Randolph."

For the second time that day, it fell on me to be the bearer of bad news. "I'm afraid that's impossible. Shirley's dead."

"Dead . . . ?" Kirby echoed.

"I'm not all that surprised," Elaine said. "Ask me, her color didn't look good. She was much too pale, too thin. Too high-strung."

Frowning, Kirby jammed both hands into his pant pockets. "What happened?"

"Shirley's body was found yesterday in a small pond about five miles out of town. The cause of death hasn't been determined yet." I stroked Casey's head more to comfort myself than my pooch.

"She might've decided to go for a swim and then had a heart attack — or an aneurysm," Elaine suggested helpfully. "Too bad, but without Shirley's expertise, maybe it's a sign to end my husband's notion of becoming a shopkeeper. Perhaps an omen for us to explore other options."

"Enough, Elaine!" Kirby's voice was sharp. "I've about had it with all your whining and complaining. You know I've worked hard and long for every dime, and I'm free to spend my money as I see fit. I've often dreamed of retiring to a sleepy Southern town, answering to no one but myself, maybe dabbling in local politics."

Before Elaine could turn away, I caught anger spark in her pale eyes and saw her mouth harden. Under a veneer of sophistication, the woman had a temper.

I was about to say something — what, I didn't know — to diffuse the tension when Vicki Lamont burst into the store.

"Hey, y'all." Ignoring me and oblivious of the couple's mood, she addressed Kirby and Elaine. "I happened to be driving by and saw your car. I've been under the weather, but I was going to call y'all tomorrow to assure you that you were in good hands with Shirley gone. Mavis Gray and I have been bridge buddies many a time. I think I might even be able to persuade her to lower her asking price."

While Kirby beamed at the announcement, his wife shot daggers at Vicki.

CHAPTER 7

Leaving Vicki, Kirby, and Elaine to debate the pros and cons of life in a small Georgia town, I returned home. Vicki, on the one hand, had painted a bucolic picture of church spires, potluck suppers, and kumbaya moments. Elaine, on the other hand, clearly wasn't interested in joining the community chorus or becoming a member of the garden club. Kirby had let the women carry on while he calmly strolled up and down the aisles, probably taking a mental inventory of the stock and cataloging changes he'd like to institute.

"Well, that was interesting, wasn't it?" I said aloud. Casey thumped his tail once or twice to show he was listening, but I could tell from his half-closed eyes that he was more interested in a nap than a discussion.

I thought about brewing a cup of tea but dismissed the idea. Tea made me think of Shirley. I wondered if she'd ever taken my advice and tried ginger tea for her bouts of indigestion. Had she received the shipment of ginger she'd ordered online? And what in blazes had caused her to show up dead — and naked — in McBride's fishing hole? I couldn't wrap my mind around the notion of her committing suicide in such a bizarre fashion. It simply didn't fit with the image she projected. Shirley was too vain. Too fastidious. No, there had to be another explanation.

Without conscious thought I opened the refrigerator and stared blankly at the contents much as the kids used to do when looking for "something good to eat." I'd once suggested — tongue in cheek — to put a television inside the fridge for their viewing pleasure. As I was about to close the door, my eyes settled on Reba Mae's take-and-go container of goulash. Lindsey might have stuck up her nose at the savory concoction of meat and paprika, but I knew who wouldn't have the same reaction. A quick phone call confirmed my suspicion.

Fifteen minutes later, I sailed into the reception area at the Brandywine Creek Police Department toting an insulated food carrier. I smiled a greeting at the plus-sized gal manning the front desk. "Hey, Precious, I brought the chief dinner as promised."

"Hey yourself." Precious Blessing's round, dark face lit up with her trademark megawatt grin. "Boss has been livin' on nothin' but black coffee all day. Maybe a good meal will cure a bad case of the funk. The man's ornery as a bear with a sore paw."

"That bad, is it?"

"Worse." She nodded, causing the colorful beads woven into her braids to clack together. "Mayor Hemmings been houndin' him all the live-long day. Refuses to give the chief a minute's peace. Mayor's mutterin' about callin' a town council meetin'. Complainin' it's been nothin' but one murder after another since the chief took office. To hear hizzoner talk, you'd think Chief was Jack the Ripper come back to life."

I switched the food carrier from one hand to the other. "Shirley's death is all people want to talk about. Most seem to think it was a suicide."

"I've heard the rumblin' and grumblin'. If Miz Randolph's dyin' turns to be self-inflicted or accidental, folks are still gonna point the blame at the chief." Precious applied a stapler to a stack of papers with the single-mindedness of a carpenter with a nail gun.

"Given time, people will find other things to gossip about. Shirley's death will be all but forgotten." Who was I trying to convince? Precious or myself?

"Folks are dang fools if they think a fine, upstandin' gentleman like the chief had anythin' to do with that woman's death. Tongues are waggin' all because they had dinner a few times. Folks gotta eat, don't they? Don't matter if they're the chief of police or a hotshot real estate lady, they still gotta eat."

Precious glanced down at the switchboard, then motioned in the direction of her boss's office. "Chief finished his call. Go on in. You know the way."

I knew the way all right. Didn't need a GPS. In fact, I'd been there often enough that I could find McBride's office during a blackout. My tentative knock was answered by a gruff, "What is it this time?"

"Food delivery." Cracking open the door, I extended the hand with the food carrier. "Someone call for takeout?"

"What the . . . ?"

"Even grumpy, beleaguered police chiefs need sustenance," I admonished, undeterred by his ill humor. "Unless you're a teenage girl dieting to fit into her prom dress, no one can refuse Reba Mae's scrumptious Hungarian goulash."

McBride gestured at his desk, which was

piled high with folders and stacks of reports. "Can't you see I'm busy? I don't have time to socialize."

"This isn't a social call. Think of this as meals on wheels." I looked around for a place to set my offering. "The goulash comes loaded with carbohydrates, guaranteed to boost your energy and increase your waistline. Man can't live on black coffee alone."

Climbing to his feet, he reluctantly cleared a space on his cluttered desk. "You're starting to sound like Precious."

"Don't blame Precious," I said, unpacking the contents of the carrier. "I know you well enough to be aware of your bad habits."

"Sweetheart," he drawled, "I've got bad habits you've never heard of."

"Really?" The idea intrigued me more than it should have.

"Yeah, really." He chuckled watching my face flush, the curse of being a redhead.

I concentrated on removing an aluminum foil–covered dish without spilling. I added a napkin, silverware, along with a dinner roll and small slice of carrot cake I'd scavenged from my freezer.

"You shouldn't have to gone to all the bother — but I'm glad you did." Picking up a fork, he peeled back the foil and dug in as though he hadn't eaten for days.

"No bother. They're only leftovers." I took one of the two chairs reserved for visitors opposite his desk. He wolfed down the meal like he did most things, with economy and efficiency. "You're actually doing me a favor by polishing off the goulash. I should thank you for removing temptation and preserving my girlish figure."

He broke off a piece of the roll. "Nothing wrong with your figure from what I've seen."

"What?" I said with a laugh. "Was that a compliment? That's hardly your style, McBride. What's this world coming to?"

"To hell in a handbasket if you want my opinion." He used the rest of his dinner roll to mop up what was left of the sauce.

"Made a fresh pot." Precious bumped the door wider with one hip. "Coffee oughta go mighty good with that slice of carrot cake sittin' there." She set a steaming mug of coffee in front of each of us, then, after giving me a broad wink, departed.

"Share it with you," McBride offered. When I indicated I wasn't interested in his dessert, he dove into the cake with gusto. When there was nothing left except a smear of icing, he pushed the plate aside. "Care to clue me in as to the real reason behind your visit? I suspect there's an ulterior motive other than trying to fatten me up with home cooking."

I feigned innocence. "A suspicious mind must be a job requirement for a cop."

"Yep." He smiled at me over the rim of his coffee mug, treating me to a glimpse of the elusive dimple in his right cheek. "Ranks right up there next to a fondness for Krispy Kremes. Now tell me what's really on your mind?"

"I didn't think my motives were so transparent." I blew on my coffee, stalling for time, trying to organize my thoughts. "I'm sure even barricaded behind your desk with Precious and Dorinda as guard dogs," I said referring to the daytime and afternoon dispatchers, "you must be aware of the rumors circulating."

McBride's expression turned glum. "I'd have to be comatose not to be. Right or wrong, folks will think what they want. Left to their own devices, they'll draw their own conclusions."

My gaze caught his and suddenly I knew with clarity why I'd come. "I wanted to reiterate that I don't believe you had any-thing — even remotely — to do with Shir-ley's death."

"Thanks," he said. "Nice to know."

I couldn't tell by his dry tone if he was

being sincere or sincerely sarcastic, so I forged ahead. "I've given Shirley's death a great deal of thought and ruled out suicide as a possibility."

McBride arched a brow and studied me. "Mind explaining to this simple country boy how you reached your conclusion?"

I leaned forward in my chair, hands around my coffee mug. "Shirley was a bit of a narcissist. She never stepped foot in public looking less than runway perfect. Hair, makeup, wardrobe. The whole ball of wax. If she'd had any say in the matter, she wouldn't have been caught buck naked and facedown in your fishing hole."

McBride nodded, whether in agreement or because of a crick in his neck I didn't know. "I think your supposition would be ruled insufficient evidence in a court of law."

"Think about it, McBride. You knew Shirley better than I did. Er, what I meant was . . ."

"No need to backpedal!" he growled. "I know what you meant."

"I didn't mean to imply —"

"Didn't think you did."

I placed my mug of coffee next to a mountain of paperwork on his desk. "If one rules out accident and suicide as the cause of death, that leaves homicide. In Shirley's line of work, she was bound to have a long list of satisfied — and dissatisfied — clients. When it came to business, she had a reputation for being a barracuda."

"And your point is?"

The gleam in his laser-sharp blues made me squirm. "I'm here to offer my assistance any way I can."

"I don't need your help!" McBride slammed his hand down on the desk for emphasis. "Remember, *I'm* the detective. A highly trained officer of the law, not some wannabe girl sleuth you read about during school vacations."

"Ouch!" I sprang to my feet and began collecting plates and silverware and stuffing them willy-nilly into the carrier. "Unless my memory is failing, you were more than happy for my assistance a time or two."

Pulling a stack of file folders closer, he flipped open the top one. "As I recall, your so-called *assistance* nearly got you killed twice — and me once."

Though it pained me to admit, I could hardly dispute the truth of what he'd said. Was he reminding me of the time he burst through my kitchen door like Eliot Ness swooping down on Al Capone and, thus, saving my life? Or was he referring to the time we both faced off an ex-mafioso in a dark street like Wyatt Earp and company at the O.K. Corral? So what was the big deal? The bullet wound he sustained had only been superficial. I pieced together my shredded pride before responding, "Like it or not, McBride, Spice It Up! has become information central. My customers like to talk, and I'm privy to a lot more than casual gossip. I already know the names of a couple persons who weren't fans of Shirley and who won't shed tears now that she's gone."

"All right, fine," he said, his tone laced with resignation. He made a show of picking up a pen and flipping to a page on a yellow legal pad.

His display of indifference, however, had come a millisecond too late. I knew the man better than he gave me credit for. I'd seen interest perk before he donned his cop mask, and I felt a perverse sense of satisfaction at making him wait for my answer. Slowly, I zipped the carrier shut, then centered it on the only available space on McBride's desk.

"Piper," McBride purred like a tiger about to pounce, "do I have to charge you with withholding information or are you going to tell me?"

"Write down Vicki Lamont's name. Vicki is . . . was . . . furious with Shirley for stealing a hefty commission right from under her nose. Vicki's been struggling to make ends meet ever since her divorce, when Kenny hid his assets in the Caymans. In my humble opinion, Vicki would qualify as a person of interest."

" 'Humble' isn't exactly how I'd describe your opinion," McBride mumbled under his breath.

I ignored his snarky comment. "Have you met the Dixons? Kirby and Elaine?"

"No, should I have?"

"The Dixons are the couple from New York — Syracuse, to be exact — who are considering making an offer on Gray's Hardware. Kirby is keen on the notion, but his wife, Elaine, is at the opposite end of the spectrum. From what I've seen, the woman has a mean temper. She's convinced that with Shirley out of the picture Kirby might change his mind about the deal. She's not wild about living in a town without a fitness center."

"That it?"

"For now. I promise I'll keep you in the loop if I learn anything else."

I was about to pick up the carrier and leave when a fax machine atop a file cabinet sputtered to life. Next thing I knew it shot out a sheet of paper like a chunk of hot dog during a Heimlich maneuver. Not giving it a second thought, I stooped to retrieve the paper, which had landed at my feet. The bold heading read: **GEORGIA BUREAU OF INVESTIGATION**. But it wasn't the heading that captured my interest.

"Piper . . . ?"

I blocked out the sound of McBride's voice as I scanned the report, my attention riveted on the concluding paragraph: *No water found in lungs. Cause of death undetermined pending further investigation.*

Wordlessly, I handed the medical examiner's preliminary summary to McBride. "If Shirley didn't drown, what happened to her?"

A lengthy silence, sticky as a spider's web, spun out between us giving me the answer.

CHAPTER 8

When would I learn? I should know better than to drink high-octane coffee late at night. And, if I did drink coffee, I needed to choose the decaffeinated variety rather than the heavy-duty stuff McBride favored. As a result, I hadn't slept well and woke up groggy and grouchy from a poor night's rest. After taking Casey for his morning walk, I filled his bowls with food and water, then left him to snooze while I opened for business.

My first order of the day was to brew a pot of coffee. Nothing like the hair of the dog that bit you, as my grandfather used to say as he downed a shot of whiskey the morning after an all-night poker game. I hoped a slug of caffeine would have the same effect on me as Jack Daniel's did for him.

While waiting for the coffee to brew, I took a feather duster from beneath the counter and made the rounds of the shelves. I dusted, rearranged a display of Asian spices, and made a mental note of which spices to reorder. My chore finished, I filled my coffee cup to the brim and retreated to the counter, where I started a list of ideas to entice customers to step out of their comfort zone and experiment with the unusual and unfamiliar. Spring meant Easter dinners, planting container gardens and window boxes, lighter meals, and spending more time outdoors. I also needed to cement plans to celebrate Spice It Up!'s first anniversary.

I was sorting through my stash of foodzines on the lookout for brightly colored photos with mouthwatering recipes when Dottie Hemmings arrived accompanied by Jolene Tucker, wife of Sergeant Beau Tucker.

I summoned a tired smile. "Hey, Dottie. Hey, Jolene. What can I do for you ladies?"

Attractive rather than pretty, Jolene, a woman her late thirties, wore her streaked ash-brown hair parted in the center, which made her round face seem all the rounder. Her brows grew thick and dark over shrewd brown eyes. She'd given me the cold shoulder ever since I unintentionally caused her hubby — aka Sergeant Blabbermouth — to be put on probation for divulging information in an ongoing case.

"Jolene wants some of your Italian seasoning," Dottie volunteered. "Gerilee swears it's way better than the brand sold at Piggly Wiggly."

"I'm making Beau's favorite for dinner tonight. Baked mostaccioli," Jolene offered, sounding unusually friendly. Apparently she was ready to bury the hatchet and let bygones be bygones.

"Sure thing." I walked over to a row of freestanding shelves and, after a nanosecond's debate, selected the larger of the two sizes I stocked. "This is a favorite of mine," I explained, handing it to her. "It's a blend of five different herbs. Use some next time you make oven-roasted red potatoes. Drizzle on a little extra virgin olive oil, mince a clove or two of garlic, sprinkle on some Italian seasoning, then bake. Your family will love them."

"Thanks, I'll give that a try," Jolene said, digging through her purse for her wallet and credit card. "Beau and the boys — typical men — are partial to roasted potatoes."

"What about you, Dottie?" I asked. "Anything you need?"

"For heaven's sake, no." Dottie giggled. "You know I'm not much of a cook. Besides, I don't plan on spending much time in the kitchen in the next few weeks."

I swiped Jolene's credit card through the machine. "Why is that? Going somewhere?"

The two women exchanged conspiratorial looks but ignored my question.

"Joey's so excited about prom. I suppose your Lindsey is, too," Jolene said, changing the subject. Her oldest son and my daughter had been classmates since kindergarten and were now high school seniors.

"Right now Lindsey's on pins and needles waiting to hear from colleges." I slid the credit card receipt along with a pen across the counter for Jolene's signature. "Does Joey know what he wants to do after graduation?"

"His daddy's been trying to talk him into following in his footsteps and joining the police force once he turns twenty-one, but Joey has other ideas. He's got it in his head to join the air force. You know how kids are."

"Piper's girl has changed her mind so many times, it makes my head spin," Dottie said with irritating smugness.

I bagged the Italian seasoning and handed it to Jolene. "Lindsey plans to take the prerequisites for a liberal arts degree — English, math, life sciences, and such — until she makes up her mind about a career."

"Joey said her SAT scores even surprised the teachers."

"Surprised herself most of all," I said.

Dottie clucked her tongue. "And here I always thought your son was the brains of the family. Can't make Chad very happy knowing his baby sister, the social butterfly, outdid him."

"Chad was a little put out at the news," I admitted. "He insists it must've been a computer glitch."

"That's siblings for you," Dottie said, patting her blond beehive.

"A cute little place you have here," Jolene commented, taking a good look around. "Too bad you don't carry fresh herbs. Dried are okay, but fresh are better."

"What a great idea, Jolene!" Instantly a vision of clay pots sprouting basil, thyme, oregano, parsley, and chives popped into mind. The front of my shop got plenty of sunlight. It would be a perfect location to grow herbs. "It's definitely worth considering. I just might give your suggestion a try."

Jolene grimaced when she glanced at her watch. "I've got to run. Mary Beth called a meeting for the heads of various prom committees. I'm in charge of refreshments."

"And I've got packing to finish." Dottie gave me a merry wave. "Toodle-oo."

Packing? Was Dottie planning a trip? Was that what she meant by not spending time in the kitchen? Before I could arrive at a conclusion CJ sauntered into my shop as though he owned the place. "Hiya, Scooter."

I cringed at the nickname I long ago thought charming but now loathed. My ex-husband had once been an idealistic young attorney, but somewhere along the way he'd strayed off course. Now, instead of defending petty thieves and miscreants, he'd discovered suing big-box stores and conglomerates far more lucrative. "No fall too big, no fall too small" was his slogan.

"What's the occasion, CJ?" I asked, admiring the expert tailoring of his navy blue suit, crisp white shirt, and rep tie. His blond hair, the same shade as on a box of Clairol's Nice 'n Easy, had been recently cut and styled.

"Got a little time to kill before a big meetin' so thought I'd stop by. Say hello."

I slid Jolene's credit card receipt into a drawer of my antique cash register. "Lindsey mentioned Amber's shopping for a new wardrobe for your trip abroad."

"Nothin' that girl loves more than a mall." He chuckled. "Unless, of course, it's me."

TMI! I decided to be charitable and cut the man some slack. After all, the couple were still newlyweds, having been married

105

over the Christmas holidays in a lavish destination wedding in the Caribbean.

"Heard from our son recently?" he asked.

Something in CJ's tone put me on high alert. "No," I said slowly. "Why do you ask?"

"Apparently our boy is in love. He and I had a long talk last night — man-to-man."

"I hope that doesn't mean he came to you for relationship advice." The thought struck fear in my heart. Based on personal experience, I didn't view CJ as a role model for the lovelorn.

CJ smiled slyly. "Aren't you interested in hearing about his girlfriend?"

"Naturally I'm interested. Just surprised is all." To the best of my knowledge, Chad has never had a serious relationship. His studies always took priority.

"The girl's from France. Her parents sent her here to immerse herself in our culture."

"Well, let's hope she doesn't return home speaking French with a Southern accent," I said. "I hope Chad's love interest won't interfere with the goals he's set for himself."

"Now, now, Scooter, don't start actin' like a mother hen," CJ warned. "Chad's not a kid anymore. He's got a good head on his shoulders."

"I suppose," I agreed, albeit reluctantly, but couldn't help worry. Logic often flew out the window when love — especially young love — flew in.

CJ peered at his watch, a Rolex I'd once given him for an anniversary gift in exchange for a wilted bouquet of roses. "Sorry," he said. "Better get a move on. Don't want to be late."

After he left and the shop was quiet again, I halfheartedly resumed flipping through back issues of *Southern Living, Cooking Light,* and the *Food Network Magazine* but couldn't seem to concentrate. It had been a strange morning. Jolene Tucker had been congenial. Dottie had alluded to a mystery trip she might be taking — and Dottie wasn't the sort who kept secrets. What entered her head came out her mouth. Then, last but by no means least, CJ, who normally liked to boast about his lawyerly prowess, hadn't divulged a clue about his "big" meeting. My intuition told me something was up. And what was all that about Chad having a girlfriend?

When Reba Mae called to say she'd had a cancellation and would I care to join her for an alfresco lunch in the town square, I couldn't agree quickly enough.

It was warm and sunny, a beautiful spring day for an impromptu picnic. Wispy clouds drifted lazily across the sky while wrens flitted in and out of the newly leafed boughs of the willow oaks. A bank of azalea bushes was weighed down with a profusion of pink blooms. I watched a gray squirrel scamper across the grass in search of nuts. From my vantage point on a wrought-iron bench, I could see the stately courthouse that anchored one end of the square. Behind me, at the opposite end, stood the Brandywine Creek Opera House.

"Hey, girlfriend. Lunch has arrived." Reba Mae settled down beside me and opened the paper sack she carried. "Hope I didn't keep you waitin'. Danny at the Pizza Palace had to show me a raft of pictures he'd taken of the twins."

I took the sub she offered me, popped open the tab of a diet soda, and tried to relax.

"My last client said the town council was meetin' in a closed session," Reba Mae said as she unwrapped her sandwich. "Think they're gonna approve plans for the new addition at the library?"

"I hardly think that calls for secrecy." I took a bite of my sub and washed it down with a swallow of soda.

"Maybe the council is votin' on a permanent replacement for Maybelle over at the chamber of commerce. Seein' how she and

Tex got hitched, she plans on makin' San Antonio her permanent residence when they're not on the barbecue circuit."

"Perhaps. . . ." I took another bite of my sub, analyzing the flavors in the owner's special sauce. Oregano, basil, and thyme for sure. But what else? Fennel? Tarragon?

"Or" — Reba Mae swung one long leg over the other — "maybe they're decidin' which plumber oughta get the contract for the public washroom down by the football field."

I happened to look toward the courthouse in time to see a group of men parade down the broad front steps. Even at a distance I could see CJ's ear-to-ear grin as he pumped the hand of Maxwell Ames, his new father-in-law. An older-model black Lincoln appeared from around the corner and drew up in front of the courthouse. A frail elderly man with a cane slowly tottered down the handicap ramp, then climbed inside the car and was driven away.

"Gracious!" Reba Mae exclaimed, following the direction of my gaze. "That's Brig Abernathy. Wonder what brought him out. These days he rarely leaves that big ol' house of his."

Sergeant Beau Tucker and McBride were the last to exit. Head down, McBride turned toward the police department. Beau, however, moved in the opposite direction, cutting across the square toward Creekside Realty.

"Hey, Beau!" Reba Mae called as he was about to pass the bench where we were sitting. "What's up?"

"Hey, ladies." He smiled and nodded. "Nice day for a picnic."

"Where you off to? Care to sit a spell?" Reba Mae patted a spot next to her.

"Can't, busy," he said. "I'm on my way to take down the crime scene tape Chief had me string at the real estate office. The place underwent a thorough search, but we came up empty-handed. Council agreed with Mr. Abernathy there's no sense keeping a local business closed for no good reason when it could be making money."

I wrapped up what was left of my sandwich and placed it in the sack. "What else did the council agree on?"

Beau avoided looking directly at me. "McBride's been placed on suspension until Shirley Randolph's case is resolved. Council says it was conflict of interest — seeing as how the body was found on his property and all."

"Whoo-ee!" Reba Mae whistled while I sat in stunned silence.

"The mayor ordered McBride to hand over his badge and service weapon," Beau continued. "I've been appointed interim chief."

Reba Mae polished off the last of her soda. "Bet that didn't go over with Wyatt."

"Like a fart in church — 'scuse the expression. McBride's packin' his stuff even as we speak." Beau swaggered off wearing a self-satisfied smile.

CHAPTER 9

It wasn't long before I learned that Beau Tucker's announcement wasn't the only surprise in store for me that afternoon.

Amber Leigh Ames-Prescott strolled into Spice It Up! shortly before Lindsey was to return from school. I'd just finished waiting on a group of senior citizens who were touring small towns listed as "off the beaten path" destinations. Fortunately, all the ladies loved to cook and excelled at outdoing one another at potluck suppers. As a result, my cash register warbled a happy tune. Cumin, chervil, and turmeric were among the spices that captured their imaginations.

"Hey there, Piper," Amber said as she bestowed her signature toothy grin upon me.

The willowy brunette was dressed in a short skirt that showcased her mile-long legs and a waist-length denim jacket studded with rhinestones. On anyone else the combination might look tacky, but somehow the former beauty queen managed to carry it off with style.

"Hi, Amber. Don't tell me you actually intend to cook a meal instead of calling for reservations?"

"Don't be silly. CJ knew when he married me that I'm not one to slave over a hot stove when I could be spending my time on hair and makeup."

"What was I thinking?" I bopped myself in the head with the heel of my hand. "Then why are you here?"

"Did Lindsey forget to tell you I was takin' her shoppin' tonight?"

Had she told me? "Um, she might have, but I've been a bit preoccupied lately."

"I know what you mean," Amber commiserated. "Our trip to Europe is months away, but it's all I can think about. For the life of me, I don't know how Melly managed to pull off both a wedding *and* a trip abroad. At her age, you'd think either one of them would've been enough to do the ol' gal in."

"Don't let Melly hear you say that. She's very sensitive about her age." I folded my arms across my chest and studied her. "Do me a favor, Amber, and refresh my memory.

113

What exactly is it you and Lindsey are shopping for?"

"Shoes, darlin'. Your girl needs an amazin' pair of heels to wear for prom. I happen to know a store in Augusta that sells knockoff designer shoes for a fraction of the cost. And as a former beauty queen," she simpered, "I can get them at an even greater discount."

I suppose I should feel grateful they were only shoe shopping. Last year Amber and Lindsey had conspired against my choice of a prom dress and instead picked a gown that exposed far more flesh than I deemed appropriate for a teen. Shoes seemed a safer route. "Fine," I said, "Lindsey ought to be home any minute."

"S'pose you heard the news about the Hemmings?"

"No, what about them?"

"Dottie and Harvey are tradin' in Brandywine Creek for The Villages in Florida. They're leavin' bright and early tomorrow mornin' for an extended visit."

So that's why Dottie acted so secretive. "How long do they plan on being gone?"

"Indefinitely. From what I gather, Harvey's had it up to his eyeballs with all the negative publicity this town's gettin'. He doesn't want to be caught in the spotlight if

114

rumor gets around about another murder. At this rate, he's worried the crime rate will surpass Detroit's."

"Detroit always gets a bad rap." I bristled at the mention of my hometown, a city where I was born and raised. Various cousins kept me up to speed on all the changes taking place there. "People tend to overlook the positive changes going on downtown. Projects like the RiverWalk, Belle Isle, and Campus Martius Park with its outdoor venue for live performances. And," I said, "what about the sports teams? The Tigers, Red Wings, Pistons, and Lions. Detroit has a lot to offer."

"Whatever." Amber dismissed my staunch support of the Motor City with a careless wave of her hand. "Dottie agrees with Harvey that they need a change of scenery, a break from the stress. Their friends rave about The Villages. Said people drive around all day in customized golf carts and line-dance all night."

"In my estimation, golf carts and line dancing are overrated." I moved toward the computer intending to check inventory on my point-of-sale software. I'd need to stock plenty of paprika — both sweet and smoky — when Reba Mae demonstrated her Hungarian goulash.

"Hi, Mom," Lindsey said as she shoved open the door. "Hey, Amber."

At hearing her voice, Casey woke from his nap in the storeroom and ran out to greet her, his toenails making happy clicking sounds on the heart pine floor. Amber shied away from the little dog as though fearful he might leap on her in a bid for attention.

Lindsey slung her backpack to the floor next to the counter and stooped to ruffle the little dog's fur, sending him into a tail-wagging frenzy. "Hey, Mom," she said, looking up at me, "did you hear about Daddy? All the kids were talking about it at lunch."

What has CJ gone and done now? I wondered. "I'm afraid not," I said. "Care to clue me in?"

"Daddy's the new mayor," Lindsey informed me proudly.

The news stopped me in my tracks. I turned to Amber for confirmation. "Is that true?"

Amber's Cheshire cat grin gave me my answer.

I tucked a stray curl behind one ear. "When did all this happen?"

"My daddy happens to be chairman of the town council," Amber explained. "He made a motion at the meetin' after Harvey's announcement. Daddy felt CJ was the best

116

qualified for the job. Our bein' married had nothin' to do with his decision."

"Of course not," I scoffed. That explained why CJ was wearing his Sunday-go-to-meeting clothes when he stopped by this morning. He knew all along the council would recommend him as Harvey's replacement. And he must have been secretly overjoyed that Wyatt McBride would be suspended as chief of police. CJ and McBride had a history dating back to high school. He'd been opposed to McBride's hiring from the very beginning.

Amber fished a small leather cosmetics case from her Marc Jacobs bag and snapped it open. "Technically, CJ is only the acting mayor — until the next election, that is, when he officially throws his hat in the ring. CJ has aspirations for a political career on a grander scale" — she inspected her reflection in the small mirror — "but everyone has to start somewhere."

"Mom," Lindsey said, "sorry, but I forgot to tell you last night that Amber and I were going shopping for prom shoes. Would you mind taking Casey for his run in the park?"

"No problem, sweetie."

"Great." Amber dropped her compact into her purse, then draped an arm around Lindsey's shoulder. "Let's go, hon. I saw

117

these fabulous shoes advertised. . . ?"

I'd just placed an order with my supplier on the West Coast when I heard the throaty roar of a motorcycle, followed by a blessed silence when the rider cut the engine. A minute later, Hoyt, my biker friend, entered Spice It Up! Dressed in black from his shiny helmet, heavy leather jacket, and chaps down to his sturdy boots, he resembled a shorter, chubbier, friendlier version of Darth Vader. Who would've guessed when we'd first met that we'd become friends? Strange, the curve balls life throws at us.

"Hey there." He grinned, removing his helmet as he came forward. "How's my favorite spice girl holdin' up these days?"

"Fine, Hoyt. What can I help you with today?"

Hoyt unzipped one of the numerous pockets of his jacket and pulled out a neatly printed list. "Gonna have my biker club buddies over for a barbecue now that the weather's turned nice. But not goin' to be the typical barbecue chicken like they're expectin'," he chuckled.

When it came to experimenting with new recipes, Hoyt dove in headfirst. I took the list he handed me and read off the items, " 'Coriander, fenugreek, ginger, garam masala.' "

He gave me a sheepish smile. "I know when it comes to garam masala most foodies make their own, but, in the interest of savin' time, I thought you might carry some already made."

"Remember Doug Winters, the vet who owned Pets 'R People before moving back to Chicago?" At Hoyt's nod, I went on, "Well, before he left, Doug gave me his formula for garam masala, which is the special blend I sell in my shop."

"Sounds perfect."

I took a small wicker basket from beside the register and filled it with the spices Hoyt had listed. He trailed close behind, stopping here or there to examine a label on a jar or scan a recipe card. "What makes your barbecue chicken different?" I asked.

"It's Indian Tandoori style. Some folks might object to a more exotic dish than the typical barbecue-joint style they're accustomed to, so I'm just calling it barbecue chicken. Wait and see. It'll be love at first taste."

The last item I selected for Hoyt was a knobby ginger rhizome. I held it for a long moment before depositing it in the basket along with the other spices. The rhizome reminded me of Shirley's quest to remedy her upset stomach.

"Hoyt," I said as a thought occurred to me, "was Shirley Randolph your Realtor when you bought the old Cooper place?"

"She sure was. Best Realtor I ever dealt with, too, and I've dealt with my share." He dropped a jar of cumin into the basket. "Told Shirley what I wanted. A property with a few acres, maybe a pole barn. Said the house didn't need to be shipshape. Since I took an early retirement, I've got time on my hands and don't mind havin' some do-it-yourself projects."

I went to the counter where I began to tally his purchases. "You sound pleased with the place she found for you."

"Yes, ma'am." He reached into another zippered pocket and produced a wad of cash fastened with a gold money clip. "The woman really paid attention to my wish list, unlike other Realtors I've dealt with who pretend to listen but don't hear a word. Ask me, that's the quality that made her so successful. Funny thing" — he rubbed his jaw — "with everything that's happened, I nearly forgot that I ran into her in Savannah a couple weeks ago."

I made change from the fifty-dollar bill he'd peeled off. "When was this?" I hoped my voice didn't betray my blatant curiosity.

"Back on St. Patrick's Day. I drove down to see Savannah's annual St. Patrick's Day Parade. You know, don't you, that it's the second-largest one in the country?"

"And you saw Shirley at the parade?"

"Considerin' the streets were jammed with people, we were both viewin' the festivities from the same street corner. How's that for coincidence?" He tucked his change back into a pocket. "I went up to Shirley, asked if she was alone or with friends, but she mumbled some excuse and left in a rush. At first I wondered if she thought I was hitting on her. But, later, I got to thinking. I came to the conclusion she ran off because she didn't want me to see who she was with. Far be it from me to know what the woman was thinking."

I handed him the sack with his purchases. "Do you think she might've been having an affair?"

"None of my business if she was. Shirley was a fine-lookin' woman, so it wouldn't surprise me none. I asked her out to dinner after I first moved here, but she said, no offense, I wasn't her type."

"Did that upset you?"

He shrugged. "Nah. I'd already figured out that the lady was too high maintenance for my taste. I'm lookin' for the type of gal who'll hop on the back of my Harley and enjoy a spin down a country road."

After Hoyt left to confer with Pete Barker at Meat on Main about some drumsticks, I couldn't stop thinking about what he'd told me. If McBride had been the one Shirley was having an affair with — and I didn't believe he was — why the need for secrecy? Both of them were single.

Unless . . .?

Unless Shirley's companion *wasn't* unattached. What if the man was married? That would be a whole other kettle of fish.

And a whole new kettle of what-ifs.

CHAPTER 10

In the last hour, I'd regressed to being a sophomore in high school. "She who watches the clock will always be one of the hands." That had been my geometry teacher's favorite saying back in the day. Mr. Corrigan would repeat it each time he caught one of his students sneaking a peek at the clock over the blackboard.

Finally, I'd had enough clock-watching. If Melly were here, she'd have a conniption knowing I was closing shop fifteen minutes early. I almost glanced over my shoulder to see if she was watching but caught myself in time. *Ridiculous!* I chastised myself. Melly was thousands of miles away, probably sipping wine in Tuscany this very minute.

Casey perked up his ears at seeing me whip off my apron and stuff it under the counter, his expression hopeful.

"Sorry, pal," I told him. "Promise I'll take

you for a run soon. Just be patient a little longer."

Casey placed his head on his paws and gave me a reproachful look as I flipped the sign on the front door to closed. If he could talk, I was certain he'd tattle my transgression to Melly first chance he got.

Locking the door behind me, I forced myself to walk sedately toward Creekside Realty, a few doors down from Spice It Up! As I passed Gray's Hardware, I waved to Mavis and she waved back. She appeared to be unloading a shipment of herbs in tiny pots. I resolved to buy some soon for the container garden I planned.

I crossed my fingers Vicki Lamont hadn't decided to emulate my bad example by closing early. Other than the fact that Shirley Randolph was beautiful and successful, I didn't really know the woman very well. Vicki, until recently, had been a good friend of hers. From what I observed, their friendship had bonded even firmer when Shirley agreed to mentor Vicki in the real estate business.

I stood inside the threshold of Creekside Realty and took a moment to gaze around. The office hadn't changed much — same two utilitarian metal desks, same dented filing cabinets — since the day I'd signed my

John Henry to a pile of paperwork making me the proprietor of a building dating back to before Prohibition. Framed photos of listings covered walls painted a neutral shade. I spotted Vicki behind a desk inside a glassed-in cubicle, but she wasn't alone.

When she saw me, Vicki ceased her conversation with a slender young man I estimated to be in his mid-thirties. He looked familiar, yet I couldn't quite place him. I racked my brain to put a name with the angular face, high forehead, and slicked-back brown hair. Both he and Vicki watched me approach.

"You probably don't remember me," the man said, sticking out his hand, breaking the awkward silence. "Zach VanFleet, mortgage loan officer at Creekside Savings."

"Right, right." I returned the handshake. "Nice to see you again, Zach." Our previous meeting had been brief, but I'd come away with the impression he was efficient and personable, a young man on his way up. Rather than take out a mortgage, however, I'd decided to purchase the building destined to be my home as well as my place of business outright with money I'd received in my divorce settlement. At least that way if Spice It Up! failed, I'd still have a roof over my head.

Vicki gave me a tight-lipped smile. "Zach knows I'm new to all of this. He was kind enough to stop by and offer his assistance."

"That's very thoughtful of you, Zach."

"Shirley had several mortgages pending, so I wanted to give Vicki an update since she'll be taking over the office in Shirley's . . . absence."

"In Shirley's absence" sounded ever so much more civilized than saying *after Shirley was found naked and dead in a fishing hole.* "I imagine you and Shirley must have worked closely together."

"Yes, we did, and I'll miss her." He slid his hands into the trouser pockets of his gray business suit, his expression somber.

My mental gears spun into action. "Worked closely together" was subject to a variety of interpretations. Exactly how close was "closely"? Was Zach VanFleet the mystery lover Hoyt suspected Shirley was with in Savannah? While Zach seemed younger than Shirley, I doubted a trivial detail such as age would have prevented her from pursuing a man to whom she was attracted. I tried to recall if he'd been wearing a wedding ring, but with no success. Zach's position as loan officer might have been enough cause for discretion. Or, perhaps, I was subject to regard every man beyond puberty as Shirley's potential love interest.

"Shirley lived and breathed buying and selling property," Zach went on. "She was the heart and soul of this company."

I nodded in silent tribute to Shirley's work ethic and noted her brass nameplate was still on the desk Vicki now occupied. An oversight, which in all probability would soon be rectified.

"I hope, Zach, people don't expect me to put in the same amount of hours as Shirley did." Vicki fidgeted with a stack of papers in front of her. "There's more to life than working 24/7. My golf handicap would suffer, and I'd have to drop out of my mixed doubles league."

"Shirley viewed her work not as a job but as a career." I regretted the words the instant they popped out of my mouth. If looks could kill, I'd be sprawled on the floor deader 'n a skunk. Before now Vicki had never held a job, and she resented the fact that her ex-husband had been miserly in the divorce, causing her to seek employment for the first time in her pampered existence.

"Ah, um . . . ." Zach edged toward the door. "Guess I'd better head back to the bank. I have a few loose ends to tie up before I call it a day. If you have any questions, Vicki, don't hesitate to call me."

He beat a hasty retreat.

"He seems quite nice," I said at last.

"He is," Vicki agreed. "It's a relief to have someone with his expertise to rely on in case I run into problems. I've got mounds of files and documents to review to bring me up to speed that I hardly know where to start. So, Piper, unless you're here on business . . . ."

I refused to take the not-so-subtle hint and leave. I'd been kicked out of better places in my lifetime. "I realize how busy you must be" — I mustered a sympathetic smile — "but I started wondering. Since you and Shirley were friends, do you know if she had a special someone in her life?"

Vicki frowned. "Why do you want to know?"

I shrugged. "There's bound to be a memorial service as soon as the medical examiner releases her body. I thought maybe there was someone who ought to be notified. Perhaps a person who might not be aware of what happened. Was Shirley romantically involved with anyone?"

"Other than Wyatt McBride, you mean?" Vicki picked up a ballpoint with the Creekside Realty logo and started clicking it. "I can't recall Shirley mentioning a boyfriend. Her life revolved around work. It was all she ever talked about — that and the big old monstrosity she planned to renovate."

"Doesn't sound like much of a life."

Click, click, click went Vicki's ballpoint until I wanted to snatch it out of her hand. "I can't wait to get out of here tonight," she complained. "All I want is a nice, hot bath and cold glass of wine."

"What's keeping you?" I asked. "Most places in town have already closed for the day."

"I still have an appointment with a newcomer who's interested in buying a single-family home in or around Brandywine Creek. He's due any minute. Then," she said, heaving a sigh worthy of Joan of Arc, "when we're done, Ned Feeney is coming to replace the lock on the back door."

"Good idea," I said. "It's probably wise to change the locks now that you're the one in charge. No telling how many people might have keys."

"That's not the reason." Vicki tucked a loose strand of hair back into her low ponytail.

I had half turned to go but turned back. "Why? What happened?"

"Nothing serious, but it has me on edge. When I arrived at the office this afternoon, my key wouldn't turn in the lock on the back door. That's when I noticed it had been jimmied. Probably kids with too much time on their hands getting into mischief."

"Was anything missing?"

"Not that I'm aware of," Vicki said, frowning. "At first I thought Shirley's computer might've been stolen; then I remembered she never let it out of her sight. She always took it home with her. It was an expensive top-of-the-line MacBook. Called it her lifeline."

"Did you report this to the police?"

"Naturally!" she snapped. "I'm not an idiot. Beau said not to worry. Being as how nothing was missing, there was no rush. Said he'd send an officer over tomorrow or the next day to take a report."

Time's they are a-changin', as Bob Dylan sang. With McBride out of the picture and Beau Tucker in charge, the police department was already falling into bad habits. "Would you feel better if I stuck around until your client arrived?"

"Thanks, Piper, but he just walked in."

I looked over my shoulder as Vicki pushed herself to her feet to greet him. I recognized the new arrival as Colin Flynn, the stranger who had stopped into my shop on Monday to inquire about Shirley. "Mr. Flynn," I said. "I thought you might've become discouraged and decided to pursue your search for real estate someplace with less notoriety."

"Hello again, Mrs. Prescott," he said. "As you can tell, I took you and your friend up on the advice to contact Ms. Lamont. And please, call me Colin."

I watched as Colin and Vicki shook hands and formerly introduced themselves.

Vicki's demeanor had noticeably brightened with the prospect of a commission. "I've got several properties lined up to show you. I hope you'll find one of them to your liking. If not, I'll keep at it until we find exactly what you're looking for."

"I'm not one to give up easily. I've been told I'm tenacious." Colin smiled, but the smile didn't reach his eyes. "People tell me it's one of my most outstanding characteristics."

"Then let's not waste any more time." Vicki lowered herself into her chair, her movements stiff, cautious, and took a file folder out of a drawer, and opened it. "I thought we'd start with these homes. . . ."

Both Colin and Vicki bent their heads over an array of photos Vicki spread across her desk while she rattled off such information as square footage, number of bedrooms, and carpeting versus hardwood floors. Neither paid any attention as I quietly exited Creekside Realty.

I walked home slowly. It was the dinner hour in Brandywine Creek. My adopted hometown was postcard pretty, peaceful, and quaint. A marble statue of a Confederate soldier, rifle in hand, guarded the town square with its crushed-shell pathways and wrought-iron benches. Businesses had all closed for the day. Main Street was virtually deserted except for a compact car sporting a sticker from a rental agency that I assumed belonged to Colin Flynn. Vicki must have parked her vehicle behind the office, which was how she'd discovered the lock had been jimmied on the back door. I hoped the incident wasn't a sign of things to come. The town didn't need to be besieged with a rash of break-ins. It had enough to contend with as it was.

But what if it hadn't been a random burglary? What if Creekside Realty had been targeted? Could the break-in be related in any way to Shirley's death? Again, I had an uneasy feeling about Colin Flynn. There was something about him that struck me as odd. Almost as though he was hiding his real self behind a fade-into-the-woodwork façade.

Crazy? Maybe, yet I couldn't dismiss the notion.

CHAPTER 11

Upon my return to Spice It Up!, I was met with an enthusiastic greeting from Casey. My furry friend bounced up and down like a yo-yo and multitasked by wagging and barking. He clearly telegraphed the fact that he had been cooped up all day and was ready to romp.

"Well, boy, consider your wish granted." I snapped on his leash, grabbed my purse as an afterthought, and headed out. I didn't expect Lindsey home from her scouting expedition for the most amazing pair of shoes on the planet until late. And I wasn't keen on a solitary dinner in a too-quiet apartment. I wanted to coax Reba Mae into sharing a pizza with me but remembered she planned to visit her aunt Ida, who was convalescing from knee surgery.

Casey and I took off at a brisk pace — too slow for jogging, too fast for a walk — which suited us fine and dandy. While I was jog-walking, my mind replayed the events of the day. First off, the town council met in a special session. As a result, McBride was jobless — placed on indefinite suspension. Then, according to Lindsey, CJ had been named interim mayor, giving Amber even more reason to gloat. Next, Hoyt offhandedly reported seeing Shirley at the St. Patrick's Day Parade in Savannah and mentioned her strange behavior. No reason for Shirley to act secretive if she had nothing to hide. So the question was, what — or whom — was she hiding? If she had been in Savannah with a lover, why keep his identity secret unless there was a good reason? Last, but not least, an unknown person, or persons, had attempted to break into the real estate office, but nothing was missing. That didn't make sense — unless they were looking for something specific but couldn't find it and left empty-handed and disappointed.

I rounded a corner of Main Street and turned down Lincoln Street. Though Shirley's death hadn't been *officially* termed a homicide, it was simply a matter of time before that changed. After all, I'd seen the fax from the medical examiner's office with my own eyes: *No water found in lungs.* My female intuition ruled out suicide. No way, Jose, would a woman as savvy as Shirley buy a big old house in the historic district, plan to spend a bundle on renovations, then jump into a frigid pond and drown herself!

But if her death was not suicide, who wanted her dead? I was positive McBride wasn't the guilty party, but who — and when? There were still too many unknowns. Some solid information would be useful, especially time of death. McBride had given his guesstimate, but knowing time of death for certain would be an invaluable way to eliminate suspects once I made my persons of interest list. All I'd have to do was find out who had an alibi and — more important — who didn't. Easy peasy.

Without conscious thought, I found myself in front of the Brandywine Creek Police Department. Karma? Far be it from me to question the ways of the universe.

"Hey, Precious," I said, grinning at my favorite dispatcher. Judging from the smell of garlic and her half-finished plate of pasta, I knew I'd caught Precious in the middle of her dinner.

Casey, the model of obedience, sat at my feet.

"Hey yourself," she returned. "How can I help you?"

"Thought as long as I was in the neighborhood I'd drop in and see if Sergeant Tucker might be able to answer a question or two." Beau Tucker might be interim chief of police, but he hadn't earned the nickname Sergeant Blabbermouth because of his discretion.

"Sorry, sugar, but Sarge already clocked out for the day."

"Oh," I said, disappointed. It hadn't occurred to me Beau might not be there. McBride worked long hours, never just nine to five. Especially when a homicide needed solving.

Precious wiped her fingers on a paper napkin. "Sergeant Tucker — he's insistin' on bein' called Chief, but I keeps forgettin' — said his wife fixed mostaccioli for dinner and he didn't dare be late. Sounded so good, I splurged and ordered me some from Antonio's. Had Ned Feeney deliver it."

My stomach gurgled in response, a reminder I hadn't eaten yet. "I'd hoped Beau could clear up a few details for me about Shirley's death. Kind of set my mind at ease."

"Things? What sort of things?"

I jumped at the sound of Officer Gary Moyer's voice coming from a hallway behind the information desk that led to a series of small offices.

Moyer scowled when he saw me. Scowled,

not frowned. There is a difference, I know. Scowling involves the entire face, brow to jowl, and this was a scowl if ever there was one. "What brings you here, Mrs. Prescott?"

"Officer Moyer," I said, recovering from my initial surprise. Moyer was a man of few words and fewer smiles. According to Mc-Bride, Moyer had served two tours with the army in Afghanistan. His rigid posture and buzz cut were also clues he was ex-military. "I, um, wondered when Shirley's body will be released." I ad-libbed, sensing he'd never divulge even a smidgen of information in an ongoing case.

His murky gray eyes gave me a probing stare, making me wonder if he'd learned the technique from McBride or if it was something taught at the police academy. "Why do you want to know?"

Precious, bless her heart, leaped to my aid. "S'pose folks want to give her a real nice send-off. Ms. Randolph seemed a classy lady."

"Yes, exactly." I shot Precious a grateful look. "Who better to know when we can schedule the service than the police department?"

"The body could be released as early as tomorrow," he said, his tone flat.

"Was the medical examiner able to determine how long Shirley had been dead before her body was discovered?" In for a penny, in for a pound. The most he could do was toss me out on my ear.

Ignoring my question, Moyer shifted his scowl from me to Casey. "What's that dog doing here? Didn't you read the sign posted on the door? Only service animals allowed."

Casey blinked his chocolate brown eyes at Moyer as if to question how anyone dare speak so harshly about his adorable self.

"Casey is a therapy dog," I said, the first thing to cross my mind.

Moyer's scowl deepened. "What kind of therapy?"

From the corner of my eye, I saw Precious roll her eyes. "Casey is an emotional support animal," I elaborated, grateful for learning about this designation recently on a nightly news segment. "Emotional support animals provide comfort and relieve anxiety. It's a highly developed skill set."

Precious disguised a chuckle behind a half cough, half hiccup.

"Just when I think I've heard it all." Moyer shook his head in disbelief, then addressed his next words to Precious: "I'm starting rounds. You know how to reach me."

"Before you go" — the words came out in a rush — "Vicki Lamont told me someone tried to break into Creekside Realty last night. Should I be worried that my shop might be next?"

"Probably just kids. Nothing was taken, so they probably got scared and ran."

"But what if the person, or persons, did gain access? What if they were searching for a particular item but left when they couldn't find it?"

"I hardly see where that's any of your concern. This is police business." He leveled a finger at me. "Stay out of it."

"Yes, sir." I tamped down the urge to salute.

"Woo-ee!" Precious blew out a breath after the door closed behind him. "That's one cold fish."

"No argument there." I patted my thigh, a signal for Casey to follow.

"Tony Deltorro sure makes a mighty fine mostaccioli. You oughta give it a try." Precious pulled her plate closer and, in the process, knocked papers sitting at the edge of her desk to the floor. "Oops! Clumsy me. Do me a favor, sugar, and pick those up while I polish off what's left of my supper."

"Happy to help," I said, bending to collect them. It wasn't my nature to return them without scanning them first, so I did. One of them was a report signed by Officer

Gary Moyer. Moyer apparently had been given the task of dusting Shirley's Cadillac for prints. Odd thing, though, according to the report I held, no prints were found. The car had been wiped clean.

"When you see the chief — the real chief, not the imposter — be sure to tell 'im Precious says hey. I'd tell 'im myself, but Sarge gave us strict orders that no one in the department speak to 'im."

"Will do," I said. "And, Precious, thanks."

Precious winked. "Us gals got to stick together."

Although it was still daylight, the shadows were lengthening. The day might have been waning, but I was still wound up and not ready to call it quits. I turned to my trusty sidekick. "I know I promised you a run, but would you trade the park for a romp in the country?"

Casey didn't seem to object, so I set my plan in motion. First stop was the Pizza Palace, where I placed an order for a large with pepperoni, mushrooms, and extra cheese. When I returned twenty minutes later driving my VW, the pizza was fresh from the oven. Its spicy aroma made my mouth water. It was all I could do on the short drive not to delve into the box and satisfy my hunger.

Ten minutes later, I drove down Mc-Bride's gravel drive. I questioned the wisdom of my visit. After losing his job this morning, McBride wouldn't be in a sociable frame of mind. No doubt, company was the last thing he wanted or felt he needed. Too bad, I decided. Hard times like this called for friends. Friends . . . ? Was that what we were? Although I tried to ignore it, an undercurrent of attraction always hummed close to the surface of our encounters. As far as I was concerned, he was the bad boy mothers warned their daughters against. Common sense told me to keep my distance. Common sense and I, however, weren't best buddies.

The beam of my headlights, which had switched on automatically, illuminated a house with almost as many varieties as my pet. Country Southern, a dash of New England Colonial, with a sprinkle of Greek Revival. A handyman special bought on the cheap.

My headlights glare summoned McBride to his front porch. Dressed in jeans and a faded gray UGA sweatshirt, he assumed a belligerent stance with thumbs hooked in his belt loops.

"C'mon, pal," I said to Casey. I grabbed

the six-pack I'd purchased on the fly at the Gas 'n Go in one hand, the pizza in the other.

McBride's expression was obscured in shadow. Was he going to ask me to leave? Or invite me inside?

"I'm the new delivery person at the Pizza Palace." I held up the pizza and six-pack for his inspection. "If you turn me away, I might get fired."

McBride watched Casey water a shrub near the steps, then shrugged. "Wouldn't want both of us to get the axe on the same day," he said, stepping aside for me to enter.

"Thought you might need sustenance after a rough day." I nodded toward the beer. "Wasn't sure of the brand, so hope this is okay."

"I drink most anything that starts with *b* and ends with *r*."

"Good." I smiled. "I must be psychic."

There had been a few changes inside his house since my last visit. Hardwood floors had replaced a plywood subfloor. A wall between the kitchen and a small dining room had been removed, creating the illusion of space. I paused on the threshold to admire the kitchen, which had been completely gutted and renovated. It now boasted white Shaker cabinets, gleaming stainless-steel appliances, and quartz countertops. A single three-legged stool stood at the breakfast bar.

"Quite an improvement!" I said. "The place looks great."

"Thanks for your help selecting the appliances. Still don't understand why I need a cooktop *and* an oven." He took the pizza box from me and made room for it on a drop-leaf table with chipped paint. That done, he pulled out a couple paper plates and ripped off a length of paper towel to use for napkins. "Care for a beer?"

I took a seat in one of the mismatched wooden chairs at the table. "Never acquired a taste for beer. Don't suppose you have a diet soda?"

He almost smiled. "I might could find one if I look real hard."

While McBride rummaged in the fridge for a can of soda, I served up the pizza. Casey found a spot under the table and made himself comfortable. "Where's that unsociable animal of yours?"

"Fraidy must've heard your voice and is pretending you're invisible." McBride chuckled.

"Figures. Don't know why that cat has it in for me." Fraidy, the cat, was a half-feral feline who had adopted McBride, and vice

143

versa. For some strange reason, she had taken an instant dislike to me. I looked around. "Don't mind my saying so, but furniture might be a nice addition."

"I'll take your suggestion under advisement soon as I win the lottery." He helped himself to a second slice. "Thanks to your ex, I've been suspended — without pay."

My appetite for pizza diminished. "That's so unfair! I can't believe anyone with half a brain thinks you had anything to do with Shirley's death."

"The council called it 'conflict of interest.' Not only did a lot of folks regard us as a couple, but her body turned up on my property — and I was the one who found it. Brig Abernathy and the rest of the council worry how it would look — if and when — word leaks that her death was a homicide."

I took a swig of soda. "Hopefully in the meantime Beau Tucker and the rest of the department will learn what happened to Shirley and find the person responsible."

"Ha!" McBride snorted. "I don't trust Beau Tucker to find his way out of the Rotary Club's House of Horrors on Halloween, much less solve a homicide. Don't get me wrong. Beau's a nice enough guy, but unless he's passing out speeding tickets he's out of his element."

"So, what are you going to do?"

"Nothing much I can do."

"I beg to differ, McBride. That's where you're wrong." My appetite had returned as quickly as it had disappeared, and I finished off my slice of pizza. "How about a little old-fashioned sharing of information?"

He regarded me suspiciously. "All right," he agreed. "You go first."

"Precious accidental-like dropped some reports off her desk, and asked if I'd mind picking them up."

"And you 'accidental-like' happened to read them on the way back to her desk?"

I nodded. "According to Moyer's report, Shirley's car had been wiped clean of fingerprints. While I'm not a hotshot detective, that doesn't sound like something a person bent on committing suicide would do."

"Have to admit that would be a first in my book." McBride took a long pull of Miller Lite. "Now my turn. Here's another thing the medical examiner found odd: Shirley had what appeared to be a fresh burn mark on the palm of her right hand."

"There's a lot to be said for teamwork, McBride. As my father always says, two heads are better than one. A lot of truth behind most clichés." I leaned back in my chair. "By the way, McBride, you do have an alibi for the weekend Shirley died, don't you?"

"Sure do." He gave me a humorless smile. "The worst alibi in the books — home alone."

CHAPTER 12

I awoke the next morning full of purpose and brimming with energy. Unfortunately, not all my days began that way, but I was determined to make hay while the sun shined — another of my father's favorite clichés. Hearing him say that time after time, one could get the impression he'd spent his life on a farm instead of working on an assembly line in an automobile plant.

Lindsey had already left for school, eager to describe her fabulous and amazing shoes to her circle of friends in minute detail. Personally, the shoes were a little outlandish for my taste. The heels were so high they practically guaranteed a broken ankle. I couldn't imagine walking in them, much less dancing, but Lindsey had no such qualms. Ah — I sighed — to be young and carefree again.

I knew Mavis Gray opened the hardware store earlier than I opened Spice It Up!

Seems the clamor for nuts and bolts began shortly after dawn. I decided to take advantage of the situation to pay her a visit. This was an ideal time to purchase herbs for the container garden I planned. As I walked the short distance to her store, I entertained the idea of buying her entire shipment. This way, I'd literally corner the market.

Mavis was behind the counter when I entered. "Good morning, Mavis," I greeted her cheerily.

She nodded but didn't return the smile. "Shouldn't you be tending to your own business instead of visiting mine?"

"I hope this isn't the way you treat all your customers, Mavis," I said.

Her unwelcoming expression rearranged itself into less harsh lines. "Sorry, Piper," she apologized. "Didn't mean to sound snippity. I'm just under a lot of pressure these days wondering whether the Dixons are going to make an offer on this place or not."

"That's okay. I understand how difficult this must be for you."

Mavis's thin mouth twisted in a tired smile. "Not a lot of folks wanting to buy a small family-run business in an out-of-the-way town. Especially not when people can get what they need — and probably cheaper

148

— at that new Lowe's out by the interstate."

"Not many places, Mavis, where a person can still buy a half-dozen threepenny nails or a single seven-eight-inch bolt. Don't forget each and every one of your customers gets individual attention. They're not at the mercy of some part-time college student who thinks a washer is the same as a washing machine. Besides, your store saves people the trouble and expense of a twenty-mile drive."

"Thanks, Piper. I've been feeling discouraged what with Shirley dead and not knowing what the Dixons are thinking."

I selected a peat pot from a carton of seedlings near an ad for pesticides. "Mmm, cilantro, also called coriander," I said, sniffing a plant with frilly green leaves. "Vicki is inexperienced, but I'm sure she'll do everything in her power to facilitate a sale. She must see dollar signs thinking of the commission it will bring."

"I suppose you're right, but when it comes to real estate, Vicki Lamont is as green as grass. Shirley, on the other hand, wouldn't let a big fish like Kirby Dixon wriggle off the hook. That woman was gifted with the power of persuasion."

"That seems to be the general consensus." I added marjoram to the cilantro. I'd en-

149

courage customers to substitute it for oregano for a less earthy flavor.

Mavis eyed her dwindling selection of herbs with satisfaction. "If it weren't for his wife, I think Kirby Dixon would've had the purchase agreement drawn up already. But, no, Elaine keeps putting up roadblocks."

"What kind of roadblocks?" I inhaled a deep breath of fragrant basil. I decided to set a plant or two aside for my kitchen windowsill. Don't know why I didn't think of it sooner. Basil was easy to grow, a good return on a modest investment.

"If not for Elaine Dixon's constant harping, Kirby would already be on board. His wife doesn't give him a moment's peace."

"Elaine does seem to have strong opinions on the subject."

Mavis folded her arms over her chest, eyes narrowed. "The woman will never be happy in a small town. She's used to big-city ways. My guess is she married Kirby for his money, thinking he'd be easily manipulated."

"Hmm . . ." Chives, mint, oregano, parsley. At this rate, I'd need a garden plot instead of a clay pot. "What do you know about the couple?"

"Not a whole lot," she admitted. "Only thing I'm interested in is them buying me out so I can go live with my sister."

I handed over my Visa. *What else do I need for my pet project?*

"Is that all?" Mavis asked.

I inventoried the dozen or more plants I'd selected. I'd gone and done it — bought Mavis's entire stock of herbs, many of which were hardly more than seedlings. "As long as I'm at it, I need a watering can, fertilizer, and a bag of potting soil." For good measure, I added a pair of gardening gloves with bright yellow sunflowers.

I waited as Mavis totaled my sales and ran my credit card. "No way you can carry all this," Mavis said as I signed the receipt. "Tell you what; Ned is coming by later to help with some cleaning. I'll ask him to make a delivery."

"Perfect," I said, "I might've gotten a little carried away."

"Sorry I vented my frustration on you." Mavis walked with me to the door. "On the bright side, however, that nice young fellow from the bank, Zach VanFleet, assured me he'd help any way he could to make sure the sale goes smoothly on his end. He knows how eager I am to move on."

I left Gray's Hardware with a bounce in my step. I may not have solved Shirley's murder, but planting an herb garden was better than sitting idle and wringing my hands.

Reba Mae arched a brow. "Home alone's the best alibi Wyatt could come up with?"

"That's what he told me." My BFF had had a late-in-the-day cancellation and chose to spend the time hanging out with me. It was near closing and the last of my customers had left. We were sipping tea — sweet for my friend, unsweet for me — and enjoying some girl talk. Lindsey had taken Casey for a run in the park, so Reba Mae and I had the place to ourselves.

"As alibis go, honeybun, home alone is pretty lame. Take it from someone who knows."

I held up my hands in mock surrender. "Don't shoot the messenger."

"Did Wyatt say what he's gonna do if he's not reinstated? Think he'll move?"

I took a sip of tea. "We didn't get into that. Finding a new job won't be easy once it's public knowledge why he was suspended. If he's under suspicion for murder, no police force in the country will hire him."

"That stinks. Granted, my friendship with Wyatt may have hit a few bumps in the road, but I'd bet my last box of rollers he's as honorable as the day is long."

I wholeheartedly agreed but worried all the same. Presumed innocent until proven guilty is all well and good. But in some instances innocent people are found guilty in the court of public opinion. I hoped that didn't happen in McBride's case.

I was about to voice my concerns aloud to Reba Mae when Ned Feeney shouldered his way through the door. "Hey, Miz Piper. Where do you want me to set all this?"

I hastily cleared a space on the counter for the tray of herbs.

"More stuff back at the store," Ned said, shoving up the bill of his cap. "I'll run right down and fetch it. Be back in a jiff."

"Don't tell me; let me guess," Reba Mae drawled as Ned hurried out. "You always secretly yearned to be a farmer?"

"Something like that. I plan to start a container garden out front where the plants will get plenty of sunlight. I think I got a little carried away."

"Gee." Reba Mae laughed. "You think?"

Ned returned, this time lugging a large cardboard box loaded with potting soil and other miscellaneous products I'd found impossible to resist. He dropped it on the floor at the end of the counter and brushed off his hands. "That oughta do it."

"Thanks, Ned. Can I offer you a nice, cold

glass of sweet tea?"

"Never refuse sweet tea. A fellow sure works up a thirst haulin' around boxes and bags for folks."

"Haven't seen you around much, Ned," Reba Mae said.

I went to the fridge at the rear and returned with iced tea, which he gulped down. "What have you been up to these days?"

"Mr. Strickland over at the Eternal Rest been keepin' me pretty busy. Mostly drivin' to and from Atlanta. Think I could find my way blindfolded to the Georgia Bureau of Investigation. Matter of fact, just brought Miz Randolph back to Brandywine Creek for burial."

Reba Mae and I exchanged looks. "Did Mr. Strickland give any indication of when her funeral might be?" I asked

"Yes, ma'am." Ned bobbed his head. "Friday."

"Friday . . . ?" I echoed. "Like the day after tomorrow Friday?"

"Isn't that a little soon?" Reba Mae asked.

"Accordin' to Mr. Strickland, her brother's goin' away — Seattle or Samoa or somewhere that starts with an *S* — and wants to have this over before he leaves. Except for an elderly aunt and uncle, the brother's the only family." Ned stared into his empty glass. "Speakin' of, I need a favor," he mumbled.

I wasn't sure I'd heard correctly. "Excuse me?"

"I need a favor from you ladies," he said, looking at us sheepishly.

"What kind of favor you talkin' 'bout, Ned?" Reba Mae probed.

"Mr. Strickland instructed me to go to Miz Randolph's house and pick an outfit for a private viewin'. Wants her to look nice for relatives. He told me Southern women always want to look their best — even if they're dead. Trouble is, I don't know the first thing about women stuff. I was wonderin' if you'd help."

"Isn't that usually a task for the family?"

"That's what I think, but . . ."

". . . but?"

"Mr. Strickland told me to stop being a wuss and just do it. Said her brother is drivin' in Friday mornin' and wants one last look at his sister before the casket is sealed. It ain't fittin' for me to go through her closet." Ned nervously tugged an earlobe. "That's where I thought you nice ladies might help me out."

I pretended to ponder the matter even though I barely restrained myself from giv-

155

ing Ned a big hug. The man had handed us an invitation on a silver platter to check the home of a murder victim. I didn't want to snoop; I wanted to investigate. Look for clues the police might have missed. I felt a rush of anticipation at the prospect.

The uncertainty on Reba Mae's face signaled she didn't share my love of adventure. "I'd like to help, Ned," she said, "but I promised my boys an old-fashioned home-cooked meal tonight."

Ned looked crestfallen at her refusal.

"Don't mind her, Ned. We'd be happy to find clothes suitable for Shirley's viewing. No reason why it can't be done after dinner, is there, Reba Mae?"

"Guess not," she said reluctantly.

"Great!" Ned beamed with obvious relief. "I knew you ladies wouldn't let me down. Be sure it's real pretty. Miz Randolph was classy-like, and I'm color-blind. If I picked the wrong outfit, I fear her ghost would come back to haunt me."

"Ghost . . . ?" Reba Mae shuddered.

"Happy to help a friend," I said.

Ned dug out a key for Shirley's house, handed it to me, then made his exit before Reba Mae and I could change our minds.

"Location, location, location," I repeated the real estate agent's mantra. I parked under the porte cochere — la-di-da — and stared out the car window at Shirley Randolph's regal Victorian, a throwback to a bygone era. The home was located in Brandywine Creek's prestigious historical district, an area where antebellum, Victorian, and Colonial-style homes comingle. Some of the homes are listed on the National Register of Historic Places while others cry out in desperate need of TLC.

"So this is the place Clay's been ravin' about," Reba Mae said in an awe-tinged voice.

Shirley's recent purchase was an imposing three-story edifice complete with fanciful gingerbread trim, scalloped shingles, and a wraparound porch that practically begged for white wicker rockers and Boston ferns. The exterior of the house was painted in vibrant earth tones that managed to appear true to the period yet modern.

"I thought this place would be smothered in crime scene tape," I commented.

"Bet it would've been with Wyatt in charge. Beau must not be considerin' this as a crime scene." Reba Mae pointed at an ivy-covered turret with a steep pointed roof at one end of the house. "Well, don't that beat all? Shirley even had her very own tower."

"Rapunzel, Rapunzel, let down your long hair." I slid out of the driver's seat. "Shirley must've felt like a fairy-tale princess living here. For some reason, though, the house seems out of sync with the impression I had of Shirley. She always struck me as the sleek and modern type."

"Location, location, location," Reba Mae singsonged, climbing of the car out to join me on the cracked concrete drive.

"Let's get started, shall we?" I extracted the house key from my purse and went up the front walk. "As long as we're here, why don't we check the fridge? There might be perishables that need to be tossed out before they spoil."

"Do you think Shirley intended to keep this place for herself once it was renovated or sell it for a tidy profit?"

158

"Guess with Shirley gone, we'll never know." A fanlight fitted with leaded-glass panes crowned a heavy wood door with an ornate brass knocker. The key slid smoothly into a lock that looked relatively new, and the door swung open. "C'mon, let's take a look-see. You must be at least a little curious."

"Maybe . . . just a bit," Reba Mae admitted grudgingly. "Bein' in a dead woman's house gives me the heebie-jeebies."

We entered a large entryway. On our right, a steep flight of stairs led to the second level. We followed a hallway past a series of rooms: parlor, library, dining room, and kitchen. We poked our heads into each one but were disappointed to find them sparsely furnished.

Reba Mae ran a finger over an oak credenza in the dining room. "Hardly any furniture, but it sure makes dustin' quick and easy. Maybe I oughta give it a try."

I headed for the kitchen at the rear of the house.

Suddenly Reba Mae grabbed the sleeve of my sweater. "Wait up," she whispered. "Think I heard somethin'."

I strained to listen but didn't hear a thing other than the sounds old houses sometimes make. An occasional groan, a mysterious grunt, an unexplained click or thud. "The house is old, Reba Mae. If we live to the same ripe old age, our joints are going to be creaking, too. Don't be such a baby."

The kitchen, I discovered, was spacious but in serious need of updating. The appliances, while functional, were old and yellowed. With a generous budget coupled with the genius of a HGTV decorator, it had the potential to be a showplace.

"Shirley wasn't big on cooking," Reba Mae said from behind me. "She was more into creature comforts and insisted the master bedroom and en suite be done first. Said the kitchen could wait."

I opened the freezer section of the fridge. "Nothing here except for a half-dozen Lean Cuisines and a bag of frozen peas." The lower section revealed a jar of dill pickles, wilted lettuce, an unopened bottle of Chardonnay, several cans of ginger ale, and two knobby rhizomes of ginger.

Reba Mae peeked over my shoulder at the contents. "What's the deal with the ginger? Shirley some kind of health nut?"

I closed the fridge. "Ginger has been used for medicinal purposes for centuries. It's thought to boost the immune system and decrease inflammation. Many use it to relieve indigestion."

"Shirley had indigestion?"

"The last time she came into my shop she complained of occasional upsets and bought some ginger to make tea." I shut the refrigerator door.

Reba Mae examined the contents of the cupboards but, other than the usual kitchen paraphernalia, didn't find anything of interest. "Let's go upstairs. I want to take a gander at her clothes closet."

"Sure," I said. I'd turned to go when I noticed the back door wasn't shut tight so I pushed on it until I heard the lock mechanism click into place. "Looks like we could have got in even without a key."

We traipsed up the stairs, several of which creaked. At the top of the landing, I paused to get my bearings. "Where do we start?"

"Clay told me that there are four bedrooms, but plans call for combinin' two of 'em into a master suite. The en suite is the next project on the renovation list. Until then, Shirley had to make do with the original bathroom."

We peeked into a guest room with a single bed that appeared too neat and pristine to ever have been slept in. Next to it was a room designated as a home office. An ergonomically designed chair sat in front of a sleek desk. A metal four-drawer file cabinet

161

stood in one corner. As I stepped farther inside, I noticed a network of fine scratches surrounding the lock. Had someone tried to break into the file cabinet? Pry the drawer open? I'm not a great believer in co-incidence, but could it have been the same person, or persons, who attempted to break into Creekside Realty?

I summoned Reba Mae for a second opinion. "What do you make of this?"

Reba Mae grasped the handle, tugged hard, and the drawer rolled out. "Empty!" she exclaimed. "Why have an empty file cabinet?"

The other drawers, as we soon discovered, were empty as well. I crossed to the desk only to find that the drawers there had suffered a similar fate. "Who do you suppose did this?"

"Beats me." Reba Mae shrugged. "Maybe Shirley emptied the drawers herself. Decided to do some spring-cleanin'."

"Either that or someone was looking for something." I placed my hands on my hips and surveyed the home office. Aside from a framed picture of a much younger Shirley standing next to a boy who bore a striking resemblance, the desktop was clear. It occurred to me that there was no sign of Shirley's pricy computer. Vicki had referred to it as her "lifeline." Was that what a thief had been after? Definitely food for thought.

"C'mon, girlfriend," Reba Mae urged. "Let's do what we came here for and blow this pop stand."

"Fine by me."

Shoving open a set of double doors, Reba Mae let out a low whistle. "Wowee kazowee!"

"Double wowee kazowee," I echoed. "Looks like we saved the best for last."

I felt like we'd just wandered into fantasyland. The master bedroom revealed an entirely different side of Shirley Randolph. For a woman who had been as romantic as a piranha when it came to business, her bedroom was feminine, luxurious, and downright gorgeous. Violet wallpaper with tiny white flowers and touches of greenery covered the walls. White sheers on the windows puddled on the floor to add to the romantic decor. A queen-size bed, nearly buried beneath mounds of pillows and covered with a fluffy white duvet, invited the occupant to curl up and cuddle. A perfect spot to snuggle on a rainy day with a good book and a cup of tea.

"I think I died and went to heaven," Reba Mae sighed. "Clay said the en suite would be even better when finished. Walk-in shower, soaker tub, double sinks. Lots of fancy tile and marble."

I gave myself a mental shake. "Well, we need to get down to business. We're not here to give an award for the most beautiful bedroom in Brandywine Creek. Let's check the closet and see what we can find in the way of an outfit suitable for Shirley's viewing."

Unlike many homes of that era, Shirley's boasted a rather large closet — probably one of the features that sold her on the property. One side of the closet was crammed with clothing; the opposite side held shelves and cubbyholes filled with shoes and handbags. Shirley's favorite scent lingered there. It wafted out, a bouquet of fragrance both fruity and flowery as exotic as the woman herself.

"I can smell her perfume," Reba Mae fussed. "This place is givin' me the willies again. Just grab an outfit, and let's hit the road."

"Don't be a ninny. We might never have a more a legitimate excuse than now to poke around."

"All right," she conceded, albeit reluctantly. "I feel like I'm in a boutique." Her eyes sparkled and her squeamishness rapidly faded at the sight of all those shoe boxes. "I bet Imelda Marcos would envy Shirley's shoe collection. Too bad they're not my size," she said after examining a shoe box. "Shirley wore a seven and a half N."

"Reba Mae Johnson!" I scolded. "Why would you want to walk in a dead woman's shoes?"

"Seems a shame all these shoes could end up at thrift store." Ignoring me, she lifted the lid on a box and admired a pair of spike-heeled pumps. "I bet she paid a couple hundred bucks for these babies. I can tell from the label they're the real McCoy and not some cheap knockoffs. Must be good money to be made in real estate."

I left Reba Mae to feast on designer footwear while I flipped through the hangers. Dresses, suits, jackets, slacks, blouses. I wasn't exactly sure what I was looking for but hoped I'd know when I found it.

"Lookin for anythin' in particular?" Reba Mae asked.

"When Hoyt stopped by Spice It Up! yesterday, he mentioned running into Shirley at the St. Patrick's Day Parade in Savannah. He said she was acting weird. He got the impression she was with someone but didn't want him to see who it was."

"Do you think her mystery man is the one who stole her files?" Reba Mae replaced a strappy pair of sandals in their box.

"Could be," I said.

"So what are you doin', looking for clues? Think whoever it was might be her killer?"

"It's possible."

Reba Mae went back to examining shoes. "What do you expect to find — a pair of men's boxers?"

"Something along those lines."

I was beginning to fear I was on a fool's mission. Then I found it. A man's charcoal gray terry-cloth robe relegated to a spot at the end of the rod. It stood out like a sore thumb among all the feminine attire. I held it up for Reba Mae's inspection. "What do you think?"

"Personally, I prefer sweats when relaxin'." After eyeing the robe, she became distracted by Shirley's assortment of purses. "Breakin' news! Michael Kors is keepin' company with Kate Spade. Who knew?"

"Reba Mae, you're not taking this seriously enough. This robe most likely belongs to Shirley's lover."

"Unlike some of us — whose names I won't mention — Shirley at least had a love life."

"Haven't you told me that the significant other — husband, fiancé, or boyfriend — is usually the murderer?"

"Well, yeah. That's how it goes on TV."

"It's a man's size Large."

"Large would fit half the men in town."

Frustrated, I yanked a navy blue dress with crisp white trim that I'd seen Shirley wear on several occasions off a hanger. "I found a dress. You find the shoes."

While Reba Mae rummaged in the closet for appropriate footwear, I decided to make a quick search of Shirley's nightstand. I couldn't help myself. I was genetically predisposed to snoop. Tissues, a couple books, both nonfiction bestsellers — and a box of condoms. All the proof I needed that Shirley, indeed, had a man in her life.

Find him, find answers. Find her killer?

CHAPTER 14

A man's bathrobe and a box of condoms. What next? I couldn't wait to find out. "Time to check out the bathroom."

"Deliver me out of temptation, girlfriend." Reba Mae reluctantly left the plethora of shoes behind and joined me on my journey to discovery.

While Shirley's house had plenty of curb appeal, except for the master bedroom, the inside was a work in progress. Even from the point of view of an amateur, such as *moi,* the bathroom was in dire need of improvement. An old-fashioned claw-foot tub, pedestal sink, and black and white hexagonal floor tiles gave off Victorian vibes. A small, modern-looking cabinet with lots of drawers that had been stuck in a corner looked out of place. It held a makeup mirror and jars of beauty products. A medicine cabinet, another add-on, hung over the sink.

"Clay said the bathroom was still untouched. It was scheduled to be the next major project, but Shirley temporarily postponed renovations."

"Why do you suppose she did that?"

"According to Clay, she wanted to consult a different contractor before goin' ahead with plans." Reba Mae began to examine the lotions and creams. "Wrinkles and fine lines didn't stand a fightin' chance against all this artillery."

I opened the medicine cabinet. Besides a lineup of the usual suspects — toothbrush, toothpaste, painkillers, Band-Aids — there were two containers of prescription drugs. I read the labels. The first was a generic I was unfamiliar with. The second prescription was for a popular brand of birth control pills — further proof Shirley had a lover. Judging from the date, the latter hadn't been refilled recently. I left the birth control pills where they were but tucked the vial of the generic pills into my pocket to Google later. That wasn't really stealing, was it? It wasn't as though Shirley would be needing her medication anytime soon. The only other item of significance was a huge bottle of antacids.

"Find anything of interest?" I asked Reba Mae when I finished searching the medicine cabinet.

169

Reba Mae seemed lost in thought, so I repeated my question. I glanced over my shoulder to see her wearing a frown. Her prolonged silence was more unnerving than her constant chatter. "Anything wrong? You're not sick, are you?"

"Somethin's buggin' me," she muttered. "Can't quite put my finger on it."

"Doesn't appear there is anything out of the ordinary." Perching on the rim of the bathtub, I swept my gaze over the room. "This place is immaculate. Not a single water spot in the sink. No soap scum around the tub. Nothing is out of place. It's ready for the white-glove test."

"I can't imagine Shirley doing her own housework."

"Me neither. Lord forbid she chip her nail polish."

Reba Mae didn't seem in a hurry to leave. While I waited, I absently ran my hand along the inner rim of the tub and felt something rough and uneven beneath my fingertips. Leaning back, I craned my neck for a better look. I was surprised at what I found. Because of the angle, I hadn't noticed the vertical black blemish about three inches long and a half inch wide. Whatever the cause, it had been powerful enough to pierce the tub's enamel finish to the cast iron underneath. When I studied it closer, it appeared more of a deep scar rather than surface blemish. A burn?

Suddenly Reba Mae snapped her fingers, making me jump. "Got it!"

"Good grief, woman." I pressed my hand to my chest to still my racing heart. "What are you trying to do, give me a heart attack?"

"I just figured out what's missin'." To demonstrate, she pulled out a cabinet drawer that housed an assortment of brushes, combs, curling irons, and a flatiron. "Lookee here," she said, brandishing a hair dryer in triumph.

"Honey," I said as kindly as I could, "you've been sniffing too many hair dye chemicals. It's affected your brain. That's a simple hair dryer, not the key to Fort Knox."

"No, don't you see?" she said, her voice animated. "Take a closer look."

I stared at the object she held until my eyes almost crossed but didn't see anything out of the ordinary. "It's like a million other hair dryers. Walmart must sell them by the truckload."

"Exactly!" She grinned at me like a proud teacher to an exceptionally slow student.

I rose from the tub and took the hair dryer from her for a better look. "I still don't get it. It's not much different from the one I own."

"Now you're cookin' with gas. This one's probably the same kind half the ladies in town use — but not Shirley. Shirley wanted only the best hair dryer money could buy. Demanded top of the line, the newest technology."

"And you know this how?" I handed her back the hair dryer.

"Because Shirley asked for my recommendation on what to buy. She claimed she didn't care how much it cost — then asked if I could use my beautician's license for a discount."

"I'm not sure I'm following you. The hair dryer you're holding is your basic, big-box store model, inexpensive, not state of the art."

"I personally ordered, then hand delivered to Shirley at her office an ionic tourmaline ceramic turbo model twenty-one-hundred-watt hair dryer. At Melly's shower, Shirley made a point to tell me how much she loved it. Said it's all she ever used."

"Where are you going with this?" I asked, but I already thought I knew.

"The new one is missin' — and this old clunker left in its place."

The tiny hairs on my arms stood at attention. The puzzle pieces were slowly starting to click into place. First, the blemish on the bathtub that on closer inspection resembled a burn. Now, according to Reba Mae, Shirley's new, high-powered hair dryer had vanished. Did one and one equal two? "I know this sounds like a long shot, but —" I moistened my dry lips with the tip of my tongue. "— I think I know how Shirley died. Hear me out. Do you think it possible Shirley might have been killed right here? In her very own bathtub? What if someone threw that fancy hair dryer into the tub — while she was in it? What if she was electrocuted?"

The hair dryer in Reba Mae's hand clattered to the floor. "Don't these things come with some kind of doohickey to shut off automatically?"

"I think so, but what if only a little jolt is enough to make a person pass out, sink under the water, and drown? Or make their heart go all wonky?"

Reba Mae paled at the thought. Bending, she carefully picked the hair dryer off the floor and placed it almost gently back where she'd found it. "We've been here long enough. I want out."

"Me, too."

I forgot all about my plan to dispose of

perishables in Shirley's fridge. All I wanted was "out." In my eagerness to leave, I'd nearly forgotten the reason we were here. Midway down the stairs, I remembered.

"Wait up!" I cried. Turning, I raced to the bedroom and retrieved the dress and shoes chosen for the viewing.

Once out on the front walk, I drew in a deep breath to steady my nerves. My relief was short-lived. As we started toward my VW, a squad car turned into the drive blocking our retreat. Reba Mae skidded to a halt at seeing it. After her recent experience as a "person of interest" in a murder investigation, she'd grown downright skittish when confronted with law enforcement.

The driver's window powered down. "Mind if I ask what you ladies are up to?" Officer Gary Moyer asked.

Reba Mae instantly mounted a defense. "Can't be breakin' and enterin' seein' how we have a key, can it?"

"Where are you going with the vic's clothes?" Officer Moyer nodded at the navy blue dress draped over my arm.

"We're here on official business," I explained. "Besides, who'd be crazy enough to believe I'd steal a dress not my size. Everyone who knows me will attest navy blue's not my best color."

174

"She's right," Reba Mae volunteered on my behalf. "Navy blue doesn't complement her skin tone."

"Thanks for the fashion advice, but you still haven't explained what you were doing in Shirley Randolph's house?"

"Mr. Strickland at the Eternal Rest asked Ned Feeney to bring him something for Shirley to wear at a private viewing. Ned didn't feel comfortable doing it, so he asked our help."

"So, you two are doing a good deed like grown-up Girl Scouts?"

"Yep, scout's honor, that's us." Reba Mae inched closer to the VW.

"Well, in that case, I better continue my rounds. By the way, Piper," he said as though it was an afterthought, "you might be interested to know the crime scene techs went over Shirley's vehicle with a fine-tooth comb. Only thing they came across was a single strand of dark hair in the trunk presumed to be Shirley's. Of course, in and of itself, that's not significant since it was her car."

"Interesting, too, that there were no prints found — since it was her car." I smoothed Shirley's dress, the fabric silky beneath my touch. "One might suspect a person, or persons, had gone to a great deal of trouble to remove all trace evidence."

"That's certainly a conclusion one might draw." Officer Moyer shifted into reverse. "Rumor has it a heat wave's heading this way right quick. Be sure to mention that to the chief should you happen to run into him."

"I'll be sure to do that — should I see him."

"What's with the weather forecast?" Reba Mae asked as we climbed into my Beetle. "Moyer plannin' to become a meteorologist?"

Heat wave? That had an ominous sound. From the rearview mirror, I watched the patrol car back down the drive and disappear from sight. "I think it was a warning of some sort meant for McBride. It's a nice night. How about we take a ride in the country?"

Reba Mae's face split into a wide grin. "I'm always up for sightseein' — especially if that sight happens to be tall, dark, and handsome."

Neither of us noticed the nondescript sedan that followed us.

CHAPTER 15

We left Brandywine Creek behind and turned onto Route 78. The sun had set, and it was growing dark. Reba Mae and I were unusually quiet on the drive to McBride's, both trying to digest everything we'd discovered at Shirley Randolph's. What were the chances of Shirley being electrocuted while taking a bath? Probably almost nil. When it came to Murder 101, guns and knives headed the list of the most popular ways to do a person in. I didn't know this for fact, but I'd guess murder by electrocution was rare. The doohickeys Reba Mae had referred to earlier were designed to prevent accidental death by small electrical gadgets. Yet Shirley's house was old, really old, and the bathroom hadn't been renovated. The wiring might never have been updated.

Finally, I happened to glance into the rearview mirror and was surprised to notice a car behind us. Years of living in a sparsely populated area had spoiled me. Oftentimes I had the roads to myself and, when I didn't, the other vehicle would soon disappear down a drive or side road. The driver of the car following us was careful to maintain a discreet distance. A little too careful, a little too discreet, for my peace of mind.

"Don't look now," I warned Reba Mae, "but we're being followed."

"What's the big deal, hon? This is a public road. News flash, you're not the only person allowed to use it."

"You're right," I sighed. "I'm just a little on edge."

"Your imagination's workin' overtime. Besides, why would anyone follow us?" Reba Mae pawed through her purse for a tube of lipstick. "I've never been inside Wyatt's house before, but Clay's always talkin' about it. Says it's really comin' along."

I shot another look in the mirror. The mystery car was still behind us, the beam of its headlights trained low and unthreatening. Reba Mae thought I was overreacting and maybe I was. But then again, maybe I wasn't.

Reba Mae pulled down the visor and applied fresh lipstick. "Clay raves about Wyatt's new kitchen. Says it's the bomb.

Nowadays, when he's not at the community college or workin' as an auxiliary cop, Clay's been helpin' Wyatt build a deck. Seems Wyatt's got his eye on a fancy barbecue grill."

"That means he's getting ready to retire his trusty George Foreman." I signaled my turn, slowed, and headed down McBride's gravel drive. I blew out a breath when the car behind me kept going.

"Cute as a bug's ear!" Reba Mae exclaimed as McBride's home came into view. "Nestled all snug in the woods like that, it could be the house where Little Red Riding Hood's grandma lived."

"And where she met the Big Bad Wolf."

No sooner were the words out of my mouth when the porch light flickered on and McBride appeared. A sheep in wolves' clothing or a wolf in sheep's clothing? I was never quite sure how I felt about the man. He kept me off balance.

"I see you brought along a bodyguard," he said when he saw who it was.

"Think I need a bodyguard, McBride?" I countered.

He shrugged but didn't smile. "Some folks might think that wise with a murderer on the prowl — and me a suspect."

"You're forgetting the self-defense course

Reba Mae and I aced. Remember? We were your star pupils."

"Hey, Wyatt." Reba Mae waved. "How do you know we didn't come prepared for emergencies? What makes you so sure I'm not packin'?"

"Reba Mae, darlin', the thing you pack best is a good lunch. Last I checked, a person didn't need a carry permit for a ham and cheese sandwich."

"Got me there." Reba Mae sauntered toward the porch steps. "So, Wyatt, you gonna keep jawin' or are you gonna invite us in? Didn't your momma tell you this was no way to treat company?"

"Sorry, I'm not feelin' very hospitable," he said. "Must've snoozed through Momma's lecture on good manners." In spite of his obvious reluctance, he swung the door wide and stepped aside for us to enter.

"Nice digs," Reba Mae commented. "I like your recliner and flat-screen TV, but furniture might add some ambiance."

"So I've been told." He shot me a meaningful look.

Figures on the TV screen were frozen in awkward poses thanks to the PAUSE feature on the remote. An opened bottle of beer stood on a metal TV tray, aka end table, next to the recliner.

"Before I get another lecture about my deplorable lack of manners, make yourself comfortable. Can I get you ladies something cold to drink? Beer, Diet Coke, Dr Pepper?"

We placed our drink orders — Diet Coke for me and Dr Pepper for my bestie — before McBride's hospitality expired and he demanded we vacant the premises. While he attended to beverages, Reba Mae and I settled into the mismatched chairs at the drop-leaf table in the dining area, which afforded an unobstructed view of the big-screen television.

Reba Mae's head swiveled, taking in the sights like a first-time visitor to Times Square. "Love the hardwood floors!" she gushed. "And the countertops. And the stainless-steel appliances. When I hit the jackpot, first thing I'm gonna do is get me a kitchen just like this.

"Those the bedrooms?" she asked, nodding at the two rooms that opened off the living space.

"Yep, but they're not part of the tour." McBride placed our sodas on the table, retrieved his beer from the TV stand, and slumped down on the lone stool at the breakfast bar.

"Gotcha." Reba Mae jerked at a loud *meow* directly behind her.

The head of a sleek black feline with one tattered ear poked her head out of a partially opened bedroom door. The cat looked dressed for a night at the opera in a white bib and tucker.

"You've just met Fraidy," I said. "She's a stray who took pity on McBride and moved in without waiting for a formal invitation. But don't expect Fraidy to roll out the red carpet. She doesn't like strangers."

As if to prove me wrong, Fraidy paraded over to Reba Mae and rubbed against her leg. Not waiting for further encouragement, Fraidy leaped into her lap and waited to be petted.

Reba Mae stroked the cat's head, making her purr with satisfaction. "Don't seem like that to me. Fraidy's actin' real friendly."

I caught the smirk on McBride's face before he hid it.

"Hey, Piper" — Reba Mae continued to pet the cat, who showed no sign of budging from her resting place — "Fraidy's eyes are the same color as yours," she teased. "Did you notice that, too, Wyatt?"

"Nope." He took a long pull from his bottle. "Never noticed."

Reba Mae snorted. "Yeah, I bet."

I felt blood rush to my cheeks at my friend's lame attempt as matchmaker. The conversation was making me uncomfortable, so I shifted to a safer topic. "Hey, McBride, what were you watching on TV?"

"A movie."

So this was how it was going to play. Every word, every syllable, had to be dragged out of him. "I don't suppose this movie you're watching has a title."

The Usual Suspects."

"I think I might've seen it years ago." I took a dainty sip of Diet Coke. "Good plot. Lots of twists and turns."

"Yeah, I know the one." Reba Mae's dangly earrings bobbed in agreement. "Butch took me to see it before the twins were born. Wasn't Alec Baldwin one of the stars?"

"I don't think it was Alec," I said. "Maybe one of his brothers. Daniel or William?"

"None of the above," McBride said, sounding a trifle smug. "The Baldwin brother in question happens to be Stephen."

I nodded. "That's right; now I remember. Kevin Spacey was in it, too, and I think Javier Bardem was one of the bad guys."

"Isn't he married to Salma Hayek?" Reba Mae took a swig of Dr Pepper.

"Nope," I said decisively. "I think you have her confused with Penélope Cruz."

"Ladies, ladies." McBride held up his hand for us to cease. "I don't know who's

183

married to whom, but Javier Bardem isn't in the cast. You're thinking of Benicio del Toro."

Reba Mae ruffled the cat's black fur. "I liked the cute Irish guy best."

"Pierce Brosnan?" I supplied, naming my favorite Agent 007.

"Hmm . . . ?" Reba Mae frowned. "That doesn't sound right. You have him mixed up with Liam Neeson."

McBride set his empty bottle on the breakfast bar with a thud. "You're both mistaken. It's Gabriel Byrne."

Reba Mae's brow puckered in concentration. "And he was once married to . . . Ellen Burstyn? Or was it Ellen Barkin?"

"Enough!" McBride growled. "If you two are here for Trivial Pursuit, you picked the wrong night. Now, care to tell me the real reason you're here?"

Reba Mae prudently kept silent and waited for me to take the plunge. I cleared my throat and hedged, "Um, Reba Mae and I just came from Shirley Randolph's."

"First of all, what were you doing in a dead woman's house? Don't you know there are laws against breaking and entering?"

"It's not breakin' and enterin' if you have a key," Reba Mae explained helpfully. "Ned asked us to find something fittin' for Shirley

184

to be wearin' when her brother gets into town. Naturally, we agreed to help 'im."

"Naturally." McBride pinched the bridge of his nose between thumb and forefinger, then rose and helped himself to another beer. "So. . . ."

"So, we know how Shirley died," Reba Mae blurted.

"Well, at least, we think we do. We came up with a theory." I wiped palms that had suddenly grown sweaty along the sides of my jeans. "We wanted to run it by you. Get your *professional* opinion."

"Feel free to tell us we're crazy," Reba Mae offered. "It won't hurt our feelin's none. It's nothin' we haven't heard before."

McBride twisted off the bottle cap, pitched it into a nearby trash can, and took a swig of his beer. "Go ahead; I'm all ears."

I explained my findings in Shirley's bedroom. He didn't seem at all surprised at my mention of a man's robe in her closet or condoms in her nightstand.

"Shirley was an attractive woman. It's not unlikely she'd have a lover," McBride said, parroting Hoyt's remarks.

"But that's not all." I could barely contain my excitement. "It wasn't until we searched her bathroom that we made our biggest discovery."

"What were you hoping to find in her bathroom of all places? Deodorant? Toothpaste? Hair spray? Jimmy Buffett's lost shaker of salt?"

"Reba Mae knows for a fact that Shirley had a fancy hair dryer, one of those ionic ceramic kinds —"

"— with two diffusers," Reba Mae interjected, "guaranteed to decrease frizzies."

"To make a long story short, her expensive hair dryer was missing and a cheaper one substituted. Then to top it off, I found what first looked like a stain along the inside of the bathtub. But . . ." I paused a beat for maximum effect. "— on closer inspection, it turned out to be a burn scar that went straight through the porcelain."

McBride paced back and forth, his beer forgotten. "Are you implying what I think you are? That Shirley was killed in her own bathroom? Electrocuted?"

Our theory didn't sound quite as plausible when he said it. I shifted my weight. The chair I sat on had become increasingly uncomfortable. Reba Mae stared at the fixed image on the TV screen while continuing to pet Fraidy, who dozed on her lap.

McBride ceased pacing and leveled his laser blues at me. "Small electrical appliances are required by law to have circuit interrupters to avoid such happenings."

"I already thought of that. Isn't it possible some people might still suffer a small jolt of electricity before the circuit interrupter thingamajig kicks on? That might be all it takes to knock them unconscious — or dead."

McBride raised and lowered the beer bottle without taking a sip. "Your scenario would explain why the ME found a fresh burn mark on the palm of Shirley's hand as though warding off a blow — or an object being tossed in the tub."

"And why Shirley was naked," Reba Mae offered.

Reba Mae was on to something. I'd have to remember to thank her later. "The perp realized it was too difficult to dress a dead woman. So instead he planted her clothes nearby to make it appear she died where the body was found."

"Staged?"

I nodded, both surprised and relieved that McBride didn't dismiss the idea. "Officer Moyer told us Shirley's car had been wiped clean. The only trace evidence was a single hair. I bet her car was used for transportation and her body dumped."

"There's a flaw in your theory," he said at length, resuming his pacing. "It's no easy task to lift and move a body — it's all deadweight, pardon the pun. The killer would have to be strong, most likely a man, to lift her from the bathtub, transport her in her vehicle, then dump her body in my pond."

I sat up straight as a sudden thought struck me. "What if more than one person was involved?"

McBride's brows knit together. "You mean, what if the killer had an accomplice?"

"More like an accessory after the fact," Reba Mae piped, then glared at each of us in turn. "Don't give me those funny looks. I saw this show once on the Lifetime channel. I know how these stories go."

"So," I said slowly, "if that's the case, we're talking about possibly two men? And what about a man and a woman? Husband and wife? Or wife and husband?"

McBride nodded grimly.

My mind immediately went to Elaine and Kirby Dixon. And what about Shirley's lover? Could he have also been the killer and his wife the accessory? The plot thickened.

I finished my drink and got to my feet. "Oh, I nearly forgot. Officer Moyer said if I saw you, I should tell you a heat wave's coming."

As if things weren't hot enough already.

CHAPTER 16

My day was just beginning when Vicki Lamont, who could've been the cover girl for dress for success in a dark business suit and pristine white silk blouse, came through Spice It Up!'s door. "Good morning, Piper."

"Good morning. You're up bright and early."

"I wanted to get a head start on the day. I'm finding the real estate business is a lot more work and a lot less glamour than I imagined." She settled her squishy leather handbag on the counter. "I was hoping to catch you before you got busy."

"Sure," I said. Close up, I noticed dark circles under her eyes that makeup couldn't quite conceal. "You look tired, Vicki. Haven't you been sleeping well?"

"No, not really," she confessed.

I slipped my apron over my head and tied the strings. "Worried that the police won't find out what happened to Shirley?"

190

"I know a lot of people think she committed suicide, but I'm not convinced. That doesn't sound like the woman I knew."

"Well, if her death is officially ruled a homicide, I'm sure whoever is responsible will be found soon and brought to justice."

Vicki stared at me as though I'd taken leave of my senses, and maybe I had. "You really believe that with Beau Tucker in charge?"

Actually, I didn't, but hope springs eternal.

Vicki ran a hand over her hair, checking to make sure loose brunette strands hadn't escaped the clip holding her low ponytail. "Jolene complains that half the time Beau can't even find the TV remote."

I grimaced. Jolene's comment about her husband's lack of detecting skills didn't bode well for a quick resolution to a murder case. "Did Shirley's computer ever turn up?" I wondered aloud.

"No. Strange, isn't it? I searched all over but couldn't find it anywhere. Shirley's computer to her was like a cell phone is to a teenager. I assume she took it home with her after work last Friday."

I debated whether to inform Vicki that the computer wasn't spotted during the recent home inspection by yours truly but decided

191

against it.

"Wish I could get my hands on it." Vicki's train of thought followed mine. "Shirley's computer would be a tremendous help. She wasn't used to sharing her clients' likes and dislikes. It's giving me a headache trying to figure out who likes hardwood, who likes carpet, who likes two-story, and who prefers ranch-style. Shirley was compulsive. She cataloged every bitty detail in that darn computer. Then, at the end of every day, she'd back up her files on a flash drive."

"Do you think whoever jimmied the lock on the door of the real estate office might have stolen it?"

"No," she scoffed. "There wasn't any proof to think they gained entrance. Really, Piper, are you playing Nancy Drew, girl detective, again?"

I shrugged. "Just saying, is all."

"I'm sure the dang thing will turn up, but, in the meantime, I'm going bananas trying to keep her clients satisfied."

"Let me know if there's anything I can do to help."

"Thanks for the offer, but I'll manage somehow." Vicki dug through her monster of a purse and pulled out a handful of business cards. "I nearly forgot the reason for my visit. I'm in the process of increasing my listings. Do you suppose Melly might be interested in putting her house on the market?"

Her question caught me off guard. "I have no idea. Cot loves to travel. He's been persuading Melly to consider downsizing, perhaps buy a condo that doesn't require as much upkeep."

"The reason I'm interested is that I have an out-of-state client who's interested in purchasing a home within easy walking distance of downtown. Melly's home is in a perfect location. All the homes in her area are impeccably maintained. Next to the historic district, hers is the most desirable part of town."

"Melly lived in that house her entire married life to CJ's father, so selling it will be a hard decision."

But where my ex mother-in-law was concerned, I'd been surprised before. She'd taken to modern technology like the proverbial duck to water. Computer, smartphone, texting, Facebook, and Twitter, she'd mastered them all. Then the biggest surprise of all — she'd fallen in love and married her old flame.

Vicki arranged her business cards in a neat little stack next to the cash register. "Don't mean to sound pushy, but I wondered if you had Melly's house key. Unless you think she'd mind, I'd like to show my client around. Should he make an offer, she'll have a nice treat when she and Cot return from Italy."

Mind . . . ? Melly would have a conniption. If bold and brassy were characteristics of a Realtor, Vicki should have a bright future. "I'm sorry, Vicki. You'll have to wait until she gets home to broach the subject with her. Until then, her house is off-limits."

Vicki smiled, nonplussed by my refusal. "Nothing ventured, nothing gained."

As pleasant as it was chatting with her, I had work to do. And planting herbs was at the top of the day's to-do list. Bending, I picked up the carton of seedlings that sat on the floor at the end of the counter.

"Oh, Piper," Vicki gasped, "do be careful when you lift anything heavy. I pulled a muscle, and my back hasn't been the same since. Matter of fact, I'm seeing my chiropractor for another adjustment this afternoon."

"I'm sorry to hear that." I felt the soil and decided my plants needed watering. "How did it happen?"

"Ned was helping me move some bankers' boxes into the storage closet at work last Saturday, and I overdid it. Since then, I leave all the heavy lifting to him. I think the man's sweet on me. He's more than willing to do anything I ask."

Heavy lifting? Pulled muscle? If I'd been a bloodhound hot on the trail, my nose would've twitched. "Ned is always on the lookout for odd jobs," I said, trying to convey nonchalance.

"Meanwhile, between my back and my job the two are wreaking havoc on my golf handicap. To make matters worse, my mixed doubles tennis league had to find a substitute for me."

I clucked my tongue in false sympathy. "It's a crime, the sacrifices working women have to make."

"Isn't that the truth?" Vicki agreed. "Gotta dash. Let me know if you need any more of my business cards to pass out."

As she exited, I noticed a subtle difference in her gait, stiffer, more cautious, than usual, lending credence to her claim of a back injury. A terrible notion had wriggled its way into my head. Could Vicki have injured her back lifting Shirley out of a claw-foot tub? Was Ned Feeney so enamored with Vicki that he assisted with disposing of a body? I mentally added Vicki and Ned to my persons of interest list.

Business was steady for the remainder of the morning, leaving me no time to plant my herbs. Things had finally quieted by midafternoon. I was about to bring out a bag of potting soil when a quartet of women, casually but tastefully dressed, burst into my shop.

"We just had the most marvelous lunch," the leader of the pack announced. I judged her to be in her sixties. The reading glasses on a chain around her neck made me wonder if she might've once been a schoolteacher or librarian.

"Our local paper carried an excellent review of Antonio's. We drove all the way from Birch Run to check it out firsthand," said the second woman, a slender, soft-spoken blonde.

"I'm Sharon, by the way," said a petite brunette. "The minestrone was wonderful."

"And the veal ravioli amazing," raved a no-nonsense type with short gray hair.

"What a cute place you have," said the schoolteacher look-alike. "I'm Joan. These are my friends Sharon, Marie, and Dolores."

"We overheard one of the waitstaff tell a coworker that Tony, the chef and owner of

Antonio's, refuses to purchase his spices anywhere but here."

You've come a long way, baby. I mentally patted myself on the back. It hadn't always been that way. Tony Deltorro used to cross the street when he saw me coming. He accused me of being too civic-minded and suspecting him in the murder of a talented but arrogant chef.

The woman, who I assumed was Dolores, plucked a dead leaf from a basil plant. "We're on the planning committee for a fund-raiser to benefit the Birch Run Humane Society. We're interested in stocking up on spices to use in various Italian dishes. Lasagna, spaghetti, mostaccioli, stuffed shells, and pizza for the youngsters."

"Basil, thyme, and oregano are among the most popular," I told her. Coming out from behind the counter, I led them to a nearby shelf and handed Joan a jar of thyme. "There are many varieties of thyme. Beside Italian dishes, it's often used in stews and casseroles because it withstands long, slow cooking."

"I tasted a hint of rosemary in the ravioli." Marie reached for a jar and read the label.

"Rosemary is another spice popular in Italian cuisine, but," I cautioned, "it has a strong, distinct flavor, so use it judiciously. Like thyme, rosemary's flavor isn't diminished by long cooking."

Sharon busily examined one jar after another. "I always add a bay leaf to my lasagna sauce."

"So do I." I nodded my approval. "Bay leaves grow wild on hillsides in Turkey. Did you know they were a favorite in ancient Greece and Rome? Bay is a member of the laurel family and dedicated to Apollo, the god of music and poetry."

"That's right." Joan beamed. "I was a research librarian at a junior college before retiring. I once read that garlands of laurel were given as prizes — hence poet laureate and baccalaureate."

"Joan knows more trivia than anyone else we know," Dolores said. "My son-in-law is Hispanic and a great cook. He uses oregano in bean dishes, burritos, and salsa."

By the time the ladies left, I'd made a tidy profit courtesy of Tony Deltorro. If he ever decided to speak to me again, I'd have to thank him. Now that my shop had quieted once more, I'd try again to plant my herbs. I hauled the rustic-looking planter I bought from Patti Sue Parker at Yesteryear Antiques for next to nothing outside to begin my project.

I had knelt on the sidewalk, humming to myself as I dumped potting soil into the container, when a pair of tan slacks came into view. Shading my eyes with my free hand, I looked up. "Hey, CJ," I said, then picked up a trowel.

"Hiya, Scooter," he said, looking inordinately pleased with himself.

His pleasant tone immediately put me on high alert. He was up to something, I could tell. "What brings you here in the middle of the day? If you're here to see Lindsey, she won't be out of school for another hour yet."

"I had to drop off a copy of power of attorney to Zach VanFleet at Creekside Savings and Loan. Thought long as I was nearby I'd say hello." He rocked back on the heels of his polished loafers. "Say, have you heard from Momma and Cot?"

I added a trowel of dirt to the planter. "No, but I didn't really expect to hear anything this soon. After all, they are honeymooners."

He frowned. "Still can't wrap my head around the notion I've got a stepfather."

"Don't look so glum." I chuckled. "I'm sure Cot won't expect you to call him Daddy."

"When hell freezes over."

"Vicki Lamont stopped by this morning."

I leaned back to better see his expression. "She wondered if your mother intended to put her house on the market. She thinks she may have a client who is interested."

CJ scowled, his mood darkening further. "I'll buy the damn place myself before I see strangers in the house where I grew up."

"Gee, CJ, I didn't know you were sentimental. Maybe you should consider selling that big mausoleum you call a home. Then you and Amber could move into your mother's place."

"That'll be the day. No way I'd get Amber to budge. She likes bein' close to the country club. Claims it saves money on transportation." His attention shifted to the partially filled planter and box of herbs as though noticing them for the first time. "What's with the weeds?"

"They're not weeds." I informed him. "I'm planting a container garden and plan to sell fresh as well as dried herbs. They ought to do well out here with all the sunlight."

"Wait just a cotton-pickin' minute. No way you're litterin' the sidewalk with a bunch of weeds in ugly-lookin' pots."

"Why not?" I could feel my temper rise but struggled to keep it in check. "I hardly think I need to ask your permission."

"On the contrary, you're forgettin' I'm the acting mayor. I don't want my first official act to be writin' a citation to my ex-wife for obstructin' a public thoroughfare. There's an ordinance in the town's bylaws against such a thing. It's considered a safety threat."

"You wouldn't," I said in a choked voice, but knew he wouldn't hesitate. My lovely plan to grow and sell fresh herbs burst like a soap bubble.

"You know me, Scooter. I've never been one to shirk my sworn duty."

I climbed to my feet, tugged off my gardening gloves, and tossed them aside. He sounded so self-righteous, so darn smug, I wanted to smack him. "Anything else you can do to ruin my day?"

Reaching into an inner pocket of his sports coat, he took out a pair of Ray-Bans and put them on. "Thought you'd might like to be one of first to know that Shirley Randolph's death is officially being treated as a homicide."

I shouldn't have felt surprised, certainly not shocked. Yet I was both. While it was one thing for me to think it, theorize about it, hearing CJ speak the words took Shirley's death out of the realm of supposition and made it frighteningly real.

"What next?" I asked.

"Beau plans to press hard to make an arrest. His career is on the line. If things go his way, he's likely to be appointed the next police chief. Everyone in town knows who's the number one suspect. McBride's in this up to his eyeballs."

I brushed potting soil off my slacks. "So far, there's nothing concrete to link him to Shirley's murder."

"Won't be the first man charged and convicted on circumstantial evidence — won't be the last." Smiling, he turned and sauntered down the street.

I stared after him, numb with the realization of the danger McBride faced. The two men had a history dating back to high school. CJ would like nothing better than to see his old nemesis behind bars.

Even if it took circumstantial evidence to accomplish it.

CHAPTER 17

Southerners place a lot a stock in a well-attended funeral. Judging from the crowded parking lot, Shirley's final act would play to a full house.

Reba Mae and I walked up the stone steps of St. Mark's Episcopal Church and entered the narthex. The first thing that caught my attention was a group of women clustered around an alcove oohing and aahing over an item of some sort.

"Let's take a gander," Reba Mae suggested. "Find out what the fuss is all about."

I started to remind my friend that the service would begin shortly, but she was already making her way across the narthex. I don't often complain that I'm vertically challenged, but in situations like this my height was a definite disadvantage. Reba Mae, on the one hand, even without the three- and four-inch heels she gravitated toward could easily tower over the heads of many of the women. I, on the other hand, was petite, a mere five foot two. Standing as I was at the back of the group, I had to weave and dodge to catch a glimpse of what the others found so fascinating.

"What is it?" I asked a trifle impatiently.

"It's a memory board." Mary Lou Lambert, a frequent customer of Reba Mae's and infrequent one of mine, informed us. "It's just the sweetest thing ever. Shirley's aunt made it and brought it with her all the way from Macon."

I darted a peek from behind a heavyset woman and caught sight of a young Shirley pictured in a Cinderella costume for Halloween.

Pinky Alexander, an adventurous cook and grandma-to-be, leaned forward giving me another glimpse of Shirley, this time in cap and gown and holding a diploma. "Oh, look," Pinky cooed. "Here's one of Shirley with a Realtor of the Month plaque. That woman sure knew how to sell houses."

Mary Lou shook her head and *tsk*ed. "Pity Shirley didn't live long enough to fix up that old house she just bought. She would've made a killing."

Mary Lou's comment had a quieting effect. One by one the women murmured excuses about needing to find seats and drifted toward the sanctuary.

"Unless we want folding chairs at the back," Reba Mae said, "we'd better find us a spot."

I swept my gaze over the memory board a final time. A photo of Shirley, dressed in an evening gown and looking happier and more relaxed than I'd ever seen her, smiled back at me. With a heavy heart, I turned to follow my friend.

The funeral concluded, Reba Mae looped her arm through mine as we headed across the church parking lot toward the parish hall where the luncheon was to be held.

"The Methodist ladies always put on a better spread than the Episcopalians. Just love all them casseroles they bring."

"Their casseroles ought to come with a warning label. They're definitely not recommended for those who recently had bypass surgery. The sodium content in the canned soups alone is sky-high."

"Um, I s'pose, but that chicken lasagna with the pecan toppin' Pinky Alexander always brings is delish. Makes my mouth water just thinkin' about it."

The parish hall was rapidly filling with people. A long table covered in white damask occupied an entire wall. A silver coffee urn sat at one end, a tea service at the other. Two members of St. Mark's Altar Guild were stationed on either end in high-backed chairs, ready to dispense coffee or tea. Nearby, a buffet table was laden with enough goodies to alleviate hunger in a third-world country.

"Don't know about you, honeybun, but I'm gonna dive in while there's still good pickin's."

While Reba Mae headed for the food, I used the opportunity to weave in and out of the mourners and unabashedly eavesdrop.

"Can't believe Wyatt McBride had the gall to show his face at the funeral," Jolene Tucker said to Gerilee Barker.

"Now, Jolene," Gerilee replied, "whatever happened to innocent till proven guilty? Can't be easy for McBride with half the folks treatin' him like a leper."

Standing next to Mary Lou, who was talking to Alvertie Hawkins, I pretended to check my cell phone for messages. "Hank and I once saw Shirley and Chief McBride sharin' a plate of chili cheese fries," Mary Lou confided. "You and I both know you don't share cheese fries with just anyone."

I bit my tongue to keep from reminding Alvertie that Mary Lou was an airhead and

206

not to pay her any mind. Instead, I moved on.

"McBride's guilty as sin, but the man's clever enough to cover his tracks," Trish Hughes, the mother of one of Lindsey's friends, said to Patti Sue Parker.

Patti Sue nibbled a cheese straw. "First time I laid eyes on him, I had him pegged as a ladies' man."

Seems popular opinion didn't weigh heavily in McBride's favor. Disheartened, I glanced around and zeroed in on Vicki, who was conversing with Zach VanFleet. "Hey, you two," I said as I joined them. "Lovely service, wasn't it?"

"Yes, indeed," Zach answered. "Very tasteful. Shirley would have approved."

Vicki smiled sadly. "Poor, poor Shirley. This is all so . . . so . . . tragic. She was a dear friend of mine and will be sorely missed."

Dear friend? Sorely missed? This from the same lips that had accused Shirley of snatching a hefty commission from Vicki's hot little hands? The very same person who stopped shy of calling Shirley a money-hungry scumbag. My, oh my. What had prompted the change of heart?

Vicki wiped an invisible tear from her eye. "I shudder to think what she must have suffered in the last moments of her life."

"Everyone is saying Shirley's death is no longer considered a suicide," Zach volunteered.

Vicki nodded. "Jolene told me a report came back from the GBI that since no water was found in her lungs, her death suggests foul play."

Leave it to Jolene Tucker to spread the news. She'd love nothing more than to see McBride discredited and her husband hired as chief.

"Shirley was a dream to work with, the soul of cooperation and integrity. But I'm sure you will be as well," Zach added hurriedly for Vicki's benefit. "Now if you ladies will excuse me, I want to grab a bite to eat before returning to the bank."

I watched him melt into the crowd around the buffet table, then turned to Vicki. "I have to confess, I'm confused. I was under the impression you were angry with Shirley for stealing a possible commission."

"Me? Angry?" Vicki's eyes widened in feigned innocence. "Shirley was my mentor. I'm indebted to her for helping me start a career. I may have been a little miffed, but . . ."

I knew the difference between "a little miffed" and "a lot angry" but decided to let it pass for the time being. "Are the Dixons still interested in purchasing Gray's Hardware from Mavis?"

"Not if Elaine has her way," Vicki retorted. "But in the meantime, I have a potential home buyer — Colin Flynn — who is keeping me busy. As a matter of fact, I'm showing him a house later this afternoon."

"Colin Flynn?" I started to search the crowd. "Is he here?"

"Stop!" Vicki hissed. "Don't stare! I don't want him to know we're talking about him. He's a very private person. If you'll excuse me, this would be the perfect time for me to confirm our appointment."

Left to my own devices, I decided holding a plate of food would make me look less of a nosey Parker. The line at the buffet table had dwindled, so I helped myself to several finger sandwiches — pimento cheese and deviled ham — then, because the sandwiches looked lonely, added a stuffed egg and a pecan tassie.

Who would be my next target? I wondered. Preoccupied, I turned and bumped into Matt Wainwright. My stuffed egg skidded across the plate and landed square on his silk necktie like an unsightly carbuncle.

"Whoa," he said, steadying me.

"Sorry," I mumbled, unable to take my

eyes off the yellow gooey mess clinging to navy and gold striped silk. "I'm so, so sorry." Coming to my senses, I dabbed frantically at the glob of egg with a paper napkin, knowing full well the mayonnaise would leave a greasy stain.

"Don't worry about it." Matt extracted a handkerchief from the pocket of his suit coat and managed to clean off most of the gunk.

"The least you can do is let me replace your tie."

"Don't worry about it," he said. "I've got more neckties than I'll ever use."

"Thanks." Looking up at him, I flashed him a grateful smile. I liked Matt. I found him nicer and easier going than his wife, Mary Beth. Tall with sandy brown hair and smoky gray eyes, Matt always had a ready smile. Today, however, his smile seemed strained and his eyes were bloodshot.

"Are you all right?" I asked. "Allergies bothering you?"

"Yeah. Must be the pollen." He wadded up his handkerchief, which by now rivaled his greasy necktie in the stain department, then walked away.

"Hey there, Piper." Amber Leigh Ames-Prescott aimed a toothy grin at me. "Another murder in our little town. This is all so shockin'. CJ swears once he's elected mayor he's goin' to put an end to the crime spree."

I was having trouble wrapping my mind around CJ being elected mayor and the "crime spree" to which Amber alluded.

She waved a French-manicured hand. "Bein' mayor is only a steppin'-stone. CJ has higher aspirations. Maybe even be governor someday. He has Daddy's blessin', of course."

"Of course," I said, knowing "Daddy's blessings" would come in the form of financial support.

"One of CJ's first duties as mayor will be to recommend Beau Tucker as new chief of police. Wyatt McBride's qualifications might look impressive on paper, but obviously the man is inept." Amber pointed at the pecan tassie still on my plate untouched. "You're not going to eat that thing, are you? Those things are loaded with calories."

"Matter of fact . . ." I popped it into my mouth for the pure satisfaction of watching her expression. "Mmm, yum," I said, licking my fingers as she stalked off to join Vicki.

"That's no way to make friends and influence people."

At the sound of McBride's voice directly behind me, I nearly dropped the plate a

211

second time. "Sheesh!" I huffed out a breath. "Do you make it a habit to sneak up on people?"

"Blame it on my DNA. I'm part Cherokee." He bit into a pickled mushroom.

"Yeah, right."

"No, it's true," he insisted. "Goes back to my great-grandfather. Cherokees, you know, were indigenous throughout the Southeast. Georgia, Tennessee, and the Carolinas. Scots and Cherokee add up to a winning combination, or so my dad used to say."

I didn't know whether he was telling the truth or pulling my leg. But the revelation went a long way toward explaining the dark hair and chiseled features. "Can't pass up an opportunity for a free lunch?" I asked, eyeing his plate, which was heaped with Southern delicacies.

"Nope." He bit into a triangle of pumpernickel bread topped with a thin slice of smoked salmon. "I wanted to give folks more to gossip about. By the way, who's the nerdy-type guy with the glasses? He must be new in town."

"Colin Flynn." I didn't even have to look. I knew immediately who he was talking about. "Shirley was supposed to show him some houses. According to him, they had never met in person."

"Seems odd." The smoke salmon triangle demolished, McBride selected a cracker spread with liver pâté to sample next. "If he didn't know Shirley, why is he here?"

I swiped an olive from his plate when I didn't think he was watching. "Good question. You're the detective. Why not go over and introduce yourself?"

"Think I'll do just that, and" — he grinned and the dimple in his cheek winked at me — "I saw you steal my olive."

Time to round up Reba Mae and get back to business. We'd been away long enough. I found her at the dessert table debating between coconut cake and double fudge brownies. "Ready to leave?"

"Soon as I sample a dessert or two." She frowned when she saw the two uneaten finger sandwiches still on my plate. "You forget to mention that you're on a diet to your best friend?"

I handed my plate off to a member of the kitchen crew who had started cleanup duties. "I almost had a stuffed egg, but it ended up as a decoration on Matt Wainwright's necktie."

"Oops." After careful deliberation, Reba Mae made her selection. "Can't never go wrong with chocolate sheet cake."

"Before we leave, let's take another look

213

at the memory board." I accepted a cup of coffee from the woman manning an ornate silver pot. "There were so many people standing in front of it, I never saw all the photos."

"Fine by me." Reba Mae took a forkful of cake. "I was talkin' to Vicki a bit ago and asked her about the banker fellow. I got to thinkin' since he and Shirley worked together maybe he was the man in her life."

"The thought occurred to me, too, even though he looks more like a size Medium than a Large." I sipped my coffee, hot and rich, just the way I liked it.

"I got the scoop straight from the horse's mouth," Reba Mae said, taking another bite of cake. "Vicki told me the guy was engaged. His fiancée works in Atlanta, and they're plannin' a fall weddin'."

"He wouldn't be the first man in a long-distance relationship to have a fling with a beautiful coworker."

"Nope, and not the last either."

Coffee and cake finished, Reba Mae and I made our way toward the entrance foyer where the memory board sat propped on an easel. It was covered with snapshots showing various highlights of Shirley's life. Pictures of Shirley and her brother as toddlers, ones of her with braces, as homecoming queen, at high school and college graduations, and as the recipient of various awards. But one photo in particular captured my attention.

Once again the photo tacked in the lower right-hand corner beckoned to me. It was the picture of Shirley I'd noticed earlier — the glamour shot of her in an evening gown. I stepped closer for a better look and this time observed a detail I had previously overlooked. I stared and kept on staring. I simply couldn't help myself.

A man's arm circled Shirley's waist. In the obviously cropped photo, only the arm of her companion was visible. French cuffs with chunky gold cuff links peeked from a sleeve of a dark suit coat. If I squinted real hard, I could make out a faint tan line on the man's hand where a wedding ring should have been. I'd seen those French cuffs, seen those same cuff links, minutes ago when Matt Wainwright wiped stuffed egg from his tie.

Shirley *and* Matt? Matt Wainwright — upstanding citizen, model husband — was Shirley's secret lover? I was flabbergasted! You could have knocked me over with a feather. I'd known Matt for years. He was a family man, devoted to his wife and his children. He and Mary Beth were as perfectly matched as a pair of brass bookends. They often finished each other's sentences.

"Hey, honeybun." Reba Mae studied me, a worried expression on her face. "You look like someone walked over your grave."

I gave myself a mental shake. "Let's get out of here."

"Good thinkin'," she said. "I've got a cut and color due in ten minutes."

We were about to pass the cloakroom when I heard raised voices from behind the partially closed door. I caught my friend's arm and held a finger to my lips. "Shh."

"I saw the photo of you two," railed a female voice I recognized as belonging to Mary Beth Wainwright.

"Hush now, Mary Beth. Don't go jumping to conclusions," Matt said, trying to placate his angry wife.

"Don't you hush me! I know what I saw," her voice rose. "I had those cuff links made especially for you. They're one of a kind."

An awkward pause followed. Reba Mae and I stayed glued to the floor, leaning forward in our eagerness to hear Matt's response.

Through a crack in the door, I saw Mary Beth wave her arm. "Just as I suspected all along. You were having an affair. I dare you, Matt, admit it — if you're man enough."

When Mary Beth's challenge was met with silence, Reba Mae and I quickly made our escape from the parish hall and ran down the steps.

"If the robe fits . . ." I paraphrased a famous line from the O. J. Simpson trial of the century.

"Yeppers." Reba Mae nodded. "Matt Wainwright looks a size Large to me."

CHAPTER 18

Impatience itched like a mosquito bite. I was sorely tempted to lock the door of Spice It Up! and play hooky. I replayed Melly's lecture in my mind on the pitfalls of being a lackadaisical business owner. I missed her. She was always ready and willing — sometimes a little too willing — to play shopkeeper at a moment's notice. Where was she when I needed her? In Tuscany, that's where, and thus far not even so much as a postcard.

The argument I'd just overheard between Matt and Mary Beth repeated through my head like a broken record until I wanted to scream. I needed to confront Matt. Wanted to hear him admit it was his bathrobe in Shirley's closet. And, most important, I wanted to ask point-blank, *Did you kill her?* If he denied it, I'd at least like to know whether or not he had an alibi for the weekend Shirley was murdered. I clearly remembered that he and Mary Beth had been noticeably absent from Melly and Cot's wedding.

To occupy my mind, I worked on plans for my one-year anniversary extravaganza. Reba Mae, bless her heart, had been persuaded to demonstrate her grandmother's recipe for Hungarian goulash. Cake and coffee were always a big draw. And I'd do a giveaway. I got out pen and paper and started jotting down ideas. A giveaway didn't necessarily have to be expensive. Maybe a nice gift basket with an assortment of spices, one of my bright yellow aprons, a pack of recipe cards, and, for good measure, I'd throw in some cooking gadgets or a cookbook. Soon I'd have to begin advertising the upcoming event. I'd start with a large sign in my window and maybe take out a small ad in *The Statesman,* our weekly newspaper. Flyers with every purchase might also serve as good reminders.

Casey woke from his nap and began pacing back and forth, alerting me to Lindsey's return from school even before I caught my first sight of her.

"Hey, Mom," she said, swinging her backpack to the floor. "Anything good to eat?"

"I thought you were on a rabbit food diet." I pulled my apron over my head and tossed it to her.

"I keep forgetting." She caught the apron one handed. "I'm craving cookies — and chocolate."

"If you keep an eye on the shop for an hour, I might be able to find one or two chocolate chip cookies stashed in the freezer."

"Deal." She grinned, stooping to rub Casey's tummy.

I grabbed my purse from under the counter and was out the door in a flash. The offices of Prescott and Wainwright, Attorneys, were located on the edge of the historic district not far from Felicity Driscoll's bed-and-breakfast and Shirley Randolph's home. Matt had campaigned heavily for the area, insisting it exuded class and success. CJ would have preferred a more contemporary environment, but, in the end, he capitulated. Shirley had brokered the deal.

As I turned in the drive and parked, I didn't spot either CJ's Lexus or Matt's Bimmer. The only car present was Wanda Needmore's Honda Accord. That worked for me. Wanda knew the ins and outs, the ups and downs, of Prescott and Wainwright better even than Prescott or Wainwright. Wanda was the firm's paralegal and had worked for CJ since he started his practice. I'd be willing to wager she knew CJ wanted a divorce from me while I was still blissfully feeding him pot roast.

I ran up the steps of a wide front porch and shoved open the door and stepped into a marble-tiled reception area. No one manned the secretary/receptionist's desk, so I went directly down a short hallway to Wanda's office.

I knocked once but didn't wait for an invitation to enter. "Hey, Wanda," I said cheerfully. "Hope I'm not interrupting anything important."

Wanda glanced up from the file she was reading. She didn't look pleased to see me, but then she never did. "What could I possibly be doing that's of any importance?"

I chose to ignore the sarcasm. Widowed, Wanda wore her gray hair in a no-nonsense style, kept her makeup to a minimum, and preferred skirts over slacks in the workplace. Her surprising concession to prim and proper was dating Dale Simons, a motorcycle rider and owner of the local pawnshop.

"I looked for you at Shirley's funeral," I said. "I saw you at the church but not at the reception."

"I failed to see the point in staying. I've eaten enough stuffed eggs and tomato aspic to last a lifetime." She applied the stapler to

221

a stack of papers. "How can I help you?"

I debated whether to pave the way with verbal foreplay or use a more direct approach. Sinking into the chair opposite her desk, I smoothed my black suit skirt, which I hadn't bothered to change after the funeral. When Wanda picked up a pen and tapped it up and down, I decided to dispense with small talk. "Did you know Shirley well?"

"No, not really," she huffed out with a sigh. "No better than most of the firm's clients."

I nodded thoughtfully. "Mary Beth mentioned that Matt had drawn up Shirley's will. Did she use the firm in her real estate dealings as well?"

"Matt's what is known in the trade as a 'dirt' lawyer. That means he specializes in anything connected to real estate."

"Then he and Shirley must've met frequently?"

Wanda frowned. "What are you hinting at?"

"Nothing." I gave her a bland smile. "Did she work exclusively with Matt or did she occasionally work with CJ?"

"CJ handles mostly litigation these days," Wanda explained.

"Yes," I replied. "I've seen his billboards

along the highway." Truth be told, I'm always so mesmerized by how white his teeth are in those ads that it's a wonder I don't drive off the road.

"Your ex is gaining quite a reputation as a trip and fall attorney. His cases bring a good share of revenue into the firm. He recently won a hefty settlement from the maker of a popular shower gel for a woman who broke her toe after dropping the bottle on her foot."

"Where does he find these people?" I asked, truly amazed by his clientele.

Wanda put her pen aside and actually smiled. "Oh, they find him. His current caseload is mostly word of mouth. His reputation is spreading like kudzu."

I heard the front door open and close. At the babble of male voices filtering down the hallway, I popped up from the chair. Although I'd extracted a couple morsels of information from Wanda, Matt was my target du jour. "Sorry for taking up so much of your time, Wanda," I said as I sprinted off.

CJ was the first of the partners to spy me. "Scooter!" he boomed. "What brings you here?"

Matt acknowledged me with a polite nod, then pulled his cell phone from his suit pocket and scrolled for messages. In the interim between the reception and now, he'd replaced his stained necktie with a similar one.

Since Matt apparently was ignoring me, I addressed my ex instead: "Hey, CJ, I didn't even get a chance to say hello to you at Shirley's funeral. Every time I looked, you were huddled with the mayor or one of the councilmen."

CJ did his cat-who-ate-the-canary imitation. "Big plans on the horizon, darlin'. Stay tuned for breakin' news."

Uh-oh. While good for CJ, this usually meant it was time for the person on the receiving end to get his affairs in order.

Finished checking for messages, Matt gave me a distracted wave and walked toward his office.

"Amber's takin' Linds shoppin' in Atlanta some weekend real soon to get her started on her wardrobe for college," CJ said, adjusting the knot in his tie. "After scorin' high on her SATs, our girl deserves a reward. Who would've guessed she was the brains in the family. Chad sure has his nose out of joint since hearin' the news."

"Chad needs to concentrate on his studies, not worry that his sister outperformed him on some test."

"I hear you." CJ chuckled. "But that doesn't do much for our boy's wounded ego."

"Guess we'll have to put a Band-Aid on his injured pride when he comes home for the summer."

CJ shot his cuffs to better view his Rolex. "That's somethin' we need to discuss, but now isn't a good time."

Instantly my mother's instinct went on full alert. "Is anything wrong?"

"Don't go gettin' your panties in a twist, darlin'. We'll talk soon enough."

"Okay." I released a breath I didn't know I was holding. "It's really Matt who I wanted to see. I . . . ah . . . have a question for him about the contract he drew up when I bought Spice It Up!" I improvised.

"I'm sure he'd be happy to put your mind at ease." CJ nodded his blond head in the direction Matt had taken. "You know the way."

Matt was on the phone when I entered but signaled me to wait. Years ago, Matt and CJ had converted the rooms at the rear of the building into two spacious offices. I took the opportunity to admire the view from the windows behind Matt's antique part-ners' desk, an anniversary gift from Mary Beth. Both his and CJ's offices overlooked a flagstone terrace and a sloping lawn mounded with pretty pink azaleas. Once or twice a year, the yard became the setting to entertain their clients on a lavish scale. Before Miss Peach Pit, the new and improved Mrs. Prescott, arrived on the scene, I'd been the hostess with the mostess at these events.

"What can I help you with, Piper?" Matt swiveled his chair around to face me. He motioned toward a pair of brass-studded leather club chairs, the rich color of fine Burgundy wine. "I overheard you say something about a clause in the purchase agreement that you don't understand?"

I took the seat closest to the door. I realized belatedly I should have taken more time to consider my approach. Being impulsive was a fault of mine. Ask forgiveness, not permission, was a philosophy that often overruled my better judgment.

Matt tapped away on his keyboard and brought up a file on his computer screen. "Brig Abernathy was the owner of record for the building you bought. He's a curmudgeon when it comes to detail. I made doubly sure all the *t*'s were crossed and the *i*'s dotted."

Shifting uneasily in my seat, I cleared my throat. If Matt turned out to be Shirley's killer, I was putting myself in his cross hairs. But I was safe here in his office, wasn't I? Should he try any funny business, I'd scream bloody murder — poor word choice — and bring Wanda and CJ running to my rescue. Gathering my nerve, I dove in headfirst. "Um, actually I'm here on another matter. I believe you're missing a certain item from your wardrobe."

Matt's expression underwent a subtle change. "Sorry, Piper, I have no idea what you're talking about."

"Does a charcoal gray terry-cloth bathrobe, size Large, ring a bell?"

He pursed his lips but didn't answer.

"I believe I found your robe in Shirley's closet," I continued, nonplussed.

"Ridiculous! What would my robe be doing in her closet?" He picked up a manila folder and flipped it open. "I don't have time for this nonsense."

If he thought I'd be dismissed this easily, he wasn't as shrewd as I thought he was. "Were you and Shirley having an affair?"

"I resent the insinuation!" he snapped.

"I'm sure you do," I said mildly, "but that doesn't answer my question."

"Naturally I deny it. C'mon, Piper, you've known me for years. You know Mary Beth and I are devoted to each other."

227

"That's what I thought until I recognized your cuff links on the man with his arm around Shirley in the photo on the memory board. Judging from the argument I overheard in the cloakroom, I know Mary Beth recognized them, too."

He studied me over steepled fingers. His expression hardened, leaving no trace of the affable man I'd considered a friend. "What if, for the sake of argument, Shirley and I were having an affair? That doesn't automatically make me her killer."

"Did either you or Shirley attempt to end the relationship? Is that what set things in motion?"

"You've overstayed your welcome, Piper. I suggest you leave."

"Do you have an alibi for the time Shirley was killed?" I fired off one final question before he could bodily evict me.

"None of your damn business." His face flushed an ugly shade of red. "Get out! Now!"

I left the office with as much dignity as I could muster. Even with a carload of possible suspects, Matt Wainwright was in the driver's seat.

CHAPTER 19

"Hey, honeybun. You'll never believe what happened." Reba Mae flounced in, plopped herself down on the edge of the counter, and pouted. "My hot-water tank quit workin' smack dab'n the middle of the afternoon."

"Oh no! That's awful!" I stopped watering my collection of herbs — herbs that, by the way, were rapidly outgrowing their tiny pots — to sympathize with my BFF's catastrophe.

"Had to cancel the rest of my appointments. Let me tell you, Mary Lou was one unhappy camper when I called to give her the news."

"What are you going to do?" I plucked a yellowing leaf from a pot of parsley. "I'd suggest having Ned Feeney take a look, but he gave himself a concussion while replacing my garbage disposal. No telling what he might do with a hot-water heater. Don't

229

want an explosion at the Klassy Kut."

"I called the store where I bought it, but they can't send a repairman till Monday." She cast a look at my container garden-to-be and pulled a face. "Those poor things are in need of some tender, lovin' care, not to mention a heap of dirt and a place in the sun."

I heaved a sigh. "I know. My dream of growing and selling fresh herbs ended when CJ threatened me with a citation for obstruction of public walkways."

"He gets elected mayor, he'll be writin' so many citations he'll end up with that carmel tunnel thing like my cousin Jake."

I tried not to smile. "I believe it's called 'carpal' not 'carmel' tunnel."

"Whatever, it ain't good. The doctor messed up the operation and now Jake's third finger is permanently pointin', you know. . . ."

I grimaced at the visual. "Not a good way to make friends."

Reba Mae nodded solemnly. "Poor guy. He's gotten into more'n one bar fight at High Cotton 'cause of that durn finger."

I tested the soil in a pot of cilantro and noted it could stand more water. "Have you decided what you're wearing to Mavis's cocktail party tonight?"

"Was gonna wear my little black dress, but Shirley's funeral was yesterday. It's against my religion to wear the same color twice in one week." She crossed one long leg over the other and let one shoe dangle. "Now that I got some time on my hands, I'm thinkin' of cookin' up a mess of tomato sauce with some Italian sausage. My boys have been cravin' lasagna. It'll make a nice Sunday supper. Sauce always tastes better if I make it a day ahead, gives the flavors a chance to get better acquainted."

"You're in luck then." I set my watering can aside. "My latest shipment of spices arrived this morning, which included oregano and basil. No self-respecting lasagna sauce is made without the dynamic duo."

"You had me at oregano."

I foraged through a box the UPS driver had delivered but I'd failed to unpack. "What's your pleasure?" I asked, holding up two jars of oregano. "Turkish or Mexican?"

"Turkish," Reba Mae replied after a second's hesitation.

"Mexican's better!" growled a whiskey-rough voice. We both looked up in time to see Hoyt remove his motorcycle helmet as he strolled into Spice It Up! "I'm partial to Mexican, less sweet, but still strong."

Reba Mae smirked. "I always use Turkish

231

for pasta dishes. It's sweet *and* strong."

"If you ever tried my chili, darlin', you'd know why I favor Mexican." Hoyt smirked right back. "When you sample my guacamole, you'll think you died and went to heaven."

"Once you taste my lasagna, you'll switch to Turkish oregano in a heartbeat."

"Deal." Hoyt grinned broadly, showing a glint of gold filling. "Let me know the time and place."

"How about Sunday? Six o'clock."

"You're on."

Well, well, well. Hoyt and my bestie flirting? In spite of their age difference, I should have seen that one coming, but I hadn't. I'd felt like a spectator at a Ping-Pong match during their exchange. Hoyt agreed so readily my jaw dropped. It'd be interesting to see how this played out, but if the biker dude hurt my friend's feelings he'd have to answer to me.

"Guess I'd better get cookin' since company's comin'." Reba Mae slid from the counter and sashayed out the door. I noticed the exaggerated sway in her hips, but, from the expression on Hoyt's face, he seemed to appreciate the scenery.

"Told you once, I was partial to redheads," Hoyt reminded me. "Your friend looks mighty fine with her hair that dark, auburn color."

"My friend looks 'mighty fine' with her hair any color of the rainbow."

"Yes, ma'am," Hoyt said with a good-natured wink. "I'm partial to rainbows, too."

I laughed. "Hoyt, you just might've met your match. Now, what brought you into my shop this afternoon?"

"Need some juniper berries. The ones I have don't smell fresh, so it's time to replace them. Better give me a small jar of cardamom while you're at it."

"Plan to do some cooking and baking, I see."

"Like to keep busy, experiment with new recipes."

I was on tiptoe reaching for the cardamom, which was on a top shelf, when the door opened and another customer entered. "Be right with you!" I called out.

"Take your time," McBride said. "I'm in no rush."

Surprised at his presence, I fumbled the jar of cardamom but managed to catch it before it crashed to the floor.

At the sound of his favorite lawman's voice, Casey roused himself from a nap in the storeroom and trotted over to greet McBride with a pathetic display of affection. McBride didn't disappoint my mutt but stooped to rub him behind his ear, sending the little dog into a paroxysm of pleasure.

"Anything else?" I asked Hoyt upon returning to the counter.

"That ought to do it." He peeled off a twenty-dollar bill from the cash he kept in his money clip, then nodded at the carton of herbs. "What's with all the plants sitting there?"

"I planned to start a container garden on the sidewalk and sell fresh herbs."

McBride frowned. "Planned . . .?"

"CJ spouted a city ordinance about cluttering and put an end to my idea." I rang up the sale. "I'm not sure what to do now."

"I've got plenty of land if you're looking for a garden plot," McBride offered.

Hoyt accepted the change I handed him. "Heck, I'll even rototill it for you if you can wait until Monday."

"Great," McBride and I answered in unison.

"Okeydokey, then. Looks like you're in the herb-growing business." Hoyt stuffed his purchases into a zippered pouch of his jacket. With a jaunty salute and a self-satisfied smile, he sauntered out.

Conscious of McBride watching me, I

went about the business of unpacking and sorting the spices I'd ordered from a supplier, baking and barbecue to one side, ethnic on the other. I was increasingly aware of the pheromones that sparked between us. McBride's testosterone beckoned to my estrogen. Casey sensing the energy, too, sat on his haunches, head cocked, button-brown eyes bright.

"You're starting to make me nervous, McBride. Seeing how you're on suspension, are you getting up courage to ask for a part-time job?" I stuffed the wrapping paper used to cushion the order back into the box. "I could use a little extra help now and then until Melly returns from her honeymoon. Do you come with references?"

A small smile played around his mouth. He picked up a jar of crystallized ginger, examined it, then set it down. "I like my salt salty and my pepper black. Will that do?"

"Gotta start somewhere. Nothing wrong with a clean slate." Gathering an assortment of jars, I moved toward a row of shelves with McBride trailing. "Your happening by saves me a phone call. I discovered who Shirley was having an affair with."

An alertness entered his cool blue eyes in variance with his casual demeanor. "This person have a name?"

"Matt Wainwright, CJ's law partner."

"You sure about that?"

"Yep." I nodded. "Positive."

"How did you happen upon this bit of information?"

"Aw shucks," I said with a sassy grin. "Nothing Nancy Drew couldn't have done."

He took a jar of cloves from me and set it on a shelf next to the Vietnamese cinnamon. "Mind enlightening me? I had to relinquish my crystal ball along with my badge."

"Blame it on the memory board at Shirley's funeral." An unruly curl fell across my brow, and I blew it away impatiently only to have it spring back. "One photo showed Shirley with a man's arm around her waist. I recognized the cuff links as the same ones Matt was wearing. Then, before leaving the reception, I overheard an argument between Matt and his wife, so Mary Beth made the connection, too."

"Lots of married couples argue," he countered. "Mary Beth might've been mad at her husband for forgetting to take out the trash. Or maybe he didn't throw his dirty socks in the laundry hamper."

"CJ used to put his dirty coffee cups in the dishwasher with the clean dishes so I'd have to run an entire cycle over again. It drove me bonkers."

"So," he drawled, his accent as sweet as a Georgia peach, "finally the real reason behind your divorce."

"The real reason" — I scowled — "is a long-legged brunette with a fondness for short skirts and older men."

"From what I've observed, Amber and CJ are two peas in a pod. They deserve each other."

"Back to the business of Matt and Shirley, I heard Mary Beth say the cuff links were one of a kind."

"Even if the man in the photo is Matt, that makes him an adulterer, not murderer."

"I know. Motive, means, and opportunity — and the greatest of these is motive. Maybe Shirley became tired of sneaking around. Maybe she wanted to take their relationship to the next level. Maybe she threatened to tell Mary Beth?"

McBride massaged the back of his neck. "Too many maybes and what-ifs to make a solid case."

"Like you said, you gotta start some-where." Folding my arms across my chest, I leaned against a row of shelves and gazed up at him. "My crystal ball is out of com-mission, too, McBride. Care to tell me what really brought you here?"

"You're not the only one who's done a bit of investigating. A friend of mine is a PI. I called in a favor. Had him do some background checks into Kirby and Elaine Dixon. Asked him to see what he could dig up."

McBride braced his arm on the shelf behind me, so close my hair brushed his forearm. My breath hitched in my throat. "So what did your friend find out?" I asked in a voice that didn't sound quite like my own.

"Kirby Dixon comes from money. After his father died, he used the money to more than double his inheritance. Before his retirement, he owned a string of car dealerships throughout central New York State. These proved a very lucrative business. On a personal note, this isn't the first marriage for either of the Dixons. This is Kirby's third, Elaine's second. The man's no fool. He insisted on an airtight pre-nup before their wedding."

"What about Elaine? What kind of work did she do before her marriage?"

McBride shot a sidelong glance at Casey, who was snoozing on the floor nearby. "You're not going to believe this." A hint of a smile played around his mouth. "Elaine was a dog groomer. She and Kirby met when she came to his house to clip and trim his poodle."

"Dog groomer to wife. That's quite a promotion."

"There's more." He paused a beat. "Elaine has a record. She served jail time some years back for larceny."

I gasped. "No way!"

McBride nodded solemnly. "I don't know for certain if Kirby was aware of this, but he did have an iron-clad pre-nup in place."

I shook my head, trying to digest everything McBride had just told me. "Being in love can have a strange effect on usually rational people."

"So I've heard," he said softly.

Reaching out, McBride brushed the obstinate curl from my brow. Instead of releasing it, however, he rubbed the strand between his thumb and forefinger, taking his sweet time examining the hue, savoring the texture. Again, he had an untoward effect on my respiration. My breathing slowed; my pulse raced; my lips parted. A powerful magnet seemed to be drawing us closer . . . and closer . . . until his mouth was a hairsbreadth from mine.

Suddenly the door to the shop burst open. "Surprise!"

Startled, we jerked apart. Seconds later the newcomer caught me up in a bear hug.

"Doug!" I extricated myself from the exuberant embrace and stepped back. I'm certain my face mirrored both shock and surprise. Doug Winters, mild-mannered vet, previous owner of Pets 'R People, and former boyfriend, smiled, obviously pleased with my reaction. Doug's prematurely silver hair was in stark contrast to a boyish face. Reba Mae once compared him to George Clooney, but personally I didn't see the resemblance.

"Let me look at you," he said, holding me at arm's length. "You're as pretty as ever."

I felt myself blush, painfully aware of McBride dissecting every nuance of Doug's effusive greeting. We'd been considered a couple until late last fall when he'd moved back to Chicago to be closer to his daughter. Although I hadn't been in "love" with Doug, I'd definitely been in "like."

McBride cleared his throat, drawing Doug's attention, and the two men shook hands. "Nice to see you again, Doug. Plan to stick around for a while?"

"Only until Monday," Doug explained. "I fly home that afternoon. I'm here only long enough to close the deal on my veterinary practice."

"I thought that was completed ages ago," I said.

"Financing for the new owners took longer than anticipated, but Zach VanFleet at Creekside Savings called to say he'd gotten final approval from the bank. Vicki knew I was coming and finagled me an invite to Mavis Gray's party this evening. I expect I'll see you there, McBride."

To his credit, McBride's expression gave nothing away. As he was the reigning pariah, his name had been excluded from the social register. "Can't make it, I'm afraid."

Doug shook his head. "What was I thinking? As a police chief with a death to investigate, you have a lot more pressing matters than a cocktail party."

"There's been a recent change," McBride said, his voice void of emotion. "Beau Tucker is acting chief of police."

Silence stretched like a wad of Dubble Bubble on the sole of a sneaker. "How well did you know Shirley, Doug?" I finally asked, jumping into the breach.

Doug removed his rimless eyeglasses and polished the lenses. "Shirley brokered the sale of Pets 'R People when I bought it. Naturally, she was the first person I called when I decided to sell and return to Illinois. Hearing she died came as quite a shock. Is it true she committed suicide?"

"It's under investigation," McBride said,

then turned and stalked out.

Doug looked puzzled but didn't pursue the issue. After extracting a promise from me to dine with him the following evening, he left to check into the Turner-Driscoll House and freshen up before tonight's party.

CHAPTER 20

Lights blazed in all the windows of the two-story Colonial. Mavis had referred to her get-together as a meet and greet. She was pulling out all the stops, determined to prove to the Dixons that Brandywine Creek was the greatest little town this side of paradise. She stubbornly refused to acknowledge that a mere week ago one of its citizens had been murdered.

I followed the walkway to Mavis's covered porch lit by the light from a crescent moon. I didn't bother ringing the doorbell. The sound wouldn't have been heard over the loud buzz of conversation. The decibel level increased as I stepped into the small foyer. Mavis magically appeared and took my wrap, then directed me to the refreshments.

The floor plan was similar to those of many Colonials. Living room on the right, dining room on the left, kitchen in the rear. Smiling and nodding, I threaded my way through the guests. I spotted Reba Mae in the dining room, trying to fit as many hors d'oeuvres as possible on a small plate.

"I think they make these plates tiny on purpose," she complained. She wedged a stuffed mushroom next to a pile of shrimp, which were nestled next to meatballs and a crab cake. Then, for good measure, she added cheese straws and a bacon-wrapped chicken tender. "This oughta hold me till it's time for dessert."

"I haven't jogged lately, so I need to go easy on the calories." I helped myself to some fruit along with crackers and a couple cubes of cheese. I really wanted a nice glass of wine but never perfected the technique of juggling hors d'oeuvres and a wineglass without spilling.

"Can you believe I'm gonna have a gentleman caller for Sunday night supper?" Reba Mae dragged a shrimp through a puddle of cocktail sauce. "I was hopin' Hoyt might be here tonight but don't see him anywhere."

"Slow down, girlfriend. Sunday night will come quick enough. You don't want to scare off a potential suitor."

"I don't think Hoyt's the type who scares easily. Can tell that by lookin' at him. Sissies don't ride Harleys."

"And real men eat quiche."

"Hoyt is the most interestin' fellow I've met since . . ."

". . . since your last admirer turned out to be in the witness protection program?" I supplied.

"You're leavin' out the good part — his Mafia connection."

"My bad."

"OMG!" Reba Mae caught my arm. "You'll never guess who just walked in."

A glance over my shoulder confirmed Reba Mae's eyesight was still 20/20. "Doug visited Spice It Up! earlier today," I explained. "He wanted to surprise me — and succeeded."

"See, what did I tell you?" She grinned. "I knew he'd be missin' you and hightailin' it back soon as he realized the error of his ways."

I rolled my eyes. "You ought to try your hand at writing romance novels. Doug's here to close on the sale of Pets 'R People. He's flying back to Chicago Monday afternoon."

"Too bad. Once upon a time, I had high hopes for the two of you." She pointed a cheese straw at a man talking to Vicki. "Who's he? I saw him at the funeral but didn't recognize him."

"Colin Flynn," I said. "He's new in town.

Shirley was supposed to show him some houses."

"He looks like a college professor, geeky but in a nice sort of way. Think I'll introduce myself. If things don't work out with Hoyt . . ."

"Reba Mae, he's way too young for you."

"Grrr!" she growled. "I might become one of them tiger ladies who like younger men."

"Cougars," I corrected, but her mischievous grin set my mind at ease.

Doug appeared at my side holding two wineglasses. "I assume you still like your wine white and your chocolate dark?"

I gratefully accepted a glass. Now I was confronted with the dilemma I'd tried to avoid — food or drink? Opting in favor of a beverage, I set the plate on an end table. "You look as though being a Yankee again agrees with you," I remarked after taking a sip of wine.

"Being back in Illinois is almost as though I never left," he admitted. "I sure won't miss the heat and humidity of Georgia summers."

"But the sixty-four-thousand-dollar question is, would you trade them for Chicago winters?"

"If it means keeping my daughter happy, then the answer is yes." He surveyed the guests, nodding and smiling at those he recognized. "I couldn't believe the news when I heard Shirley died. I was even more surprised to learn McBride's been suspended."

"Her death is being treated as a homicide — with McBride the number one suspect."

Doug let out a low whistle. "Were Mc-Bride and Shirley an item?"

"The two of them had a quasi relationship and, since McBride doesn't have a solid alibi, he's considered a person of interest. It doesn't help matters any that her body was found on his property."

Doug's brow furrowed. "Do you think it's wise spending time with him until things are sorted out?"

"Doug Winters!" I scolded. "I gave you more credit as a judge of character. You ought to know better than to think McBride had anything to do with Shirley's death."

He had the grace to look shamefaced. We chatted about the weather, our children, our jobs, but avoided the more personal. In the past, talk always flowed freely; now, however, it seemed . . . awkward. I already dreaded keeping the conversation ball afloat during our dinner date tomorrow night.

"I'm still having a hard time believing Shirley's dead," he said, staring into his wineglass as though expecting to find answers.

"Can you recall the last time you spoke to her?"

"A couple weeks ago, I guess. She called to tell me a date had been set for the closing." He sipped his wine, a faraway look in his eyes. "I still recall a conversation we had just before I left Brandywine Creek."

Something in his tone caused the needle of my curiosity meter to twitch. "Tell me about it," I said.

"Shirley knew I wasn't an MD but wanted my medical opinion anyway. Seems a friend of hers has a heart problem. Apparently this 'friend' read a magazine article that said a preliminary study from some university suggested ginger is helpful in certain cardiac conditions. When I assured Shirley that the friend's condition could be easily controlled with medication, she seemed relieved."

"Hmm. I don't suppose this friend of hers had a name."

"No." He shook his head. "I assumed he, or she, might have been a client."

"Probably," I sighed, disappointed. *Another piece of useless information? Another dead end?*

Vicki glanced over in our direction and motioned for Doug to join her. "Better go find out what she wants," Doug said. "I'll catch up with you later."

Matt and Mary Beth, I observed, were among the last guests to arrive. Neither appeared to be happy breathing the same air as the other. After briefly greeting their hostess, they gravitated to opposite ends of the house. Matt singled out Kirby Dixon at the buffet table while Mary Beth joined Gerilee Barker and Amber, who were huddled in a corner of the living room.

"Done with your plate, Miz Prescott?" asked a tall, attractive young woman with skin the color of café au lait. She indicated the unfinished plate of hors d'oeuvres I'd set on an end table.

"Lakeisha!" I said, instantly recognizing my son's former high school classmate. She and her auntie, Precious Blessing, shared the same bright smile and sunny disposition. "Georgia Southern know you're home for the weekend?"

"Yes, ma'am. Mrs. Gray called my momma and said she could use help serving." She stacked my plate on a tray she carried. "A friend told me Chad is thinking about taking a gap year before starting med school."

My brain froze. *A gap year?* Did that mean what I thought it did?

249

"My friend," Lakeisha continued, unaware I'd been mortally wounded, "said Chad wants to backpack around Europe."

Speech deserted me. I drained my wine, then snatched another from Lakeisha's tray. My son, the nose-to-the-grindstone student, planned to delay his education in favor of becoming a vagabond in a foreign country?

"Nice seeing you, Miz Prescott." Lakeisha smiled and moved on.

Did CJ know what our boy was contemplating? I needed to find out — the quicker the better. My gaze darted from group to group until I found my ex at the makeshift bar, his hand plastered to the small of Amber's waist. Much as it pained me to admit, Amber looked stunning in a formfitting red dress that showed off her assets — both God given and man-made.

I advanced like a determined General Patton leading his troops across France and tapped CJ on the shoulder. "We need to talk."

"Darlin', judgin' from your tone — and the look on your face — this is hardly the time or place for a showdown. Why not call my office for an appointment like most folks."

Amber gave me a smile sweet enough to induce a diabetic coma. "Now that CJ's

250

actin' mayor, he hardly has a minute's peace without bein' perstered for favors."

"Boo-hoo!" I snapped. "CJ, did you know Chad intends to take a year off before entering med school?"

"The boy might have mentioned it in passin'." CJ accepted a glass of Wild Turkey from the bartender. "I told him he deserved time off to sow some wild oats."

My voice rose. "You actually *encouraged* our son to drop out of school and backpack across Europe?"

CJ forced a smile. "Not just Europe, Scooter darlin', Chad wants to visit Thailand and India, too."

My head was reeling; whether from the news or downing too much wine too quickly I didn't know.

"Chad has a girlfriend, you know." Amber smiled slyly. "She's French. Her name's Brielle. I think he's in love."

"Why am I the last to know?" I asked, though I didn't expect an answer.

I didn't need CJ or Amber to explain what I already knew. Chad didn't want to confide in me because he didn't want to deal with my reaction. I felt heartsick at the idea of him abandoning the hopes and dreams he'd worked so hard for. Love shouldn't make you less; it should make you more. Yet I'd

251

dropped out of college before my senior year to marry his father and support him through law school. Next came two children whom I adored. During the ensuing years, I devoted myself to being the best wife and mother possible. How could I criticize my son for being blinded by love when I had done the same?

"Fine," I said at last to CJ. "We'll talk later."

Amber tugged on CJ's arm. "C'mon, Pooh Bear," she simpered. "We need to mingle."

No longer in the mood for a party, I went in search of my wrap. While daytime temperatures were pleasant, evenings required a sweater or light jacket. Tonight, I'd chosen my favorite paisley shawl to ward off the chill. Mavis had taken it from me when I arrived. My best chance of finding it was in an upstairs bedroom.

I had no sooner retrieved it from a pile of garments on a bed in a guest room and started down a hallway toward the stairs when I met Elaine Dixon coming out of the powder room. Elaine had dressed for her role as guest of honor in an apricot silk cocktail dress. Diamonds sparkled in the studs in her ears and from the eternity necklace circling her throat.

"Damn inconvenient having your guests

climb a flight of stairs to freshen up," she complained.

"It's a problem with a lot of older homes."

Elaine smoothed her pencil-slim skirt. "In my opinion, these fossils make better museums than homes. Shirley kept trying to sweet-talk Kirby into buying a house in your historic district. It made me furious listening to her raving on and on about it."

"I gather that you didn't like Shirley very much."

"What's to like? She was a beautiful woman who wouldn't hesitate to use it to her advantage. I saw the way she flirted with my husband. She was doing her best to persuade him to buy a business and settle here. Never in my life did I picture myself the wife of a hardware store owner in a town so small you need a magnifying glass in order to find it on a map."

"Do you miss being a dog groomer?" I don't know what made me ask, but the words seemed to pop out of their own volition.

Elaine's eyes widened, then narrowed. Under skillfully applied foundation, her complexion turned an ugly red that clashed with her apricot-colored dress. "I don't know what you're talking about," she fairly spit between clenched teeth.

I'd poked a sleeping bear with a sharp stick. Not a wise move on my part. I edged around her toward the stairs. "On the contrary, Elaine, you know exactly what I'm talking about. If Shirley and I could find out about your past, surely others can, too." I'd made a wild stab in the dark about Shirley discovering Elaine's past. Since she was reputed to be a savvy businesswoman, it might not be too farfetched to think she'd done a background check.

"Shirley, the bitch, thought she could use my former occupation against me." Elaine jabbed me in the chest with the sharp tip of a manicured nail, and I instinctively grabbed the banister. "Well, Shirley was wrong. I warned her to back off; now I'm warning you. Don't tangle with me, spice girl. I can fight dirty if I have to, so don't get in my way."

I fled down the stairs, the pulse pounding in my ears. Elaine Dixon had revealed herself as a formidable enemy. There was a moment when I'd feared she'd actually shove and send me tumbling down the steps. She was livid that I knew she'd been a dog groomer. What would her reaction be like if she knew I'd learned about her criminal past?

And what lengths would Kirby Dixon go

to in order to shield his wife from a murder charge?

I drove home in a daze. Lindsey still hadn't returned from the movies by the time I arrived home. My encounter with Elaine had left me more shaken than I cared to admit. I'd glimpsed a side of the woman, I'll wager, only a select few ever saw. Combine a mean, vindictive streak with a hot temper and it added up to a dangerous woman. I could easily envision Elaine tossing a high-powered hair dryer into a woman's bathtub — and afterwards persuading her husband to help cover up the crime.

After exchanging my party duds for a comfy nightshirt, I curled up on the sofa with a cup of herbal tea. Casey jumped on board and made himself comfy near my feet. In my hurry to leave, I'd neglected to say good-bye to Doug, so I'd have to apologize over dinner tomorrow. I replayed my conversation with him. He'd remembered Shirley's concern for a friend with a heart condition and how relieved she'd been when he reassured her it could be easily controlled with medication.

Medication . . . ?

I jumped from the sofa so suddenly my tea sloshed in the cup. Casey raised one ear and regarded me with a puzzled look. After rummaging through my purse, I resettled on the sofa with my laptop and a brown plastic pill vial. It was the vial I'd taken from Shirley Randolph's medicine cabinet. Clicking on my browser, I carefully typed in the generic name of the drug. Numerous references instantly appeared on the screen. I clicked on a link belonging to a prominent pharmaceutical company and discovered the mystery drug was classified as a beta-blocker. Further research revealed it was frequently prescribed for people with an irregular heartbeat.

Leaning back against the throw pillows, I processed this bit of information. Shirley had been worried about her own health, not that of an anonymous friend. Next I scrolled through the list of side effects and learned they included stomach cramping, nausea, and vomiting. No wonder Shirley sought the medicinal properties of ginger whether in the form of ginger root, ginger ale, or ginger tea. But what, if anything, did this have to do Shirley's death?

CHAPTER 21

Monday. I went about the business of being a shopkeeper half-heartedly. I kept glancing at the regulator clock on the wall. I'd seen turtles move faster than the hands on that darn clock. Soon Doug would board a plane in Atlanta and fly off to Chicago. By now he'd have signed his John Henry to a stack of papers at Creekside Savings transferring the deed of Pets 'R People to its new owners. I doubted our paths were likely to cross in the future.

I picked up a feather duster and began making the rounds. Dinner last night had been anticlimactic. At evening's end, we'd exhausted our supply of small talk and were both ready for our final good-byes. As I stood on tiptoe and kissed his cheek, I'd felt a slight tug on the heartstrings.

A slight tug, then nothing. I wished him well.

I ran the duster over and around jars of

dried herbs, which served as a reminder of my plan for fresh herbs. Hoyt had phoned to report that my garden plot at McBride's awaited planting. Hoyt, bless his heart, said he'd even fenced it with chicken wire to keep the "varmints" out. As soon as I closed shop for the day, I intended to transfer plants from their pots into organically enriched soil.

"Hey, Miz Piper." Ned Feeney loped into Spice It Up! and gave me a wide grin. "Things are slow over at the Eternal Rest since Miz Randolph passed. Wondered if you might have any chores needed doin'? I'm real handy, you know."

Ned had a heart of gold and a God-given talent for complicating even the simplest task. "Thanks, Ned," I said, "but not at the moment."

He shoved up the bill of his ever-present ball cap with its Georgia bulldog logo. "Well, whatever you do, don't get it into your head to lift any heavy boxes like Miz Vicki. She hurt her back somethin' fierce on a Saturday afternoon and couldn't see her doctor till Monday. Lucky for her, the doc prescribed some heavy-duty pain pills."

I paused to stare at him. "I don't suppose you remember when this happened."

"Yes, ma'am, sure do. It was the weekend

Miz Melly and the judge got hitched. I remember because I stopped by Miz Vicki's house on my way to the weddin' Sunday afternoon to see how she was feelin' and found her sound asleep on a heatin' pad. She said them pain pills the doc ordered knocked her for a loop. She was still dressed in the same clothes she'd been wearin' the day before. Hadn't been for me droppin' by, she'd've missed the weddin'."

Ned had jogged my memory. With everything else that had been happening, I'd nearly forgotten Vicki talking about a pulled muscle. Sadly for my suspect pool, Ned had just unwittingly confirmed that Vicki would have been in no condition to kill Shirley, drag her body out of the bathtub, and transport it where it could be found on McBride's property. I mentally scratched Vicki's name off my persons of interest list.

After Ned departed, I plugged in the vacuum and vented my frustration on stray dust bunnies hiding in corners and beneath shelves.

"Piper — ?"

I almost jumped out my skin at a tap on my shoulder. I whirled around to find Mary Beth standing behind me. I had no idea how long she'd been there. The drone of the vacuum had drowned out the sound of her arrival. Switching off the vacuum, I busied myself rewinding the power cord. "Hey, Mary Beth."

"Sorry I startled you." Mary Beth extracted a three-ring binder from the side pocket of a sleek leather tote. "I meant to come by earlier, but I've been tied up in meetings with the various prom committees all afternoon."

I couldn't help but wonder if she was here as a result of the conversation I'd had with her husband after Shirley's funeral. "Is there something I can help you with?" I asked warily.

"Actually, there is." She opened her binder and consulted her notes. "Last week you agreed to serve on a prom committee if needed. Are you still willing to help?"

"Sure," I said, envisioning myself knee-deep in tissue paper flowers. Or wasn't that sophisticated enough for teens in this day and age? High school gyms had lost their popularity, too, as prom venues. Lindsey's class, partly due to CJ's recommendation, had booked the country club for the event.

"Great," Mary Beth said with a nod of approval, making a check mark next to my name. "I'm short on chaperones. Prom is a black-tie affair. And, Piper, we prefer couples. Do you suppose you can round up a date for the evening?"

"Umm . . . ," I hedged.

"Wonderful." She frowned when my clock bonged the hour. "Have to run if I don't want to be late for my kickboxing lesson."

"Kickboxing?"

Mary Beth tucked her notebook back into her carryall. "You ought to give it a try. Punching and kicking is a great way to rid yourself of stress — and builds muscles you didn't know you had."

After she left, I flipped the CLOSED sign and locked the door. Mary Beth had provided food for thought. The woman was physically fit, active in sports, and game to take on new challenges. What if she — not Matt — had killed Shirley? She might've suspected their affair, confronted the "other" woman, and, in a rage, turned a hair dryer into a lethal weapon.

After all, men didn't corner the market on murder. It was entirely possible Shirley's killer had been female. And both Elaine Dixon and Mary Beth Wainwright topped my short list of suspects.

"Let's go plant us some herbs," I said aloud to Casey. "Nothing like some good honest labor to help give us some perspective."

■ ■ ■ ■

Thirty minutes later with Casey along as my trusty sidekick, I turned down McBride's drive. It was déjà vu all over again. It appeared I wasn't McBride's only visitor. Squad cars were parked willy-nilly on his newly mowed lawn. I wedged my Beetle into a space behind a Crown Vic and newer-model Ford Taurus, climbed out of my car, and clipped on Casey's leash.

Uniformed men could be seen moving back and forth inside McBride's house. I spotted McBride lounging against the hood of his pickup, cradling his cat, Fraidy. I approached with caution. "Just a crazy guess, but I'd say Beau convinced a judge to sign a search warrant."

He zapped me with a look from his laser blues. "You here to gloat?"

"C'mon, McBride. You know me better than that." I settled beside him, imitating his casual stance minus the cat. Casey, as though sensing McBride's dark mood, lay down quietly at my feet. "What happened a year ago is water under the bridge," I continued. "You were only doing your job."

McBride grunted; Fraidy snarled.

"What do they expect to find?"

"I asked Beau the same question."

"And what did he say?"

McBride's shoulders rose and fell. "Said he'd know when they found it."

"You're a cop, McBride. Make a wild stab at it. What do you suppose they're looking for?" I peered up at him, but his features appeared carved in granite.

"Tucker might be inexperienced when it comes to homicide investigations, but he isn't stupid. My best guess is that he's looking for something — women's clothing, toiletries, jewelry, or the like — to link me to Shirley. He's trying to prove we were having a hot and heavy affair."

"And will he find any of those things?" I despised myself for asking but couldn't seem to help myself.

"Our *relationship* was strictly business," he reiterated. "Don't know why folks made such a big deal over the two of us grabbing a bite to eat a couple of times. Far as I know, it's not a federal offense to share a meal while discussing pros and cons of buying or selling property."

"I wonder if this is the heat wave Officer Moyer warned about." I nodded toward the collection of police vehicles. "I doubt the Weather Channel or Doppler radar could've been more accurate."

"Moyer's a good guy, a good cop. Probably his way of sending a message." McBride absently stroked Fraidy's glossy black fur. "So, if you didn't come to gloat, why are you here?"

"Hoyt called and said my garden plot was ready, so I brought my herbs to plant." I deliberately omitted telling him my visit had a secondary motive. This didn't seem an ideal time to ask him to be my date for senior prom.

"Leave the herbs. I'll plant them tomorrow. These days, I've got more time on my hands than I know what to do with. I'd rather keep busy."

After this exchange, we fell silent, content to stand side by side, waiting and watching. Officer Gary Moyer came out on the porch, talking into a cell phone. He glanced in our direction, then gave us an almost imperceptible nod before resuming his conversation and returning inside. At last, the men began to troop out of the house and down the steps. They piled into their patrol cars amid much door slamming and drove away. All of them, especially Reba Mae's son Clay, avoided eye contact with McBride. Beau Tucker, looking particularly glum, was the last to leave.

His round face creased into a scowl at the

sight of McBride and me leaning against the pickup. Hitching up his pants, he swaggered toward us. "Place is all yours, McBride," he said. "Didn't collect any evidence, but that's not surprising. You've had plenty of time to dispose of anything that might be incriminating. Only girlie thing we found was a six-pack of Diet Coke."

"There wasn't any evidence to find — not then, not now."

"Doesn't mean you're off the hook. Way I see it, you and Shirley got into it, argued, matters got heated, one thing led to another. Shirley ended up dead. Crime of passion, plain and simple."

"Nothing simple about it," McBride said calmly. "How do you account for the fresh burn mark on the palm of her hand?"

Beau's scowl deepened. "Your guess is as good as mine. Likely had nothing to do with getting herself killed. She might've burned herself grabbing a hot pan out of the oven or pot off the stove. Happens to my wife all the time."

"That might be the case with Jolene, but Shirley never cooked," I informed him. "She was a takeout or pop-a-frozen-dinner-in-the-microwave sort of woman. What did the ME give as cause of death?"

Fraidy started to growl, low in her throat,

so McBride petted his cat's head to soothe her.

Beau shot a worried look at Fraidy as if the feline might spring out of McBride's arms any second and attack him. "Verdict's still out," he said, nervously clearing his throat. "Can't comment on an active investigation as you damn well know. Hope you're not planning to leave town anytime soon, McBride. You might could be called in for further questioning. See you around."

Beau didn't try to hide his smile as he turned on his heel and strode toward his vehicle. It was plain as day he enjoyed having the upper hand at McBride's expense.

McBride didn't move a muscle, but Fraidy's good ear twitched.

"Let's go inside," I ventured after a lengthy silence. "I'll help you clean up."

"Appreciate your offer, but no thanks." Pushing away from the pickup, McBride drew himself upright. "Nothing personal, but I've had enough people pawing through my belongings for one day."

"I understand," I replied. And I did. I knew from personal experience what it felt like to have my cupboards and drawers ransacked by persons looking for evidence that might connect me with a murder. McBride was a proud man. My heart ached knowing it was worse for him since the search had been conducted by men he'd once directed — and ones who had trusted him.

"Hey, McBride, wait up!" I called as he started to stride off. I'd suddenly remembered the secondary reason for my visit. Now was as good a time as any to pop the question. "You busy Saturday night?"

He stopped and turned. "Why? You asking me out on a date?"

"Not an ordinary date . . . the prom." I shifted my weight, scrounging up courage that had skittered off. "I thought, maybe, if you had nothing better to do, you could take me to the senior prom."

"You can't be serious."

"Serious as a heart attack." Nervous, I tucked an errant curl behind one ear. "Mary Beth's committee is short on chaperones. She prefers couples."

He studied me for what seemed an eternity; then one corner of his mouth curled in a smile. "Sure, I'll be your date. Nothing better to do."

"Great," I said, releasing a long breath. "Oh, McBride, there's one more thing."

Master of the pregnant pause, he lifted a brow and waited.

"It's black-tie," I blurted. "Don't suppose

267

you own a tux . . . ?"

"Might could rustle one up if I tried real hard." This time his smile was genuine, not the dimple-teasing favorite of mine, but a smile nonetheless.

"Good, that's good." I wiped my sweaty palms on the sides of my jeans. "See you Saturday."

Once McBride disappeared inside his house, I had the presence of mind to set my box of herbs on the lawn where he was sure to see them. I drove home feeling both elated and depressed. On one hand, I was excited as a teen for having a date for senior prom, but on the flip side, I was scared silly. Beau Tucker might not be the sharpest tack in the box, but he was as tenacious as a pit bull. He was determined to see McBride arrested for Shirley's murder. And equally determined to be appointed Brandywine Creek's next chief of police. My resolve hardened anew. All I had to do was find the guilty party.

Easy peasy, right? Who was I kidding?

CHAPTER 22

When I arrived home from McBride's, I found Lindsey working on her laptop. Textbooks, spiral notebooks, and highlighters were scattered across the kitchen table. She eyed my worn jeans and T-shirt with disgust. "Where have you been?" she asked. "It's late."

"It's not that late," I said after darting a glance at my wristwatch. "I went to Chief McBride's to plant my herbs."

"Well, you should have left a note. That's what you're always reminding me to do."

"You're right; I should have." I headed toward the fridge. "Hungry?"

"I already ate." She returned to tapping on the keyboard. "I saved you some salad."

Properly chastened, I took out a bowl covered in plastic wrap and a jar of my homemade poppy-seed dressing. After scooping dog food into Casey's dish, I cleared a space at the table and sat down.

"Mrs. Wainwright stopped in today to ask a favor. You'll never guess what it was."

Lindsey didn't look up. "I'm not in the mood for guessing games tonight, so just tell me."

I speared a forkful of lettuce and studied my daughter's face. I didn't have to be clairvoyant to know something was troubling her. I hoped my news would cheer her up. "I'm going to be one of the chaperones at your prom," I announced merrily.

"You're what?" Lindsey ceased typing. Her eyes widened in surprise.

I smiled at her reaction. "You heard me. Mrs. Wainwright said she prefers couples, so I asked Wyatt McBride to be my date — and he accepted."

"Mother!" she wailed. Shoving away from the table, she jumped to her feet. "How could you do this to me?"

"I didn't do anything *to* you," I protested, dismayed. "I simply volunteered to help Mary Beth any way I could."

"How will it look that my mother is at prom — with a date, the chief of police of all people — while I sit home?" Lindsey made a wild sweeping gesture. "What will the kids say? It'll be all over school."

I rose from the table. "What do you mean, I'll be there while you 'sit home'?" I asked, choosing my words carefully.

"Sean and I had a fight. All he's done lately is complain about how much money prom is costing — renting a tux, buying flowers, hiring a limo. When he suggested we have dinner before prom at Billy's Buffet Barn, I told him I'd had enough." Lindsey sniffed back tears. "We broke up."

I wrapped my arms around her. "Oh, Linds, honey. I'm so sorry."

"Now you've got a date, and I don't," she blubbered, resting her head against my shoulder. "And even if we do make up before prom, my face is breaking out. I'm getting a zit!"

A zit? The ultimate tragedy for a teenager before prom. I patted my girl's shoulder, rubbed her back, and tried with limited success to convince her that the world wasn't coming to an end.

She was mopping up tears with a wad of tissues when her cell phone rang. "It's Sean," she said upon reading the display. After letting the phone ring a respectable number of times before answering, she finally picked up.

"I'm sorry, too," I heard her say as she wandered into her bedroom and closed the door for maximum privacy.

No longer hungry, I refrigerated what

remained of my salad to have for lunch the next day. Although it wasn't early, it wasn't exactly late either. I hadn't jogged in what seemed like ages, and the idea of working off some steam appealed to me. Before I could change my mind, I slipped into my running shoes and zipped a hoodie over my T-shirt.

When I opened Lindsey's bedroom door to inform her of my plan, Casey bounded inside and leaped up on her bed. "I won't be long," I said, patting my pockets to make sure I had everything, including a canister of pepper spray.

Lindsey gave me a thumbs-up and went back to her conversation with Sean. From the snippits I overheard, Sean and Lindsey's coupleship was back on track. I ran downstairs and outside. After a few warm-up exercises, I started out slow but gradually increased my pace and found a rhythm.

It was a lovely night for jogging. Clouds lazily floated across a waning sliver of a moon, and the air smelled . . . fresh . . . that unique scent of buds and blossoms bursting into life. I chose a route through the residential streets. Melly's house appeared buttoned up tight, no pile of unread newspapers, no overflowing mailbox, to indicate her absence. Only that morning,

I'd received a brief text from her: *Loving Italy.* I guess those two words said it all. Lights were on in Mavis Gray's house and I could see the television flicker through the living room window. The only sounds were crickets chirping in the bushes and the slapping of my soles against concrete.

Motive, means, and opportunity. The holy trinity of crime solving. My feet hit the walkway in time to the beat. I already knew the means, so that left motive and opportunity. Mary Beth and Matt Wainwright had motive, but what about opportunity? Did they have alibis for the weekend Shirley was killed? And then there was Elaine Dixon. Elaine was a prime suspect in my book. She felt threatened by Shirley, blamed her for Kirby's continued interest in a dusty old hardware store in Podunk, USA, and had a hot temper. Any one of them could be guilty.

Ahead, a child's bike lay sprawled on its side in a yard, partially obstructing the sidewalk. I managed to skirt around it in time to avoid a nasty spill, but it threw off my stride. I found it again, but the brief interruption was enough to make me aware of footsteps thudding counterpoint to mine. I rarely encountered other joggers and, when I did, it was generally during one of my early-morning runs. Nerves fluttered in my stomach, and I blamed it on McBride. Ever since attending his self-defense course for women last November, I tended to be hypervigilant whenever alone. I told myself I was being foolish, yet in the back of my mind I kept hearing McBride's advice to always trust our instincts. To pay attention to our surroundings. He referred to situational awareness as the gift of fear. Picking up my speed, I decided to experiment to see if the person behind me did the same.

He did.

I slowed and whoever followed me did likewise. I neared the corner of Jefferson and Maple streets and knew from previous runs that a huge magnolia tree stood in a homeowner's yard. Rounding the corner, I stepped off the sidewalk and concealed myself in the tree's dense shadow. My hand automatically went to the pocket of my hoodie for a container of pepper spray not much bigger than a lipstick.

From my vantage spot, I watched the jogger slow to a halt, stand with hands on his hips, and turn in a semi-circle as though looking for someone, namely me.

I stepped away from my hiding place — perhaps not the wisest thing to do — the can of pepper spray held at arm's length, my finger on the trigger. "Freeze!"

The person tensed but didn't attempt to flee.

I advanced slowly, my adrenaline pumping. I was Wonder Woman, Supergirl, and Xena: Warrior Princess, all rolled into one. Me and my pepper spray felt invincible. "Who are you?" I demanded boldly. "And why are you following me?"

A wispy cloud drifted off, and the pale moonlight revealed Colin Flynn's narrow face and slender build. "Put the pepper spray away, please, before you accidentally set off a blast. That stuff is nasty."

"Not until you explain what you're doing out here!"

"Same as you. I run every day."

I was beginning to wonder if I had overreacted. "Then you're not the same as me," I muttered. "I only run to burn off the calories from eating too much pizza."

Colin shoveled his fingers through thinning medium-brown hair. "You are aware, aren't you, that there's a killer on the loose? It's not safe for a woman to be out alone after dark."

"You're a fine one to talk, since you're the one on the business end of my pepper spray." Sensing the threat level lessen, I lowered the canister marginally but didn't release my grip. "You mysteriously showed up in town around the same time Shirley was murdered. How do I know you aren't the killer?"

"How many times do I have to tell you that I never met the woman? Why would I want her dead?"

I didn't have a ready answer, so I tried a different tack. "It doesn't make sense why a man your age would want to settle in a small town where you don't know a soul. Why not pick Atlanta, a city with shops and clubs and plenty of people your age?"

"I'm a novelist," he said. "I need a quiet place to write my book."

"Okay," I muttered for lack of anything pithier. So, Colin Flynn was a writer. That sounded harmless enough. I tucked the pepper spray back into my pocket. Somehow, though, his story didn't ring true. It sounded too rehearsed, too pat. McBride's "trust your instincts" speech reverberated in the back of my mind. My skepticism might be another instance of my hypervigilance.

"See you around," Colin said as he continued down the street.

I watched until he was almost out of sight, then changed my route. No more dark, shadowy residential streets for me when I could just as easily head for the bright lights of Main Street — Main Street and the Brandywine Creek Police Department.

Out of breath, I pushed through the police department's double doors. Precious stopped munching a MoonPie. "Hey, Piper," she said, grinning. "Looks like somethin's got you all hot and bothered — and I know it can't be the chief 'cause he ain't here."

Bending forward, I placed my hands on my knees and tried to bring my breathing under control. "Thought I'd come by . . . ask if you'd heard anything about that new guy in town."

"This new guy got a name?"

"Colin Flynn. He claims he's a novelist." I straightened and wiped sweat from my brow. "According to him, Shirley was supposed to help him find a house in the area. He said they never met, that their only contact was in the form of emails and texts."

"Name don't ring a bell. Guess he must be keepin' a low profile by stayin' out of trouble." Precious brushed MoonPie crumbs from her ample bosom. "Why you askin'?"

"I can't quite put my finger on it," I admitted. "There's just something strange about him. First time we met, his jeans were so new they practically squeaked when he walked. If I had to wager a guess, I'd say he held some kind of a desk job until recently. He gave me some line about him needing peace and quiet," I said, shaking my head in disbelief. "Doesn't everyone with a keyboard claim to be a writer these days?"

"If that's true, honey, I must be a crime writer seein' how I spend my time inputtin' the deeds of felons and miscreants."

"Well, if you should hear anything unusual about Mr. Flynn, I'd appreciate a heads-up." I looked around to make certain we were alone but didn't see anyone. "Are there any new developments in the investigation into Shirley's death?"

My paranoia must've been contagious, because Precious shot a quick glance over her shoulder, then lowered her voice. "The ME puts Ms. Randolph's death between late Saturday, early Sunday mornin'. Her bein' half in, half out of the water makes it harder to estimate. By the way, your ex and the city council are puttin' the thumbscrews to Sergeant Tucker to make an arrest. Let me tell you, Sarge was mighty unhappy the search at the chief's place turned up empty."

The front door swung open behind me, and Precious quickly swept what remained of her MoonPie into a desk drawer. "Can I help you gentlemen?" she asked the man and two young boys who accompanied him.

"My sons found a computer in a field behind our house," the man explained. "It looks expensive, so I told 'em we ought to turn it in to the police. See if someone might've lost it."

I stared hard at the sleek, thin laptop the man set on the counter in front of Precious. The once shiny silver case looked scuffed and dented; whether on purpose or by accident I had no way of knowing. "Mind if I take a closer look?"

The two boys, whom I guessed to be around seven and nine, exchanged unhappy glances.

"No, ma'am, go right ahead," the man said. "Don't suppose you know who it might belong to?"

Opening the lid, I pressed the ON button and when nothing happened flipped the laptop over and saw that it had been eviscerated. A space gaped in the spot where the circuitry and motherboard were normally housed. I couldn't say with 100 percent certainty, but the computer appeared disturbingly similar to Shirley's high-end Mac-Book.

"Let me have you fill out some paperwork." Precious rifled through a file drawer and produced a form, which she handed to the father.

"Can we keep the computer if no one wants it?" the older of the boys asked.

"Yessir." Precious bobbed her head. "No one claims it within ninety days, it's yours. Considerin' the shape it's in, probably not worth much."

I ran my hand lightly over the abused case. "Don't be too disappointed, boys, but someone already stole all the best parts."

I left the man filling out forms while Precious treated each of the boys to one of her MoonPies. Thoughts swirled through my head during the short walk home. None of this made any sense. Why go to all the trouble of stealing an expensive computer, then rip out the insides and toss what was left into a vacant field? What secrets had Shirley's computer held? And what, if any, secrets had it given up? However, maybe it was nothing more than a vengeful act by the killer with no significance whatsoever.

But I didn't believe that.

CHAPTER 23

"Conclusion by exclusion." I think I heard the term used on one of those investigative news shows — *20/20, Dateline,* or *48 Hours.* All morning, I'd tried to concentrate on preparations for my first-anniversary gala, which would be held at the end of the month. I'd toyed with BOGO — buy one, get one — then decided against it for a more profitable route of buy one, get one for half off. Flyers advertising the event were ready to print. I'd also started to gather items for my giveaway gift basket. But somewhere along the way, my enthusiasm stalled.

My mind kept circling back to McBride and his predicament. It was impossible for me to stand on the sidelines and watch him face a murder charge. I needed to do *something,* to be more proactive. I had to find out whether Shirley died at the hands of her lover, her lover's irate wife, or an enraged woman who viewed the Realtor as a threat to her marriage and obstacle to her happiness. Until recently I'd considered Vicki as a possible suspect, but Ned had confirmed her story about injuring her back, thus providing her with an alibi. And I also wanted to discover how, if anything, a stolen computer with a battered case entered into the equation. Knowing whether my suspects had alibis or not would be a perfect place to start. For no particular reason, I decided to make Matt Wainwright my target.

Today was Wednesday, the day CJ and Matt had a long-standing date for lunch at the country club followed by eighteen holes of golf. The pair often invited clients to join them, but if no one was available they'd play the round as a twosome. CJ insisted that more business was conducted on the golf course than in a boardroom. I told him to save his arguments for a jury.

The throaty rumble of a motorcycle drew my attention to a world outside my shop. As luck would have it — good luck in this case — Hoyt picked that moment to saunter into Spice It Up! "Mary, Mary, quite contrary, how does your garden grow?" he singsonged, looking mighty pleased with himself.

"If you're referring to my herb garden, I've been told it's doing quite well under

McBride's supervision."

"It's hard to grow things in this Georgia red clay, so I added some topsoil to help give those babies a head start."

"We had a nice rain early this morning, so that should also help."

"McBride's a good guy. Sorry he's going through a rough patch."

I shoved a stray curl off my brow. "Yes, well, let's pray this all gets sorted out soon and life gets back to normal."

"Sure hope so," he said, wagging his head. "Talk is that Beau Tucker had the entire Brandywine Creek Police Department searching McBride's house with a fine-tooth comb but came up empty-handed."

"Beau's under pressure to make an arrest. Since he lacks the imagination to look elsewhere, he's pinned a bull's-eye on Mc-Bride."

"Not that I think McBride's guilty, you hear, but you gotta admit it doesn't look good him finding her body — and on his property."

"McBride's isn't stupid. If he murdered someone, he'd have enough smarts to hide the body where it wouldn't be easily found — not in his fishing hole."

"Yeah, that's a good point."

"Shirley was McBride's Realtor," I continued my rant. "Just because they met for dinner a few times doesn't mean they were lovers."

"You're right again." He chuckled. "Sharing chips and salsa at North of the Border or a plate of chili cheese fries at High Cotton doesn't constitute an engagement. Too bad they had half the town as an audience each time they dined."

We both turned as the front door opened.

"Hey, honeybun." Reba Mae sailed in waving a sheet of paper. "Here's the recipe as promised for Meemaw's goulash. Hoyt —" She stopped short at seeing him. "— I didn't expect to find you here."

I ducked my head to hide my smile. Reba Mae's feigned surprise was as phony as a three-dollar bill. Only a blind person would have failed to notice the shiny maroon Harley-Davidson at the curb.

"Hey there, darlin'," the bewhiskered biker switched on the charm. "Seein' you just made my day. I swear you get prettier every time I see you."

Reba Mae made a show of fanning herself with the paper she carried. "This ol' country boy sure knows how to turn a girl's head."

"Don't let the secret out," Hoyt said, addressing me, "this little gal makes the best darn lasagna I ever tasted. Her cooking would put Tony Deltorro's eatery out of business in a heartbeat."

Reba Mae beamed at the compliment.

My head swiveled from one to the other. I sensed a romance taking root and couldn't be happier. Reba Mae had been a widow ever since Butch drowned during a bass-fishing tournament. With nary a complaint, she'd raised her boys, learned a trade, opened a business, and kissed a number of frogs without finding her prince.

"Wish I could hang out with you guys," Reba Mae said, "but Mary Lou Lambert is too vain to admit she needs glasses real bad. She misread the instructions on a box of hair dye and left the developer on too long. Now she wants me to fix it."

"Go!" I made a shooing motion. "Take care of your emergency."

"See you, Friday!" Hoyt called after her.

"You two have big plans for Friday night?" This time I didn't try to hide my smile.

Hoyt rocked back on his boot heels. "Thought we'd drive down to Augusta. Try this Thai restaurant a friend recommended. Reba Mae's got an adventurous streak. The gal's not afraid of new and different."

"No, there's not much that scares her." *Except ghosts and things that go bump in the night.* "Say, Hoyt," I said as an idea occurred to me. "If you're not real busy could you keep an eye on Spice It Up! while I run an errand? I know this is an imposition, but you have my word it won't take long. I'll be happy to compensate you for your time."

"Heck, why not?" He treated me to a broad grin with a glimpse of a gold tooth. "That mean I get to wear one of those cute chili pepper aprons?"

"You bet." I untied the one I was wearing and tossed it to him. "Here, use mine."

The apron didn't completely cover his girth, but he didn't seem to mind. Grabbing my purse from beneath the counter, I hurried out the back door. Melly would lecture me on my shortcomings as a shop-keeper if she ever found out I left my shop in the middle of the day in the care of a man I hardly knew. But, at the moment, I had more pressing things to worry about than one of Melly's reprimands.

Fifteen minutes later, I passed through wrought-iron gates that guarded the entrance of Brandywine Creek Country Club. Nothing much had changed since the days I'd come as a member and not a guest. The gently rolling lawn looked as though the blades of grass had been cut with manicure scissors rather than a lawn mower. Mounds of bright azaleas added splashes of color. I drove down a tunnel formed by Bradford pear trees that were surrendering spring's lacy blossoms to the pale green leaves of summer.

"Good afternoon, Miz Prescott." Jackson Barber, the valet parking attendant on duty, greeted me with a friendly smile. "If you're meeting Mr. Prescott, he called to say he's runnin' late. Had me tell Mr. Wainwright he'll be along shortly."

"Thanks, Jackson." I didn't bother to correct the man's misconception.

Crossing the spacious foyer, I went directly to the Grille Room. I spotted Matt sitting alone at a table near one of the floor-to-ceiling windows overlooking the eighteenth green. I sat down uninvited and waved off the waiter. "Hello, Matt."

Two vertical lines formed between his brows. "What are you doing here?"

Since I didn't know how much time I'd have before CJ's arrival, I got straight to the point. "I thought you might be interested knowing a couple kids found what appears to be Shirley's computer in a vacant field. It's trashed. Whoever stole it removed the motherboard."

"Shirley never went anywhere without her laptop. She called it her brain/memory bank." Matt's frown deepened. "Who would want to steal her computer, then destroy it?"

"That's what I've been wondering." I took a sip from the water glass meant for CJ. My ex was bound to appear any second and bring my interrogation to a premature end. It was now or never to ask the hard questions. "You and Shirley were lovers. Why try to deny it?"

"True." Matt pinched the bridge of his nose and sighed wearily. "I cared for Shirley a great deal. She wanted to take it to the next level, but I couldn't do that to Mary Beth. Furthermore, I wasn't willing to subject my family to a divorce. Especially not after seeing what it did to yours."

I sucked in my breath. Matt's words stung. I know my divorce from CJ had been hard on our children, but it hurt to hear it from another's lips.

"Face it, Piper," Matt said. "Lindsey acts out from time to time. The girl's had a series of boyfriends and can't make up her mind about a career. Chad rarely comes home and now wants to backpack around Europe instead of applying himself to his studies."

"I didn't come here to discuss the pitfalls of divorce," I reminded him in an effort to get our conversation back on course.

After casting a sweeping glance over the room to make sure the other diners weren't within earshot, Matt leaned forward and spoke, his voice low, urgent. "Look, Piper, Shirley and I had an on-again, off-again affair that lasted several years, but I'd never do anything to harm her. Never," he repeated fiercely.

I believed he was telling the truth, but my interrogation still wasn't finished. "One last question, Matt, do you have any idea who might have wanted her dead?"

"No, but I hope they find the bastard who did this and hang him out to dry."

Out of the corner of my eye, I saw CJ enter the Grille Room and pause to speak to the bartender. "Do you have an alibi for the weekend Shirley was killed?" I asked as I rose to my feet.

"You said one question, Piper; that makes two." Matt picked up his menu, a signal it was time for me to leave. "This dining room is for members only and their guests. As far as I know, you're neither."

I manufactured a smile. "Sorry, my memory's not what it used to be. Must be old age creeping up on me."

"Hey there, Scooter." CJ flashed his megawatt smile as I passed him on my way out. "What's the occasion? Homesick for your old stomping grounds?"

"Nice shirt," I said, eyeing his pink golf shirt with its purple stripes and collar. "Amber pick it out?" The CJ Prescott I used to be married to wouldn't be caught dead in such girlie colors.

"Amber said it lent me a more youthful flair." He picked up a tumbler the bartender handed him, which I assumed contained Wild Turkey. "I told Lindsey to invite some friends over for a post-prom party and to spend the night. This way we don't have to worry about her bein' on the road knowin' some kids been drinkin' and partyin'."

"Sounds like a good plan," I said, nodding approval. "Be sure you and Amber keep a visible presence and put the brakes on before things get out of hand."

He took a swig of bourbon. "Got plenty of food ordered, house has a good sound system, and the pool's heated, so the kids can bring their swimsuits for a dip."

"That ought to earn you Father of the Year Award. Just remember to hide the key to your liquor cabinet — unless you want a repeat of last year."

I had the satisfaction of seeing my parting remark wipe the insufferable grin from his face. My satisfaction faded quickly with the realization Matt still withheld his alibi.

Conclusion by exclusion had failed to rule him out as a person of interest this round. But I refused to go down for the count.

CHAPTER 24

All of a sudden it was prom night.

"I wish your grandmother could see how pretty you look." I stepped back to admire my daughter's reflection in the mirror. That afternoon, Reba Mae had fashioned Lindsey's long blond hair in a soft, romantic do that she referred to as "messy" chignon. Lindsey's dress was a deceptively simple princess style, strapless with a flowing floor-length chiffon skirt. Simple on a hanger, but stunning on the wearer. "She'd be happy you choose a gown that shade of blue."

"It brings out the color of my eyes."

We burst out laughing at Melly's familiar phrase whenever she referred to her favorite silk blouse.

I reached for my camera. "Now slip into your shoes and let me take some pictures."

Lindsey, careful not to wrinkle her gown, sat on the edge of the bed and donned a pair of shimmery open-toe sandals with a thin ankle strap. Then she stood and twirled ready to pose for pictures.

Snap! Snap!

The shutter of the camera clicked and captured Lindsey's shocked expression as she toppled to one side. She managed, barely, to break her fall by grabbing on to the dresser. "My shoe," she gasped.

We stared in openmouthed horror at a glittery heel no longer attached to the sole of the shoe.

"I'm jinxed!" Lindsey wailed. "Ever since you offered to chaperone prom, I knew that I was headed for disaster. Why is this happening to me? First Sean and I almost broke up — now this?"

I picked up the heel and examined it. "Maybe if we try gluing . . ."

"And then what? Have it fall off on the dance floor?"

"What about a pair from your closet?" I suggested, trying to halt the tsunami I saw building. "You have a long dress. No one will notice your shoes aren't perfect."

"M-Mother!" she wailed again, louder this time, "I don't believe you said that! I can't go to prom now; that's all there is to it. The whole night is ruined. Ruined!"

Casey, who observed the drama from a

rug on the floor, rested his head on his paws, one ear cocked sympathetically.

"Honey, calm down. We'll think of something."

Lindsey plopped down on the bed, no longer concerned about wrinkles. "This will teach me never to buy knockoff Stuart Weitzmans at a discount shoe store."

"Let's focus, all right." I paced back and forth. Sad to say, but there was nowhere near Brandywine Creek to purchase fancy dress shoes at a moment's notice. "Maybe you could borrow a pair. Let's call Reba Mae."

"Her feet are bigger than mine."

"Right, right. What about your friend Taylor?"

Lindsey's eyes pooled with tears. "Taylor's feet are small; so are yours."

"How about Amber? She must have a closet filled with shoes."

"I wear a narrow; her feet are wide." A big, fat tear rolled down Lindsey's cheek.

Too big, too small, too wide, when what we needed was "just right." I was trapped in "The Story of the Three Bears." Sinking down next to Lindsey, I covered my ears to block out the chorus of "woe is me."

"Sean will be here in half an hour," she said, sniffling. "What am I supposed to do?

Go to prom barefoot?" She unbuckled the offending sandal and hurled it across the room.

Casey yelped and dove for cover under the bed.

Then the solution struck me like the proverbial bolt out of the blue. Amber Leigh Ames-Prescott wasn't the only person who had a closet filled with shoes. I knew of someone else who did — Shirley Randolph. And if I remembered correctly, she wore a size 7 1/2 N, the same size as Lindsey.

"Dry your eyes," I said, racing from the room. "I'll be back in a jiffy."

Minutes later I was at Shirley's. Thankfully, I still had the house key Ned had loaned me days ago. I let myself in the front door and ran upstairs. Even in my haste, I noticed the stuffy, unlived-in odor. I made a mental note to come over, clean out the refrigerator, and air out the place. Upon reaching Shirley's bedroom, I threw open the closet door and heaved a sigh. Her abundant supply of shoes had been undisturbed since my previous visit — and they were, as I remembered, 7 1/2 N. All that was left for me to do was find a pair that would complement Lindsey's prom dress.

Red shoes, blue shoes, flats, and heels. Wedges, pumps, and sandals. I was nearly ready to admit defeat when I found what I was searching for in a far corner. I opened the lid of a shoe box and discovered the answer to my prayers. Nestled inside protective coverings were a prom-goer's dream — the real McCoy, not knockoffs. I carefully removed one of the shoes and inspected it. Glittery, strappy, stiletto heels. The only drawback as far as I could tell was this pair had toes while Lindsey's were sandals. I turned the shoe over and examined the sole. The shoes were brand-new, never worn. A small, black plastic object dropped on the floor. Thinking it a gadget used for quality control or a gizmo to protect against shoplifting, I absentmindedly stuck it in the pocket of my jeans. As I hurried home, I made a silent pledge I'd return the borrowed-not-stolen shoes the very next day.

With disaster narrowly diverted and Lindsey and Sean on their way to dinner at Antonio's — not Billy's Buffet Barn — it was time for me to get ready for my "date." I'd offered to meet McBride at the country club, but he wouldn't hear of it. Instead, he insisted on escorting me.

I'd no sooner finished showering when Reba Mae pounded up the back staircase determined to tame my unruly curls into submission.

"I have to hand it to you, girlfriend, you're a magician when it comes to hair," I told her as she shoved another pin in my updo.

"Damn straight," she replied. "Now sit still and watch me morph from hairdresser into makeup artist."

"Go easy," I cautioned. "I want McBride to recognize me."

"Never fear, hon." Reba Mae picked up a bottle of foundation and a small sponge and went to work.

My friend knew her stuff. When Reba Mae stepped back to inspect her handiwork, I gazed at myself in the bedroom mirror. The woman staring back was still me, but a new, improved, glamorized version. Nary a freckle peeked through the expertly applied foundation. And my smoky eyes rivaled those of a runway model.

"Now let me see you in your dress."

I donned an evening gown I'd been saving for a special occasion. Thanks to jogging, the dress fit better now than the day I bought it. The moss green sheath made from shimmery fabric draped low in the back, nearly to my waist, and had a thigh-length slit up one side. Elegant yet simple. I'd bought it for a bar association dinner dance. Instead of dancing the night away with my husband, after CJ announced his need for "space" I'd sat out the evening at home — alone.

Reba Mae gave a maternal nod of approval. She handed me a pair of sparkling chandelier earrings. "A dress like that doesn't need much jewelry."

I fastened on the earrings, slipped into silver heels, then hugged Reba Mae. "Thanks to you, I feel like I'm eighteen again, not forty-something."

Casey, who had been watching from the foot of the bed, thumped his tail against the floor in a show of approval.

At a knock on the door, I spritzed on my favorite perfume. "Showtime," I said, grabbing my evening bag and a wrap.

"Lead the way, honeybun."

With Reba Mae following close behind, I carefully navigated the stairs conscious of my long dress and high heels. I didn't want a detour to the emergency room to mar my grand entrance.

"I brought my camera along to take pictures of the good-lookin' couple."

"Hush!" I hissed. "We're chaperones, not teenagers going to prom."

Reminding myself there was no need to feel nervous, I opened Spice It Up!'s front door. My pulse kicked up a notch at the sight of McBride in a tux.

"My, my, my," Reba Mae drawled. "Don't you look all 007."

"I like my martinis shaken, not stirred, but prefer a cold beer." He flashed that dimple-winking smile that never failed to make me weak in the knees and handed me a plastic florist's box. "I didn't want you to be the only girl at the prom without a corsage."

I felt blood rush to my cheeks. "You shouldn't have," I protested.

Reba Mae clicked off a series of pictures as I slipped on a wrist corsage of deep red sweetheart roses and baby's breath. "You two better get a move on or you're going to be late. Don't worry about the shop, Piper; I'll lock up. You kids have fun, you hear."

McBride offered his arm. "Your chariot awaits."

Distracted by McBride in a tux and the sweetheart roses, I'd failed to notice a late-model Lincoln sedan waiting at the curb. I'd expected to be practically airlifted to reach the seat of his Ford F-150 pickup, not riding in luxury. "So what's the deal, McBride? You take up grand theft auto to supplement your income?"

"Now there's a thought." McBride saw

me settled into a cushy leather seat, then rounded the hood of the car and climbed inside. "I happen to have a very generous friend who decided my date should ride in style."

"Does your generous friend have a name?"

"S. W. Hoyt."

"My Harley-Davidson buddy?"

"One and the same." McBride chuckled. "Sebastian W., commonly known as Hoyt, was CEO of an electronics firm before he sold his company for a substantial profit and retired early."

I was still processing this piece of information when we arrived at the country club. McBride valet parked, then came around to open the passenger door. "You do know, don't you," he whispered, "that you're going to be the center of attention in that dress. You look . . . beautiful."

To lighten the mood, I batted my lashes and vamped it up with my best Mae West imitation: " 'It's better to be looked over than overlooked.' "

Behind us, a parade of limos dispensed laughing and happy couples. Conscious of McBride's hand resting on the small of my back, I made my way into the main dining room.

"I always wanted to visit Paris. Looks like

I finally get my chance." In keeping with the *Midnight in Paris* theme, bistro tables had replaced the regular dining tables. Reasonable facsimiles of the Eiffel Tower and Arc de Triomphe, courtesy of the industrial arts department, stood at opposite ends of the room. A giant crescent moon was suspended from the ceiling; pots of ficus sparkled with hundreds of miniature LED lights. Red-and-white checkered tablecloths had transformed the adjacent Grille Room into a sidewalk café. "The students did an amazing job."

"I see Mary Beth waving at us." McBride steered me to where a small group of parents had gathered.

Mary Beth, clipboard in hand, put check marks next to our names. "I'm happy y'all heeded my advice and wore formal attire. The object is to blend in, to be as inconspicuous as possible. I've assigned each set of chaperones a specific quadrant to patrol. Keep an eye out for liquor. Boys like to sneak in a flask and spike the punch. Be on the lookout for couples sneaking off. We won't tolerate any hanky-panky."

"Hanky-panky . . . ?" McBride echoed in a voice low enough for my ears alone.

"It's a technical term," I whispered back. "She means fondling or groping."

301

"Spoilsport," he grumbled.

Mary Beth's sermon over, the chaperones drifted to their assigned locations. Matt Wainwright was present, too, but maintained a healthy distance from his wife. At a signal from Mary Beth, the DJ stepped up to the mic, and the prom was in full swing.

"Let me get us some punch."

If I wondered that McBride might be out of his element at a high school dance, I was mistaken. He seemed as at ease in a tuxedo as in worn denim. I noticed more than one teenage girl watching his progress and casting envious glances in my direction.

I caught sight of Lindsey and Sean bobbing about on the dance floor along with their friends Taylor and Joey. Brittany Hughes, another friend of Lindsey's, waved when she saw me. Mary Beth flitted about, stopping here and there to speak to various people. She looked tense and unsmiling.

McBride returned with two plastic glasses of pale pink liquid and handed one to me. "Cheers," he said, tapping his cup to mine. "Here's to our first date."

"Cheers," I said, taking a sip. "I hope you didn't go to a big expense renting a tux. You were lucky to find one that fits as though it were made for you."

"It was." He watched the dancers bounce

302

and gyrate. "The tux is a holdover from my years with Miami-Dade PD. A starlet, Jennifer Jade, had received death threats. I was assigned to be her escort for the premiere of her new movie. Her publicist objected to her 'bodyguard' being photographed in an ill-fitting rented tux, so the studio sprang for one. Haven't had much call to use it since — until tonight."

The DJ shifted gears from rock to romantic. "All right, you guys," he spoke into the mic. "Time for you to step up and let your dates know that you're with the prettiest girl in the room."

The sexy, seductive, yet upbeat strains of Frankie Valli's hit "Can't Take My Eyes off You" drifted from the speakers. "Shall we?" McBride asked. Not waiting for an answer, he took my empty cup and set it on a nearby bistro table.

Mutely, I let him lead me onto the dance floor and slide his arm around my waist. I could feel the heat of his palm burn through the thin fabric of my gown as we swayed to the music. He'd once claimed he wasn't a dancer. Maybe he didn't do the shag or polka, but he wasn't a novice when it came to a slow dance. He moved with a natural athleticism.

"I often wondered what this would be

like," he said.

I smiled up at him. "A prom?"

"No," he said, then paused as though searching for the right words. "I wondered what it would be like, just the two of us, enjoying each other's company like a normal couple."

My smile wavered. "I hope you're not disappointed," I said in a voice that didn't sound quite like mine.

"On the contrary . . ."

I didn't want the song to end. A haze seemed to descend over the room. I forgot I was in a room filled with teenagers. I was acutely aware of McBride's body pressed against mine, the citrusy scent of his aftershave, the —

"Just a freaking minute!" a woman shrieked.

McBride and I jerked apart in time to see Mary Beth physically separate two boys who were about to come to blows.

"Not on my watch, you don't!" She grabbed the larger of the boys by the scruff of his neck, the other by his ear, and marched them off the dance floor. Although both boys easily towered over and outweighed her, they were no match for her fury.

McBride and I looked at each other as the

same thought crossed our minds. The woman was strong as an ox. *Strong enough to lift and move a body?*

At last, the prom wound down and it was time to leave. McBride and I were both quiet on the short ride to my apartment. McBride parked at the entrance to Spice It Up!

"Care to come in for a nightcap?" I asked, wanting to prolong the evening.

"Thought you'd never ask." He sprang out of the car and came around to the passenger side. Taking my hand, he helped me to my feet and escorted me to the door . . .

. . . and kissed me.

Kissed me right there on the sidewalk. Did the earth quiver? Crazy, but I could swear that I saw fireworks, shooting stars, and skyrockets. Longing flooded through me like a storm surge after a hurricane, bringing with it the sense of being in exactly the right place with exactly the right man. The kiss ended leaving me giddy. My hands shook slightly as I unlocked the door and led him inside.

"Are you sure?" he asked with uncharacteristic hesitation.

I smiled. "I'm positive."

A chill gust of wind blew through Spice It Up! From the rear of the shop, a door slammed against the wall sounding like a gunshot. Upstairs, Casey burst into frenzied barking.

McBride pushed me behind him. "Stay put and call nine-one-one."

CHAPTER 25

"But —"

"Stay put!" McBride withdrew a pistol no bigger than a squirt gun from a holster at the small of his back. "And call nine-one-one."

"Be careful," I whispered, but too late; he was already gone. Frantic, I dug through an evening bag large enough only for my phone and a lipstick.

It seemed an eternity for my 911 call to be rerouted to the officer on duty. Apparently no one manned the front desk at this hour. At last, a groggy-sounding Beau Tucker came on the line to assure me he'd be there shortly.

"All clear!" McBride shouted.

I followed the sound of his voice and hurried through my shop and upstairs as quickly as my long skirt and high heels allowed. I froze on the threshold to my apartment. My home had been trashed. The contents of the kitchen cabinets were strewn everywhere. Whoever did this was obviously looking for something and had been angry they hadn't found it.

"Hate to tell you this, but your bedroom's even worse." McBride replaced his weapon. "Only place not ransacked is your daughter's room."

Casey chose that moment to peek out of Lindsey's doorway. My little mutt was overjoyed to see me. In a single mighty bound worthy of a superhero, he leaped into my arms.

"At least your pooch is unharmed. I found Casey locked in Lindsey's bedroom. Looks like he tried to claw his way out. You'll probably have to refinish or replace the door."

"Doors can be easily replaced; pets can't." Holding Casey tightly, I maneuvered through the disaster zone in a daze. Cushions and throw pillows littered the living room floor. The drawer of an end table had been dumped on the carpet, its contents scattered. "I'm glad Lindsey's spending the night at CJ's and won't see this mess."

My bedroom had taken the brunt of the attack. Sheets and bedspread had been ripped off and tossed on the floor. The mattress rested at an odd angle on the box spring. My clothing lay in untidy heaps everywhere. The drawer of my computer desk had been emptied, then smashed into smithereens.

"Any idea who might be responsible?"

I was aware that McBride watched me closely. Was he afraid he'd have to comfort a hysterical female? Watch me dissolve in a puddle of tears? Truth be told, hysterics and tears might have brought some relief. Instead, I felt numb and shocked by what a stranger had done to my home — my sanctuary. "No," I said, shaking my head. "I have no idea who might have done this."

McBride wrapped his arms around me. "It's all right. We'll figure this out."

Slowly, my world righted itself. I rested my head against his shoulder and allowed myself to be comforted. McBride tightened his embrace until Casey yelped in protest, making me smile. "Sorry, pal," I told him.

Flashing red and blue lights from the street below bounced across the apartment walls. "Police!" Beau Tucker bellowed.

"Upstairs!" McBride shouted back, then released me.

Tucker's heavy footsteps pounded on the stairs. We met him in the kitchen. He frowned when he saw that I wasn't alone, but if he was curious why McBride was with me — and dressed in a tux — he kept his

309

comments to himself. He stood for a long moment surveying the chaos, then shoved up the bill of his cap. "Place is a mess. Who did you piss off this time?"

McBride drilled him with a look. "If that's an example of your interview technique, Sergeant, you need to return to the academy for a refresher course."

Beau's face colored at the reprimand. "Anything missing?"

"No," I murmured, "but I won't know until I get a better look."

"On my way upstairs, I checked your cash register. Looks like the perp jimmied the drawer with a crowbar or some such tool. Took the bills, left the coins."

"Oh no," I groaned at hearing this. "Saturday is my busiest and my most profitable day. I was distracted helping Lindsey get ready for prom, so I postponed depositing the day's receipts."

"Any reports of recent break-ins?" McBride wanted to know.

"Some joker attempted a B and E at the Gas 'n Go a few nights back. Must've spotted the security cameras and got scared off." Beau took a notebook out of his uniform pocket and flipped through the pages. "A hunting cabin got vandalized last week. Probably kids lookin' for booze."

"What next?" I absently petted Casey's head. He rewarded me by slathering my chin with doggy kisses.

"I'll send Moyer over in the morning, have him dust for prints. In the meantime, take a look around, but don't touch anything until the scene's been processed." He snapped his notebook shut. "You have someplace to spend the night? Might be best if you stay away until Moyer's done his job."

I nodded. "Thanks."

He turned to leave. "The perp gained entry by kicking in the rear door. Have James Bond here secure it before you leave."

I blew out a sigh after hearing him drive off. "And as they say, that's that."

"C'mon," McBride said. "Grab whatever you might need. You're spending the night at my place. Tomorrow will be soon enough to tackle this project."

I stared at him, unsure I'd heard correctly. "I'm sure Reba Mae won't mind letting me sleep on her sofa."

He placed both hands on my shoulders. "Look, it's late. Surely you don't want to disturb Reba Mae and her boys at this hour. Bring your mutt along. He'll be good company for Fraidy. She's been an only pet for too long."

I had neither the energy — nor inclination — to muster a refusal. "Okay, but what about the door? The burglar might come back. I can't leave it wide open."

"Tell me where you keep a hammer and nails. I'll fix it while you gather your things."

McBride was as good as his word. By the time I returned downstairs with a few items hastily stuffed into a pillowcase, he had the door securely fastened.

"Let's go."

I woke the next morning to the smell of coffee brewing. I lay quietly for a moment, naked and content in McBride's king-size bed. No regrets. No embarrassment. Only an overwhelming sense of well-being.

I heard McBride moving about, so, yawning and stretching, I rolled out of bed. I decided to take advantage of the opportunity to shower. I emerged smelling of pine-scented soap and my hair a riot of curls. I had no idea where the pillowcase containing my belongings might be — for all I knew they could still be in Hoyt's Lincoln — so I made do with what was available.

When I came out of the bedroom, I found McBride hunched over his laptop at the breakfast bar. A wide grin spread across his face when he looked up and saw me standing there. "My tuxedo shirt looks better on you than it does on me."

"Oh, I wouldn't say that. I saw the way girls were giving you the eye." I walked over to the coffeemaker and poured coffee in a cup he had had waiting.

"So this is how you look first thing in the morning."

I dragged a hand through my tousled hair. "What you see is what you get."

"I like the freckles. It was one of the first things I noticed about you." He got up and sauntered toward me, coffee mug in one hand. "I confess, I'm not much of a cook, but I know how to fry an egg."

"Give the caffeine time to jump-start my brain; then I'll raid your refrigerator and see what I can come up with."

"I spoke to Moyer while you were in the shower. He said it could take a while to do a thorough job. So there's no need to rush. . . ."

So we didn't rush. Instead, we took it slow and easy.

"Sure you don't want my help?" McBride asked.

"Thanks, but Reba Mae offered to tackle the job. She knows my home almost as well as her own."

Reality hit like a sucker punch. We were in Hoyt's Lincoln, which McBride would return in exchange for his truck. McBride kept his eyes trained on the road as he talked. "Tucker's convinced you angered some person who took out his or her aggression on you. Moyer, conversely, hasn't ruled out a random act of vandalism."

"What do you think?" I studied his profile, but it didn't give a clue to the thoughts.

"Both theories are valid, but I got the impression that whoever did this was looking for something specific."

"Like cash or jewelry?"

"Do you keep anything of value in your apartment?"

"I sold all the expensive jewelry CJ had given me over the years to help finance Spice It Up!" I confessed.

"Could someone be sending you a message? A warning of sorts?"

"I don't know why. I've asked questions of a few people but haven't discovered anything worthwhile."

He turned down the street behind my shop and switched off the ignition. "You've gained a reputation as an amateur sleuth. You might be making someone nervous." He rested his arm along the top of the seat, his hand cupping the back of my neck.

"Promise you'll be extra careful."

"Promise." I tried to sound carefree and nonchalant, but carefree was impossible when he started to stroke my throat with his thumb. My pulse bucked like a bronco beneath his touch.

The reaction didn't go unnoticed. Mc-Bride's mouth curved in a smile of pure male satisfaction seconds before he leaned across the console and claimed mine for a kiss with enough heat to fog the windows.

It might have grown even steamier if Reba Mae hadn't chosen that moment to knock on the driver's side window. "All right, you two, break it up!"

Snatching my belongings from the backseat, I scrambled out of the car.

"Hiya, Wyatt." Reba Mae grinned ear to ear. "Nice day, isn't it?"

"You bet." With a jaunty salute, he drove off.

Reba Mae draped her arm over my shoulders as we trudged up the path leading to my rear door. "Makin' a fashion statement?" she asked, laughing. "Silver stilettos and blue jeans. And what's with the T-shirt? Looks big enough to fit McBride."

My cheeks flushed. "In all the confusion last night, I only had time for a grab and go. Besides, all my clothes are going through

315

a wash cycle before being put away. It gives me the willies knowing some creep handled my things."

"Wyatt called Clay first thing. Told him about the break-in and how you needed a new door with a sturdy lock."

"I don't know how Clay managed it, but I owe him big-time," I remarked, spying a door so new it needed a coat of paint.

"Don't worry about a thing. My boy's got contacts in the construction business." Reba Mae slid a key into the hefty stainless-steel lock and opened the door. "Clay said be sure to remind you that you need to do a thorough inventory for your insurance company."

Reba Mae let out a low whistle when she entered my kitchen. Bending down, she picked a whisk and set of measuring spoons off the floor. "I'll start here. You take the bedroom, and we'll meet in the livin' room. Then" — she winked — "you can tell your BFF all about your sleepover."

I tried to set my mind on autopilot as I went about restoring order out of chaos. My washing machine and dryer worked nonstop as I did load after load of laundry. I was double-checking the pockets of various pairs of jeans before tossing them in the wash when I pulled out an oblong piece of plastic barely an inch long. I held it in the palm of hand and stared at it, puzzled. Then it dawned on me. It was the same object that had fallen out of Shirley's shoe yesterday. On closer examination, I realized it wasn't a device used to deter shoplifters but a flash drive.

But what was a flash drive doing in the toe of an expensive pair of designer shoes? First a stolen computer, now a hidden flash drive. Like McBride, I wasn't a believer in coincidence. The two had to be connected, but how? And what, if anything, did this have to do with her death?

I hurried into the kitchen, where Reba Mae was sorting cutlery into a drawer. "Reba Mae, have you seen my computer?"

"Nope, but I'll help you look for it."

We searched high and low but couldn't find it anywhere. "Guess a missing computer goes on my inventory list," I said, feeling discouraged.

"Doesn't Lindsey have a laptop?" Reba Mae plumped a seat cushion before setting it on an armchair. "Maybe the home wrecker missed it."

"Let's check." I went into Lindsey's bedroom with Reba Mae close behind. Buried beneath a mound of clothing on Lindsey's dresser, her laptop was seemingly untouched. After powering it on, I plugged the flash drive into a USB port. "This was tucked into the toe of one of Shirley's shoes," I explained, scrolling through my options. I found the drive with the USB, clicked on it, and waited.

Nothing happened.

Reba Mae watched from over my shoulder. "Why isn't it workin'?"

I straightened, more puzzled than ever. "Because the flash drive's password protected, that's why. Whatever's on it, Shirley wanted to make sure it was for her eyes only."

CHAPTER 26

Usually I felt a certain sense of satisfaction with every sale, but today was an exception. My antique cash register — of which I was extremely fond — had been abused. Its cash drawer had been battered by a burglar. Instead of rolling out smoothly, it now had to be pried out with a coat hanger or nail file. Officer Gary Moyer had dusted it for prints but nada, nil, zero. From Moyer's comments, I knew Beau Tucker considered mine a run-of-the-mill break-in and entry no different from the one at the Gas 'n Go or Creekside Realty.

In between customers, who were prompted to visit more by curiosity than an urge to purchase salt or cinnamon, I filled out the inventory form the insurance agent had supplied. I'd promised him I'd drop it at his office by the close of the business day. Aside from Saturday's cash profits, a few pieces of costume jewelry and my laptop comprised the list.

And the recent robbery wasn't the only problem on my mind. I was also concerned about my children. How would Chad and Lindsey react when they found out their mother was . . . involved . . . with Wyatt McBride? I doubted they'd welcome the news. Lindsey was intimidated that, even though suspended, McBride was still technically the chief of police. Chad hadn't met McBride yet, so no telling if he'd be pro or con about our . . . involvement. Before he started college Chad and I had shared a special mother-son bond, but our relationship had undergone a subtle change. I wasn't sure whether to blame the estrangement on our divorce or the physical distance separating us. Until recently, I'd been under the impression he was focused solely on being accepted by one of the top-ranked medical schools. Then I started hearing talk of a girlfriend and a gap year.

On impulse, I reached for my cell phone and punched in a familiar number. "CJ, we need to talk. When's a good time?"

After some hemming and hawing on his end of the line, we agreed to meet at his office at the end of the day.

The insurance agency had already closed by

the time I reached their office, so I slid the inventory form under their door where they'd be sure to find it first thing tomorrow morning. My final stop was the offices of Prescott and Wainwright, Attorneys. I squeezed my VW into a space between CJ's Lexus and Matt's Bimmer. Wanda's Honda was present, too, even though it was after the paralegal's usual quitting time. For a reason that escaped me, the woman had never been a member of my fan club. Now that I was no longer married to one of her employers, she often let her dislike be known.

Straightening my shoulders, along with my resolve, I marched up the walk and into the reception area. No one manned the front desk, which wasn't unusual. The young and inexperienced receptionists CJ and Matt kept hiring tended to treat the job as a revolving door.

I proceeded down the hall toward CJ's office. A quick peek through Wanda's half-open door found her scowling at a computer printout. She appeared clearly unhappy, and I was glad I wasn't the object of her wrath.

I found CJ, his shirtsleeves rolled to the elbows, his tie loosened, behind a massive desk. When he saw me, he removed a pair of reading glasses with sleek black designer frames and motioned me to take a seat.

"What's with the glasses, CJ? Old age creeping up on you?"

He had the grace to look shamefaced. "Amber's been pesterin' me to ditch the eyeglasses and have laser surgery."

"Better to project that boyish charm of yours?"

"You might say that." Opening a desk drawer, he brought out a bottle and poured two fingers' worth of Wild Turkey into an Old Fashioned glass. "I'd offer you one, but I know you've never been partial to fine Kentucky bourbon. Havin' dinner tonight at Amber's parents' house. Need to fortify myself before an evenin' with Amelia and Max." He studied me over the rim of his glass. "So what's with all the talk about you and McBride? Matt said you two were actin' pretty chummy at Lindsey's prom."

Instantly I went on the defensive. "No concern of yours, CJ. We're both adults."

He pointed the raised glass of whiskey at me. "Heed my advice, darlin': McBride's nothin' but white trash. Always was, always will be. You can do a whole lot better."

I bit my tongue to keep from asking, *Better than what? An ambitious, ambulance-chasing, skirt-chasing man like the one I married?*

322

"McBride's a likely suspect in a murder investigation. Have to hand it to him, he's a wily devil. Thinks he's covered his tracks, but you wait; he'll trip himself up. And when he does, Beau will be waitin' with an arrest warrant."

"McBride didn't have anything to do with Shirley's death, and you know it as well as I do." I clasped my hands in my lap to keep them from shaking — or punching him. "I didn't come here to discuss McBride. I'm here to find out what's going on with our son. These days you seem to be the parent in the know."

CJ leaned back and savored a sip of bourbon. "Our son didn't want his momma makin' a fuss about him wantin' to take a gap year is all. Lots of kids do it."

"Chad has been working like crazy to make good grades for the sole purpose of getting into a top-ranked med school. Now suddenly he wants to gallivant all over Europe? I don't get it. What's changed?"

"Her name's Brielle and, from everythin' Chad's said, she's quite a looker."

"But —"

"Chad's love life is only part of it," CJ cut me off. "He feels he's been missin' out by keepin' his nose to the grindstone. He wants to experience life from more than the pages of a textbook. Needs to spread his wings. To kick up his heels."

Seemed like a lot of spreading and too much kicking to suit me. "Call me a fuddy-duddy, CJ, but exactly how does Chad plan to finance this . . . this . . . journey of discovery?"

"I told him not to worry. To consider it a loan from his old man."

"Swell." My voice oozed sarcasm. "I hope he plans to spend some time at home before jetting off to explore the world."

CJ's cell phone rang, ending further conversation. "It's a client. Mind closin' the door on your way out, darlin'."

And just like that I'd been ousted.

I started down the hallway but paused when I heard raised voices from Matt's office. I stepped behind an artificial ficus and tried to look like a leaf.

"How stupid do you think I am?" Wanda demanded. "Don't try to pull the wool over my eyes. Do you honestly expect me to believe these charges were work related?"

"I'm telling you, they were."

"According to the expense report you turned in, the charges are for two people — not one. Sounds like you and Mary Beth took a second honeymoon and expect the firm to pay for it."

"Take my word for it, Wanda, a honeymoon couldn't be further from the truth."

"Hmph!" Wanda snorted. "Why else would you spend a weekend at the Marriott in Augusta? The amount you charged for food is outlandish — pan-seared duck breast and grilled ahi tuna — when you could have ordered Domino's."

"I worked the entire weekend," Matt insisted angrily. "Now sign the damn voucher so I can get reimbursed."

"I will, but repeat this scam I'll go straight to CJ."

Wanda stormed out and down the hall. I waited until she returned to her own office and slammed the door before stepping out from behind the potted plant. I started past Matt's office, but the door was ajar. Unable to resist peeking inside, I saw Matt slumped at his desk, his head in his hands. He looked so dejected, so disheartened, I simply had to find out why.

"Hey, Matt," I said from the doorway. "Are you all right?"

He raised his head. "I suppose you heard everything."

I entered his office and quietly closed the door behind me. "No need to worry, I won't mention the conversation I just overheard to CJ. Do you want to talk about it?"

"Sorry you had to witness the scene with Wanda," he said tiredly. "She's only doing her job. Can't fault her for that. I told Mary Beth not to pursue this, to consider it an out-of-pocket expense, but she's a stickler when it comes to our personal finances."

"If it was a legitimate, work-related expense, you deserve to be compensated."

He rubbed his eyes with the heels of his hands. "Right now, my life's one hot mess."

I advanced farther into the room. "Is Shirley partly to blame?"

"Yes." Matt blew out a breath and stared up at the ceiling. "Shirley was fantastic, but she wanted more than I was willing to give."

"Things such as marriage, maybe a family?"

Matt nodded, his expression downcast. "Shirley's biological clock was ticking. She wanted to get pregnant, have a baby."

"And you didn't."

"Hell, no." He barked out a laugh. "My son's ready to enroll in college. Why would I want to start all over with diapers and three A.M. feedings?"

"Was Shirley the reason Mary Beth followed you to Augusta?"

"Yeah, indirectly." Matt made what sounded like a half laugh, half sob. "Mary Beth suspected I was having an affair, but until that photo appeared on the memory board at Shirley's funeral she didn't know with whom. She discovered I had planned a weekend getaway and where I was going to stay. She burst into my hotel room like gangbusters, dead certain she'd find me and the 'other' woman flagrante delicto."

I hitched the strap of my purse higher on my shoulder. "So, what did she find?"

Matt smiled but without humor. "She found me flat on my back — alone — except for a nearby ice chest. I'd just come from having a vasectomy at my urologist's office."

I was momentarily stunned speechless. I don't know what I expected to hear, but this definitely wasn't it.

"Strange as it sounds, Shirley's the reason I had the procedure done. During an argument, she threatened to stop taking her birth control pills. I didn't want to chance that happening."

"No, of course not," I murmured.

"I have to hand it to my wife. She's an old-fashioned Tammy Wynette stand-by-your-man kind of gal. When she realized what I'd gone and done — and how much pain I was in — she never ventured from my side the entire weekend. She'd make one hell of a nurse."

"Exactly when did your vasectomy take place?" I had to ask, had to know, but was afraid he'd tell me it was none of my business.

"Ironically, the same weekend Shirley's body was found — the weekend of Melly and Cot's wedding. And —" He thumped his desk for emphasis. "— Wanda's got the damn receipts to prove it."

After leaving the law office and returning to Spice It Up! I went upstairs to make dinner. I opted for one of my daughter's favorites — spaghetti casserole. While it baked and with Casey along for companionship, I walked the short distance to Creekside Savings and Loan and dropped the green zippered bag of cash into the night depository. Zach VanFleet spied me as he headed for his car and gave me a friendly wave.

Zach seemed a personable sort, I mused on the way home. Much more forthcoming than the secretive Colin Flynn, who had magically appeared with some cockamamie story about needing peace and quiet in which to write the great American novel. Did the man think I was born yesterday? Just wearing glasses and having a professorial air didn't make one a writer.

328

Lindsey had already finished setting the table by the time Casey and I came home. "I made a salad — but only a small one — to go with the spaghetti," she announced. "I've eaten enough lettuce in the last two weeks for a herd of bunnies."

"I didn't know bunnies came in herds." I took the casserole out of the oven and set it on a trivet.

She shrugged. "It was a question once on a general science exam. A group of young rabbits with the same parentage is referred to as a litter, and a group of domestic rabbits is sometimes called a herd."

I poured each of us a tall glass of milk. "I'll try to remember that in case I'm ever a contestant on *Jeopardy!*"

Dinnertime was filled with Lindsey's endless chatter about prom and the after party her father and Amber hosted. CJ had not only a pool but also a pool table, a state-of-the-art sound system, and a media room. I could hardly compete with his array of techno toys. To be honest, though, it was a much pleasanter topic than that of having our home vandalized by a thug in search of . . . drugs, money, valuables? Was the BCPD any closer to discovering the culprit's identity? I needed to check with Beau Tucker to see if he'd made any progress on the case.

"All my friends think Chief McBride is really hot — especially for being a cop and an older dude." Lindsey sliced off another serving of spaghetti pie. "Some of the guys wondered if he was packing. Was he?"

I speared a cherry tomato with my fork. "Yes, he was, I'm happy to report. He had his weapon drawn and ready when he went upstairs to make sure the burglar was gone."

Lindsey shuddered dramatically. "I feel safer knowing Clay installed a new door and a heavy-duty lock. Even so, it gives me the creeps to think someone broke into our home." Then, without missing a beat, she changed the subject. "I can't wait to meet the girl Chad fell head over heels for. I can't believe he wants to take a year off to go trekking around Europe. It doesn't sound like my saintly brother. I never would have guessed he'd postpone med school."

"Me neither." I scooped up the last bite of casserole on my plate and gathered the dirty dishes. "It will seem strange this fall with both of you gone. I'm already suffering the onset of empty-nest syndrome."

"I should hear soon from the colleges I applied to; then we can do some serious shopping." Without waiting to be told — which I interpreted as a sign of maturity —

Lindsey loaded the dishwasher. "Promise you, I'll get home more often than Chad. It'll be almost like I never left."

After Lindsey went off to study for finals with her friend Taylor, the apartment seemed unnaturally quiet. I roamed room to room giving each one a cursory inspection. I'd put in long hours yesterday restoring order, but, except for having to replace the drawer of my computer desk, everything had pretty much been returned to normal. I was about to pass Lindsey's bedroom, which had been spared the intruder's wrath, when I spotted the box containing Shirley's designer shoes on the foot of the bed.

"Sorry, Shirley," I said aloud. "I didn't steal them; I only borrowed them. Certainly you wouldn't begrudge my girl the loan of a pretty pair of heels for her senior prom."

But the shoes just sat there, a silent rebuke that I'd pledged to return them along with a grim reminder of the flash drive I'd found hidden inside one of the toes. And not an ordinary flash drive either, but a password-protected one.

CHAPTER 27

Earlier that day, Reba Mae and I had rehashed finding a flash drive in, of all places, a pair of shoes but failed to come up with a satisfactory explanation for what it was doing there. Maybe three heads were better than two when it came to solving the riddle. Since it wasn't late and seeing as I had nothing better to do, I decided to solicit a third opinion. I hadn't heard from McBride since he'd dropped me off yesterday morning. I didn't relish the notion of sitting around and waiting like an insecure teen for the phone to ring. How pathetic was that for a woman my age? So we had made love, not once, but twice. No big deal, right? After all, we were two single, consenting adults. No reason to feel awkward or embarrassed the next time we saw each other. Still, I couldn't stifle a tingle of anticipation at the thought of seeing him again.

I tucked the flash drive into the pocket of

my jeans, then packed up what was left of the spaghetti casserole, snatched the shoe box off Lindsey's bed, snapped on Casey's leash, and started out. Thanks to daylight savings time, the sun was just starting its descent, spreading a rosy-golden glow across the western sky. Before driving to McBride's, however, I detoured to the historic district.

Upon reaching Shirley's, I sat in her drive for a long moment admiring the graceful lines of the old Victorian. Until recently, Brandywine Creek's historical district had been a closely guarded secret. Due to the state's off-the-beaten-path marketing strategy, the town had been discovered. As a result, the plan was bringing more tourists into my shop as well. Felicity Driscoll's bed-and-breakfast and the Brandywine Creek Opera House were also popular destinations for folks wanting to escape the hustle and bustle of their daily lives.

I rolled down the passenger side window for my pet. "In and out," I told him. "Five minutes max."

I wrinkled my nose the instant I entered the foyer. The house had acquired even more of that musty, unlived-in odor since my previous visit. The place needed tenants who would complete the renovations Shirley intended and lavish it with TLC. I made a mental note to ask Vicki what Shirley's brother planned to do with the place. The location was prime, so I doubted it would remain on the market long.

I unlocked the front door and started up the stairs but caught myself repeatedly glancing over my shoulder. The fine hairs at the back of my neck prickled. Something felt . . . off . . . almost as though I was being watched. *Strange.* Logic told me that I was here alone. Yet I couldn't escape the feeling that something was amiss.

Shadows skulked in the upstairs hallway, filling it with gloom, and adding to my unease. *In and out,* I reminded myself. Five minutes max as I'd promised Casey. Going directly to Shirley's bedroom, I threw open the closet door . . . and stared in mute surprise.

A veritable mountain of peep toes, platforms, pumps, wedges, and sandals lay in a jumbled heap on the floor. I might not have been the epitome of tidy in my frantic search to find Lindsey a suitable pair of shoes, but this wasn't my handiwork. I shivered. Someone other than me had been here — and when they didn't find what they were looking for my home had become the next target. I felt that with unshakeable certainty. I practically threw the box of borrowed footwear at a now-empty shelf and fled the house as if chased by the hounds of hell.

Casey greeted me with a flurry of tail wagging, eager to be off on our next adventure. "Let's blow this pop stand, puppy dog," I told him as I cranked the engine, shifted into reverse, and backed down the drive.

The episode left me rattled. Yet, at the same time, it lent an odd sense of exhilaration. I sensed I was getting closer to the truth. Was the tiny storage device I'd found the key to unlocking the mystery of Shirley's murder? If so, the secret was safe from everyone except a skilled computer hacker. I was still mulling this over when I pulled into McBride's drive.

Self-doubt belatedly kicked in. What was I doing, coming here? A man as good-looking as McBride must've had his fill of women vying for his affection — the brazen hussies. But I was neither brazen nor a hussy, I rationalized. I simply wanted to exchange information and brainstorm theories. So what if I'd brought along food? Man can't live on pizza and fried eggs alone. Besides, it wasn't as if I'd made spaghetti casserole with him in mind.

I climbed out of the VW with Casey nipping at my heels and went up the porch steps. I knocked, but when no one answered I was tempted to do an about-face. I'd no sooner taken a half step back when the door swung open.

"I . . . um . . ." Words deserted me.

McBride, naked to the waist, stood toweling his wet hair. He grinned at seeing me. "This is a nice surprise. I wasn't expecting company."

My mouth suddenly dry, I swallowed and held out the foil-covered dish. "Supper."

He peeked under the foil. "Perfect timing. I was just about to crack open a can of soup. C'mon in."

Before I could reply, Casey scooted through the open doorway. I spied Fraidy, who had deigned to come out to inspect McBride's visitors. Seeing who it was, the cat took one look at me, lifted her tail high in the air, and disappeared into one of the bedrooms.

I followed McBride into the kitchen. "Don't read too much into this, McBride. It's only leftovers."

"Never apologize for bringing leftovers to a starving man." He snagged a denim shirt from the back of a chair and shrugged it on. "Join me?"

"Thanks, but I ate earlier with Lindsey."

336

"So this is all for me?" He sliced a generous wedge of spaghetti pie onto a plate, slid it into the microwave, and set the timer. "Unless you've developed a taste for beer, all I can offer is coffee or Diet Coke?"

"Soda will be fine," I said, taking a seat on the lone stool at the breakfast bar. "I hope you don't get the wrong idea about my coming here tonight."

Taking a can of diet soda from the fridge, he popped the tab and placed it in front of me. "Like get the notion that you're after my fine body?"

I tried not to stare at his hard-muscled chest visible courtesy of the unbuttoned shirt. "That's not funny, McBride," I said, trying to sound stern. "I'm here in an official capacity and can't stay long."

"I was afraid of that."

My heart did a strange little tap dance at hearing this, making me wonder if palpitations like Shirley had complained about were contagious. "Button your shirt, for heaven's sake, before you catch a cold."

"Nothin' you haven't seen before, sweetheart," he said with a trace of pure Georgia in his drawl, more amused than offended.

I felt a warm rush of color to my cheeks. *Would this blushing like a schoolgirl ever cease?* "Understand, it's not a complaint

337

but a distraction. Bottom line —" I cleared my throat. "— I need to get home before Lindsey does. I don't want her coming into an empty house until the person or persons responsible for trashing my home have been found."

The microwave *ping*ed just then. McBride removed the casserole with one hand and ripped off a length of paper towel to use as a napkin with the other. I slid off the stool and took silverware from a drawer. "Beer?" I asked, knowing his fondness for the beverage.

He nodded. "A woman after my own heart."

"Okay, now eat before it gets cold." Realizing how that must have sounded, I shoved an impatient hand through my hair. I placed a bottle of Yuengling on the table and sat opposite him. "Sorry. I didn't mean to come across as your mother."

"For the record, my mother wasn't the Betty Crocker variety. If it didn't come out of a can or a box, it wasn't considered food." He dug into his meal as though he hadn't eaten all day. "So if it wasn't a mercy run for a starving lawman, why are you here?"

"A couple things." I let out a sigh, then proceeded to tell him about my visit to the law office and the ensuing conversation with Matt Wainwright. "I think we can cross Matt and Mary Beth off our persons of interest list," I concluded.

Finished with his meal, he pushed his empty plate to the side. "You said 'a couple things.' What else is on your mind?"

Shifting my weight, I dug the flash drive out of the pocket of my jeans. "This fell out of a pair of designer shoes that I borrowed from Shirley."

"You borrowed a dead woman's shoes?" he asked with a bemused smile.

"It was an emergency. I don't plan on making it a habit."

"Good to know." He held the flash drive in the palm of his hand and studied it. "Have you checked to see what's on it?"

I huffed out a breath. "Of course, I did. It's password protected, or maybe even encrypted. I'm not computer savvy enough to be able to tell the difference. But I do know that whatever's on it must be pretty darn important for Shirley to go to those lengths."

Our eyes met for a long moment; then McBride nodded slowly. "I agree that you're on the right track. We might've been going at this all wrong."

"What do you mean?" I asked even though

339

I'd already guessed the direction this conversation was heading.

"It's possible we've been mistaken about Shirley being killed by a lover, an enraged wife, or an irate client. What if her death was related to something else entirely?"

"Such as her job?"

The corner of his mouth twitched. "In spite of my initial misgivings, you might could have the makings a first-rate detective."

"Aw shucks, Chief." I gave him a saucy smile. "You sure know how to turn a girl's head."

He chuckled, then turned serious. "Piper, promise me you'll be extra careful. Whoever killed Shirley knows your reputation as an amateur sleuth. Your ransacked apartment was his or her way of letting you know they're watching."

At hearing this, I felt as though an icy-cold finger trailed down my spine. Maybe the unease I'd experienced when I returned the shoes hadn't been the result of an overactive imagination. I decided against telling McBride about the incident — or the messy pile of shoes — but vowed to be increasingly vigilant.

I drew concentric circles on the frosty can of soda with a fingertip. "We still need to rule out Elaine Dixon. She's got a short fuse and viewed Shirley as a threat. Who knows what she's capable of?"

"Keep your pretty nose out of it." He held up his hand to forestall the protest he saw forming. "Beau Tucker can't see beyond me as a suspect, but if it makes you feel better, I'll have Gary Moyer question the woman. See if he can find out whether the Dixons have an alibi for the time of the murder. In the meantime, I know a computer hacker who might be able to help us with the flash drive, but it'll take time."

"Good," I said, getting to my feet. "I really have to go home."

McBride walked me to my car. Without waiting for an invitation, Casey jumped inside and curled up on the passenger seat. As I half turned to bid McBride good night, he rested his hands lightly on either side of my neck. I'm certain he could feel my pulse leap beneath his touch. "Look, Piper, with me being under suspicion for murder, this . . . us . . . is the worst possible timing."

My breath caught in my throat. I tried, and failed, to read his expression in the moonlight. "Are you trying to say what happened between us was nothing more than a one-night stand?"

"That would be the wisest course of ac-

341

tion, except ...."

"... except?"

His mouth hovered over mine. "Except I care about you more than I should."

"Being wise is overrated." I rose on tiptoe, and our lips met in a kiss that spoke more eloquently than words.

On the ride home, I couldn't stop smiling. It wasn't until I'd driven several miles down the winding county road that I glanced into the rearview mirror and was nearly blinded by the bright headlights of the car behind me.

A car followed too close for comfort.

Had I been daydreaming, driving at a snail's pace, and irritated another driver? Stories of road rage flashed through my brain. I pressed on the accelerator to put more distance between the two vehicles. The driver of the car behind me did the same. That's when I knew I was in trouble.

CHAPTER 28

"What the . . . ?"

My grip tightened on the steering wheel. Casey snapped to attention, his little body so tense it fairly vibrated. I took a deep breath and ordered myself to remain calm.

The first tap on my rear bumper was almost gentle — a teasing, taunting kind of tap.

Catching my lower lip between my teeth, I darted a nervous look into the rearview mirror but couldn't see beyond the glare of the headlights.

I knew this stretch of road well. It was narrow and curvy with almost no shoulder and no guardrails. Steep ditches ran parallel to the roadway before the land slanted upward to the tree line. The few homes along this stretch were widely spaced on lots that boasted acreage such as McBride's. I reached for my purse, which was on the seat next to Casey, and fumbled for my cell

phone just as my Beetle was struck again —
much harder this time. My purse tumbled
to the floor, its contents scattered.

Casey growled deep in his throat but other
than that could offer little help.

"Hold on, pal," I said through clenched
teeth. Not knowing what else to do, I
jammed the pedal to the metal. My valiant
VW surged forward, but it was no match
for the more powerful car that was on my
tail.

Bam! My skull slammed against the head-
rest from the force of the next blow. Before
I had a chance to recover, the driver
switched tactics. He veered sharply to the
left, gunned the engine, and pulled up
beside me, running me off the road.

Standing on the brakes, I clung to the
steering wheel for dear life. *Stop! Stop,
please stop!* This was a crazy carnival ride
to end all crazy carnival rides. I caromed
down a grassy slope, bounced across a
muddy ditch, then up an embankment. For
one terrified moment I feared the little car
would flip on its side. The VW jolted over
the uneven terrain. Bushes scraped the
undercarriage. Metal screeched as we side-
swiped a veritable stockade of pine and
hardwood. Finally, the Beetle rolled to a
halt, but not before a massive oak crumpled

my fender as easily as an empty water bottle.

I sat stunned. I was quaking like an aspen, my pulse racing. What had just happened? The entire incident seemed surreal. It had taken only minutes from start to finish. Minutes from the first love tap to heartlessly being forced off the road, hurtling across a gulley and into the woods. I barely had time for more than a glimpse of the driver, who appeared to be wearing a hoodie pulled low to conceal his features.

"Casey . . . ?" I called, a tremor in my voice.

My furry sidekick let out a frightened yelp as he crawled out from beneath the dash. Casey leaped into my lap, narrowly avoiding impaling his small body on the gearshift in his frantic scramble to comfort — and be comforted.

I felt something warm and wet trickle down the side of my face. Raising a trembling hand, I touched my forehead. My fingers came away sticky from where I must've gashed my head on the edge of the mirror. Since I hadn't hit any objects head-on, the airbags hadn't deployed. I didn't know if this was a good or bad thing. The VW's headlights speared through a copse of trees. A deer appeared out of nowhere, stood spotlighted, then just as quickly vanished.

Slowly, my racing heart returned to normal, and brain cells woke from their stupor. Unfastening my seat belt, I clutched Casey under one arm, then used the other arm to grope the floor on the passenger side for my cell phone. My fingers curled around it and held on tight. The adrenaline coursing through me ebbed, leaving me drained and shaky. It took several tries before I succeeded in punching in 911.

I almost sobbed with relief at hearing Precious Blessing's voice on the line. "Hey, Precious. . . ." After I gave a jumbled explanation of what had happened, she assured me help was on the way.

"Sure you're okay?" Precious asked. "You don't sound okay. Should I call EMS? Or the chief? The real chief — not the lazy-ass imposter we got now."

I smothered a hysterical giggle at her description of Beau Tucker. "Thanks, but the danger's over. There's nothing McBride can do. Besides, he has enough on his plate without worrying about me."

"Change your mind, hon, give me a holler. In the meantime, tow truck's on its way."

After disconnecting, I leaned back to await the arrival of Brandywine Creek's finest and

Caleb Johnson's tow truck. I resisted the urge to phone McBride and have him come to the rescue of a damsel in distress. I didn't want to be viewed as a weak, needy female, who yearned for a big strong man to bail her out of trouble. I was woman, hear me roar. I could bring home the bacon, fry it up in a pan. Song lyrics and TV commercials summed up the philosophy I'd embraced since my divorce. I didn't need a man to take care of me. I could take care of myself. But who was I kidding? I'd love having McBride here this instant.

News about my "accident" spread faster than kudzu over a parked car. Except for a Band-Aid on my forehead and being stiff and sore, I was still standing. My poor Beetle, however, had suffered more serious injuries. Caleb had reassured me the damage was nothing a good mechanic and skilled body repairman couldn't fix. My car would soon be as good as new. In the meantime, he'd given me a loaner, a 2005 Ford Focus with a stick shift. I hadn't driven a stick shift in years, but Caleb assured me it was like riding a bike. Once mastered, forever remembered.

A group of ladies from New Bethany Presbyterian Church in Tylerville, a small town thirty miles to the south, had no sooner departed for a guided tour of the opera house when McBride stormed in. Seeing his expression, the last straggler shot me a worried look, then hurried to catch up with her friends.

"Why didn't you call me last night?" McBride kept his voice low, controlled, but his blue eyes shot daggers. "Instead, I had to hear about it from Reba Mae, who heard it from Clay, who heard it from Caleb, who heard it from Precious."

"There was nothing you could've done." Instinct prompted me to be a moving target rather than a stationary one. Taking the feather duster from beneath the counter, I began to circle the shelves. "I reported it to the police, and Caleb arrived with a tow truck. End of story."

I ran the duster over an assortment of salt and pepper mills — wood and acrylic — that were a recent addition to my stock. "I'm a big girl, McBride. I'm accustomed to taking care of myself."

A muscle ticked ominously in his jaw. "Did you get the number on the license plate? What about the make or model of the car? Can you give a description of the driver?"

"No, no, no, and no." His rapid-fire questions were giving me a headache. "I already answered these questions when Officer Moyer took my statement."

"You don't get it, do you?" McBride snatched the duster from my hand and flung it to the floor, where it landed with a clatter.

Gerilee Barker chose that moment to make her entrance. She stared round-eyed at the two of us, who had squared off ready to go another round, and took a step back. "Um, I need to see Pete about a chuck roast. I'll come back when you're not so busy."

I placed hands on my hips and glared at him. "See what you've gone and done, McBride? You ran off one of my best customers. How am I supposed to earn a living if you keep doing that?"

McBride glared back. "You could've been killed."

"But I wasn't. Except for a few aches and pains, I'm fine. Nothing Tylenol won't fix."

"You've got a tiger by the tail with whoever killed Shirley." Frustrated, he shoveled his fingers through his hair. "Unless you solemnly swear you'll be more careful, I'll camp out right here in your shop."

I sketched a cross over my heart. "Promise."

He took my shoulders in a firm grip so I couldn't wander off. "No more going out alone at night. Keep your cell phone handy and charged at all times. Remember to observe situational awareness. Make sure your locks have the dead bolts on. Understand?"

"Yes, I get it."

"Stay away from Shirley's house," he continued. "Stop asking questions. Let the police do their job."

"No need to be upset."

"I'm not upset. I'm . . ." He pulled me into his arms and held me close. "I just don't want anything to happen to you."

I opened my mouth to reassure him, but he silenced me with a kiss that ended much too quickly. Releasing me, he turned on his heel and strode out. *So much for the strong, silent type,* I thought watching him leave.

I needed to work off some steam after McBride's visit. Since it was a lovely spring afternoon, I decided to walk across the square and buy one of the chuck roasts Pete Barker advertised as a mid-week special at Meat on Main. It had been a while since Lindsey and I had pot roast. And as long as I was out and about and in need of fresh air, I'd take the long way instead of cutting across the square.

The long way encompassed walking one block down Main Street, skirting the square, and going up the other side of the street. I wouldn't be gone more than fifteen or twenty minutes tops. I felt only the smallest twinge of guilt as I flipped the CLOSED sign.

I waved to Patti Sue as I passed Yesteryear Antiques and nearly ran over Mary Lou Lambert coming out of Second Hand Prose carrying an armload of romance novels.

"Oh, Piper!" Mary Lou exclaimed. "I heard all about your terrible accident. Shouldn't you be home in bed restin'?"

I kept on going. "No call for alarm, Mary Lou. I'm fine."

I was about to sail past Creekside Realty but for some reason slowed my step. I peered through the window and saw Vicki wasn't alone. Zach VanFleet from the bank and newcomer Colin Flynn stood at her desk. Right then and there, I decided to pay them a visit.

"Hey, y'all," I sang out as I entered. "Hope I'm not interrupting a meeting of some sort?"

Zach smoothed his necktie and gave Vicki a paternal smile. "I've been negligent on congratulating Vicki on her handling of the closing of Pets 'R People. She was the

351

consummate professional. No one would have guessed she was a newbie."

Vicki beamed at the praise. "Zach has been extremely helpful. I don't know what I would have done without his guidance."

Since Vicki and Zach were basking in mutual admiration, I turned to Colin Flynn. I wondered if he bore me any ill will after the pepper spray incident. "What about you, Mr. Flynn? Has Vicki found you a place to live while writing the great American novel?"

"Finding the perfect property is often quite difficult," Vicki replied. "Mr. Flynn has a very specific list of must-haves."

Colin smiled thinly. "Ms. Lamont was about to show me a place that has possibilities."

"Becca Dapkins' children are tired of renting out their mother's place and are eager to sell."

Zach nodded knowingly. "Renting property from afar is risky business."

"Anyhow" — Vicki shuffled a stack of papers — "I just finished showing Colin comps in the area."

Taking off his eyeglasses, Colin polished the lenses with a handkerchief. "If the price is right, it's worth taking a look."

I still didn't trust the man. And it was

more than the brand-new jeans or the unconvincing lines about him being a wannabe novelist. Ignoring McBride's advice, I asked, "Have you been bunking with relatives while you search for the perfect house?"

"I've a room at the Beaver Dam Motel."

"The no-tell motel?" I asked, the picture of innocence. "I understand they finally have the roach problem under control."

Zach turned his head to hide a smile at seeing the younger man wince.

I started to leave but paused. "By the way, Vicki, did Beau Tucker ask you to identify the computer that some kids found in a field? I think it might've belonged to Shirley."

Rising from her desk, Vicki placed the comps in a leather portfolio and zipped it shut. "I told him it looked like hers, but it was too beat-up to be certain."

We stopped chatting as Kirby and Elaine Dixon, tanned and fit, breezed into Creekside Realty. Vicki quickly walked over to greet the well-heeled newcomers. It might have been my imagination, but I thought I saw dollar signs flash on her eyeballs. "Kirby, Elaine, what a nice surprise!"

When Kirby slid his arm around his wife's waist, Elaine smiled, looking pleased as the

Cheshire cat. "Is this a bad time?" she inquired sweetly.

Vicki frowned. "Did I forget we had an appointment?"

Elaine and Kirby laughed as though she'd just cracked a joke. "No," Kirby said, "but Elaine and I thought it only fair that we give you our news in person."

News? What news? I stayed rooted to the spot. Zach and Colin, I noted, suffered from the same temporary paralysis.

Vicki nearly clapped her hands in joy. The woman was practically salivating at the prospect of a hefty commission. "I knew you'd come around. You're here because you want me to present a written offer to Mavis. And what about the Granger house? It would be perfect, absolutely perfect, for the two of you."

Kirby had the grace to stare at the floor. His wife, however, didn't share his reticence. "That's just it, Vicki. We made an offer, but it's not on Gray's Hardware. We decided to purchase a condo on Hilton Head Island instead."

"We visited old friends on Hilton Head a couple weeks ago — the weekend of Cot and Melly's wedding, actually. A property we saw then has recently become available."

"And the buyers accepted our offer."

Vicki seemed on the verge of tears. "I see."

The weekend of Melly and Cot's wedding? My stomach dropped to my toes at hearing this. That was the weekend that Shirley had been killed. It meant the Dixons were hundreds of miles away at the time. They couldn't possibly have been in two places at once. It had happened again. Another suspect bit the dust.

"A condo with an ocean view suits our lifestyle much better than life as a hardware store owner in a town most people have never heard of," Kirby explained.

"We're absolutely thrilled at the prospect of moving to Hilton Head permanently!" Elaine gushed. "First-class shopping, fine dining, and even a center for the performing arts."

"You forgot to mention the championship golf." Kirby chuckled.

"After all the work I've done?" Vicki whined. "What will I tell Mavis?"

"That's not our problem, dear," Elaine informed her with a cold smile.

"I'm certain the right buyer will come along one of these days and fall in love with this charming little town." Kirby glanced at his Rolex. "We'd better finish packing, dear, before Felicity charges us for another day."

The Dixons left behind a subdued group,
each of us lost in our own gloomy thoughts.

I slid into a booth at North of the Border across from Reba Mae, who had margaritas waiting along with the ubiquitous salsa and chips. The lively mariachi music flowing through the speakers grated on my nerves. A dirge would have better suited my mood. Maybe doom and gloom were by-products of last night's accident. Or perhaps, seeing as how the Dixons had alibis, I was experiencing an acute case of lack-of-murder-suspects-itis. Above all, I was terrified that Beau Tucker had McBride lined up in his sights and an arrest was imminent. I cared for McBride much more than I was ready — or willing — to admit.

"Hey, hon." Reba Mae shoved a margarita closer. "What's with the long face? You look like your puppy dog just died."

I mustered a smile. "You're a bad influence on me, Reba Mae Johnson. I had every intention of staying home and making this an early night."

Reba Mae raised her glass and clinked it against mine. "Time to celebrate, honey-bun."

I took a cautious sip, savoring the drink's sweet-tart taste. "Celebrate what? The fact that I have no willpower whatsoever when it comes to Mexican food and drinks laced with tequila?"

"We're celebratin' you bein' all in one piece, that's what." She dunked a chip in the salsa and took a bite. "Caleb said you have the makin's of an Indy car driver."

I shuddered remembering my wild ride the previous night. Disney could add it to their repertoire at one of their theme parks — oh, right, Disneyland already had Mr. Toad's Wild Ride. "I thanked my lucky stars. It could have been worse."

Nacho, owner and our favorite waiter, arrived at our table, pad in hand, then disappeared with our orders.

"Betcha Wyatt had steam comin' out of his ears when he heard about the accident."

"You might say that." I swirled a chip through salsa rich in cilantro. "He doesn't want me asking any more questions. He says it's too dangerous."

"Probably good advice." Reba Mae nodded, setting the gold hoops in her ears swaying. "Did you see who might've been behind the wheel?"

"Don't have a clue."

I watched a young family of four seated several booths away. While the mom tended to an infant in a baby carrier, a curly-haired toddler climbed out of a booster seat and snagged a red and yellow sombrero off the wall. The tyke peeked out from beneath the brim of the giant hat, looking quite pleased with himself. The child's mother, not amused, announced, "Time to go."

Our meals arrived just then — a beef burrito for Reba Mae, a chicken chimichanga for me. Lindsey was at softball practice and, afterwards, she and her teammates were going out for burgers. My bestie's dinner invitation had spared me a solitary meal with a tuna sandwich for a companion.

Reba Mae tucked into her burrito. "So," she said, "you believe the Dixons' story about buyin' a condo on Hilton Head? Sure hope they get hurricane insurance. Take me, on the other hand, I prefer livin' on an evacuation route rather than being the evacuee."

I sliced off a small portion of my chimi. "Elaine and Kirby were already considering Hilton Head. If the condo they were interested in hadn't become available, Kirby might very well have decided to settle in Brandywine Creek instead."

"Since the Dixons and the Wainwrights have alibis, where does that leave us?"

"It leaves our suspect pool in the midst of a drought, that's where."

We ate for a while in silence — a highly unusual feat where the two of us were concerned.

My mind kept revisiting the flash drive I'd discovered in the toe of a shoe and the battered MacBook the two boys had found in a farmer's field. The two were related, but, for the life of me, I didn't quite know how. Vicki hadn't seemed overly interested when I mentioned the laptop. Come to think of it, Zach VanFleet and Colin Flynn had shown more of a reaction.

Reba Mae scooped up a forkful of refried beans. "Think Shirley's death might have been job related?"

Like many longtime friends, our thoughts often traveled parallel paths. "That's exactly what I've been wondering. When it comes to detective work, we're amateurs, not professionals. Even McBride thinks we've been going about this all wrong." I lowered my voice. "Reba Mae, you've lived in or around here all your life. Who owns Creekside Realty?"

Reba Mae's brows drew together in a frown. "Don't know. Never gave it much thought. I always assumed it was part of a corporation. A company with a string of offices in small towns across central Georgia."

Finished with my meal, I pushed my plate aside. "I've never given it a lot of thought either, but Shirley had to be accountable to someone. But who?"

"I can ask around." Reba Mae polished off the last of her burrito, then wiped her hands on a paper napkin. "Uncle Joe might know. After all, he was Brandywine Creek's chief of police for more 'n two decades before retirin'. He and Aunt Ida are probably at Tuesday night Bible study over at First Baptist, but I'll call 'im first thing in the mornin'."

Afterwards, our conversation drifted to more mundane subjects such as Reba Mae's upcoming cooking demo. Talking goulash and debating the merits of various paprikas acted as a welcome return to normal and an escape from harsh reality. True to the promise to myself, when I returned home I took a long, hot bubble bath and fell asleep the instant I heard Lindsey's key in the lock.

Reba Mae phoned early the next morning. "You sittin' down, sugar? You won't believe

361

what I'm about to tell you."

I sank down on a corner of my bed. "Shoot."

"Brig Abernathy, the ol' buzzard, owns Creekside Realty — as well as a half-dozen other real estate agencies sprinkled over the South. Even though Brig's older than dirt, he likes to keep his finger in every pie. Specially if it's a moneymakin' pie."

"Should've known," I said with a sigh. "Don't know why you're so surprised. So, Shirley had to report to Brig, keep him in the loop about the listings and closings."

"Guess so. Brig's slowin' down some, so Uncle Joe thinks Brig trusted Shirley to run the show while he watched from the sidelines. Gotta go," she said. "My first client just walked through the door."

I sat for a time mulling over what Reba Mae had told me. It made perfect sense Brig Abernathy was the proprietor of Creekside Reality — along with half the buildings along Main Street. The man dabbled in acquiring businesses the way many gamblers bet on the ponies — always hoping for a long shot to deliver.

First chance I had, I'd pay Brig a visit. The sooner the better. I'd ask Lindsey to take over the shop the minute she dropped her backpack, I thought, then remembered she was spending the night at her father's. Apparently CJ had just purchased a foosball table and invited some of Lindsey's friends over for some good-natured competition. I'd have to default to Plan B. Only problem was, I didn't have one.

Ruby Phillips and Joanie, her best friend from high school who was visiting on her way home from Florida, spent nearly an hour in Spice It Up! Ruby's friend turned out to be a foodie with a penchant for down-home cooking Southern-style. After listening to my spiel on the benefits of using fresh spices to brighten family favorites, Joanie confided some of her spices dated back to the Beatles and purchased a large selection of replacements. Before they took their leave, however, my favorite bearded biker dropped in.

"Howdy, ladies." Hoyt held out a brown bag he carried. "Boiled peanuts. Help yourself. Bought them from a fella in the vacant lot next to the Gas 'n Go."

Ruby's friend eyed them with suspicion. "Er, no thanks."

"What, no takers?" Hoyt looked crestfallen.

"Sorry, I never acquired the taste." I smiled to buffer my refusal. "I prefer my peanuts dry roasted and lightly salted, not green or raw that have been boiled to death."

He dug into the sack and pulled out a handful. "You ladies don't know what you're missing. Boiled peanuts are a favorite snack food here in the South."

The two women said hurried good-byes and left.

"Last chance, darlin'." Hoyt offered the peanuts to me a final time. "These things are downright addicting. Of course, they go better with a nice, cold beer, but thought I'd get a head start."

"Hoyt . . . ?" I gave him a speculative look. "I wonder if you'd mind the shop for a bit while I run an errand."

"Be happy to," he said with a broad grin. "You can give me a jar of your apple pie spice as payment."

"Deal." Before Hoyt could crack another peanut I'd whipped off my apron, snatched my purse, and was out the door.

Brig Abernathy lived in a stately antebellum home in the historic district not far from Felicity Driscoll's bed-and-breakfast where Melly and Cot had been married. Although the sky was overcast with the possibility of showers later that evening, the ride was a pleasant one. Bright yellow daffodils and perky red tulips sprouted from flower beds in carefully maintained lawns.

I turned into a circular drive that once upon a time had been used by carriages and gentlemen on horseback. A gigantic magnolia tree, probably as old as the house itself, occupied pride of place in the side yard. In another month, its dinner plate–size blooms would be showstoppers. Brig's home could have been the set for Tara in *Gone with the Wind.* The stately white two-story house was complete with black shutters, Doric columns, and wide porch. It was meticulously maintained and practically reeked of old money.

It wasn't until I let the heavy brass knocker fall that I began doubting my impulse to visit. Nervously I smoothed my hair and wished I'd taken the time to freshen my lipstick — or at least peek into a mirror. What was I doing here? I asked myself. What did I hope to gain from talking to a shrewd old man who could trace his ancestors back to the *Mayflower?* Then the answer crystallized, as clear and bright as a ray of spring sunshine. Brig Abernathy was possibly my connection, my link, to unearthing a killer.

The door was opened by a slender black man of indeterminate age with snowy white hair and coal black eyes. "May I help you?"

I plastered on my friendliest smile, hoping I wouldn't be mistaken for an Avon Lady. "I'm here to see Mr. Abernathy."

"Is Mr. Abernathy expecting you?" he asked, unimpressed by my friendly-stranger act.

"No, he isn't, but I promise not to take up much of his time."

"If you give me your name, I'll see if Mr. Abernathy is receiving guests."

"I'm Piper Prescott. I own the spice shop on Main Street." When that failed to elicit a flicker of recognition I hurried on, "He doesn't know me, but tell him I was once married to Attorney CJ Prescott and I'm friends with his mother, Melly Prescott-Herman."

"Wait here." He closed the door in my face. Though it couldn't be characterized as a slam, it was definitely a close relative.

I mentally reviewed a litany of questions while I cooled my heels. Who, what, when, where, and why. I intended to pick Brig Abernathy's brain cleaner than a turkey buzzard on roadkill.

"Follow me," the manservant said upon his return, then stepped aside to allow me entry into the hallowed halls. "Mr. Brig will see you in the library."

He led me down a broad central hallway, past two rooms that had probably served as a formal parlor and less formal one for the family's use to a library at the rear. As I passed, I got the impression of dark, stuffy rooms with high ceilings and old-fashioned furniture. The library was a bit cheerier with lots of natural light spilling across the honey-hued heart pine floors. A walker rested against a window frame. Glass-fronted mahogany bookshelves were weighted with volumes both incredibly old and remarkably new. The glaring concession to the twenty-first century was a two-foot-wide computer monitor resting on a massive antique desk.

"My great-great-grandfather oversaw his varied business ventures behind this same desk. I like to think he'd be proud I carried on the tradition." Brig Abernathy peered at me over wire-rimmed spectacles. A bulky-knit cardigan hung loosely on his skeletal frame. Though his body might be frail, his faded blue eyes were eagle sharp. "To what do I owe the honor of this unexpected visit?"

Did I imagine it, or did he put subtle emphasis on "unexpected"? "Thank you for agreeing to meet with me on such short notice."

"Short notice?" he snorted. "No notice at

367

all if you ask me. You young people think it's perfectly acceptable to barge right in. Well, what's so all-fired important?"

I didn't know whether to be flattered at being considered young or insulted at being reprimanded for my poor manners. I'd ponder that later; right now I had an interrogation to conduct. "I hoped you'd answer a few questions for me."

He pointed a gnarled finger to the grandfather clock in one corner. "*Tempus fugit,* young lady."

My Latin was a bit rusty, but I think he was telling me to hurry. I glanced at the wingback chair in front of his desk but didn't get an invitation to sit, so remained standing. "It's my understanding you own Creekside Realty."

"That a question or a statement?" he growled. "Why do you ask? Are you interested in buying it?"

"Are you interested in selling?"

"Time's come for me to downsize my holdings. Thought I had a buyer, but she . . . died."

"Shirley Randolph wanted to buy your real estate agency?"

"Isn't that what I just said?" Brig snarled. "Are you dim-witted?"

"Um, no, not usually." Fidgety, I shifted

my weight from one foot to the other. "Mind if I sit?"

His thin lips turned downward. "Go ahead, sit if you must, but don't take that as permission to linger."

All righty then. "I'm investigating Shirley's murder. Do you know if she made any enemies in the real estate business?"

"My dear girl, every businessperson, man or woman, makes enemies. You'll find this out for yourself if your little store stays around long enough."

I tucked this advice away for future reference. "Let me rephrase, do you know of anyone who wanted her dead?"

He studied me over steepled hands liberally dotted with liver spots. "No, most folks liked Shirley. She worked hard. Her goal was to save up and buy me out. That's why she put a halt to those extravagant renovations on that house of hers."

I nodded. That explained why she postponed remodeling her master bath — including bringing the electrical up to code. "Shirley had expensive tastes. Car, clothes, house. Do you think her real estate commissions were her only source of income?"

"Truth is, I often wondered that myself. Some things weren't adding up."

"Did you trust her?"

"Yes and no," he said after a lengthy pause. "I was considering hiring the services of a forensics accountant to go over the books. Unfortunately, Shirley died before I got around to it. If you're curious about Shirley's real estate dealings, Mrs. Prescott, my advice is follow the money."

Follow the money? That's precisely what I intended to do.

CHAPTER 30

I thanked Brig Abernathy for his time and fled. Back in my loaner, I phoned Hoyt and asked — make that begged; I'd grovel if necessary — him to continue his duties as my sales clerk. Hoyt assured me he was having a fine time chatting up customers and ringing up sales. He even suggested the idea for a monthly recipe exchange. He explained that his brainchild would encourage women to brag about their favorites and tempt others to experiment with the tried and true recipes of friends and neighbors. And, in the process, they'd stock up on spices not currently residing on their pantry shelves. I concluded our call knowing Spice It Up! was in capable hands.

During our final dinner together, Doug Winters had confided the amount he'd received for the sale of his veterinary practice. Since Shirley was the Realtor of record who had handled all the negotiations and paperwork, I was curious to see if the amount on the deed corresponded with the figure Doug had mentioned. He hadn't been thrilled with the final offer, but, not knowing when a better one might come along, he'd accepted it.

My next stop was the Brandywine County Courthouse situated at the far end of the town square. Mayor Hemmings always liked to boast that the courthouse bricks had been made from the Georgia red clay the building stood on. I parked next to a battered pickup with a rusted bumper and faded red paint. Most county offices, I knew, were open nine to five, which gave me plenty of time to check on a recent deed.

I ran up the concrete steps at the rear entrance. Once inside, I stood for a moment to let my eyes adjust to the dimly lit interior. The heavy smell of floor wax competed with an underlying stale odor that older buildings sometimes acquired. I spotted a directory tacked to a wall with the offices listed. Recorder of Deeds seemed to be my preordained destination. When I asked a man in bib overall for directions, he aimed his thumb over his shoulder.

The floorboards creaked beneath my feet as I walked past a series of offices with impressive titles neatly stenciled on frosted-glass doors. COUNTY TAX ASSESSOR. AUDITOR. PLANNING AND ZONING COMMISSION. ECONOMIC DEVELOPMENT. Finally, I arrived at the Recorder of Deeds. Taking a deep breath, I shoved open the door.

The office was small, cramped, but maybe it only appeared that way because of the mountain of paperwork. Ledgers on utility shelves were piled nearly to the ceiling. Behind a counter, a harried-looking black woman manned a desk with an ancient computer. The desk's surface was nearly buried beneath manila folders and colorful binders. On a stand next to a printer/copier, stackable letter trays brimmed with papers yet to be filed.

The woman looked up from a computer screen when she heard me clear my throat. "Yes, can I help you?"

The nameplate on the counter read: HAZEL BLESSING. "Hey," I said, donning a smile I hoped would erase the frown from the woman's face. "You must be related to Precious. I'm her friend Piper."

Her expression cleared as she rose from her desk to greet me. She was slender, half the size of Precious, with streaks of silver in her short dark hair. "You must be the spice lady my sister-in-law keeps going on about.

The one who's always playing detective. Nice to meet you, Mrs. Prescott."

"Nice to meet you, too, Hazel, and call me Piper. Which one of Precious's brothers is your husband?" I knew the Blessing family had had five boys until Precious came along, thus the reason her mother named her baby girl Precious.

"Married Levi. He's the eldest. Excuse the mess my predecessor left behind." She flung out her hand to indicate the chaos. "I'm trying best I can to get it organized, but my assistant's out on maternity leave. Now, what can I do for you?"

"I was wondering if I could see the record for a recent sale. My friend Dr. Doug Winters called from Chicago and asked if I'd make sure that the deed for his practice had been properly filed. Seems his lawyer is questioning the efficiency of transactions south of the Mason-Dixon Line." As lies went, that was a whopper. All it lacked was a sesame-seed bun.

"Hmph!" Hazel sniffed angrily. "Dr. Winters can assure his big-city lawyer that even though we can't compare with the likes of Chicago, we strictly adhere to local, state, and federal laws."

"I'm sure you do, Hazel, but I'm only doing a favor for a friend. One quick peek and

I'll be out of here."

"Deeds are a matter of public record." Hazel went to her desk and came back with a thick, black three-ring binder. Flipping it open, she rifled through the pages until she found what she was seeking. "Here, see for yourself."

Follow the money. My ears buzzed; my chest felt tight. I sensed I was on the brink of something; whether disaster or success I would soon find out. I drew a calming breath — in through my nose, out through my mouth — then studied the page Hazel Blessing indicated.

I stifled a gasp of surprise, blinked, then reread the document. The amount Doug had quoted for the sale of Pets 'R People and the amount on the deed didn't jibe. The recorded deed reported a considerably higher dollar amount than Doug had stated. According to this, Creekside Savings had agreed to a loan in excess of the purported selling price.

And Zach VanFleet had been the mortgage loan officer.

"Find what you're searching for?" Hazel asked. "You're looking a mite peaked."

"I'm fine," I told her, but I wasn't fine. Not really. Shirley's name had appeared on the papers Doug had signed. She'd prepared them before her untimely demise. I could only draw one conclusion: Zach and Shirley had been in cahoots. They were co-conspirators in a mortgage and real estate fraud that had culminated in Shirley's death.

"You be sure to tell Dr. Winters no need for him to lose any sleep. The deed and title are in good order."

"I'll do just that." I thanked Hazel for her time and left her office, dazed by what I'd discovered. I returned to my car and then sat there, drumming my fingers on the steering wheel, trying to process everything. Was the discrepancy on a single document enough to prove my theory? I felt certain that if it happened once investigators would surely find similar discrepancies.

What had I stumbled across? This was more than a simple misdemeanor. Probably a crime on a federal scale. The proper authorities would have to be notified and an investigation initiated. Eventually, charges would be filed and one of those would be for murder. I was willing to bet that Zach VanFleet killed his partner in crime.

Now what? I wondered. Who should be contacted first? Acting chief of police Beau Tucker? The notion of Beau, on the one hand, taking me seriously was laughable.

McBride, on the other hand, was another matter entirely. He was smart, savvy, competent. All the things Beau wasn't. McBride would know what to do next. He'd be able to advise me on an appropriate course of action and, what's more, I trusted his judgment. Before leaving the courthouse's parking lot, I called Hoyt to inform him I'd been further delayed.

"No sweat, darlin'. Your shop's in good hands. If you're not back by closing time, I'll see to it that it's locked up so tight not even Houdini could get in."

Hoyt had turned out to be a diamond in the rough. I made a mental note to make it up to him with a basket of barbecue seasonings. I shifted into reverse, the transition fairly smooth as I was still reacquainting myself with a stick shift, and maneuvered out of the lot. In spite of a few jerky stops and stalls, Caleb had been right about remembering how to drive a car with a manual transmission.

Usually I enjoyed the five-mile ride in the country, but not this afternoon. I paid scant attention to the budding trees or the daffodils growing by the roadside. Clouds had been gathering all day, and a light rain was beginning to fall. Groping along the dashboard and steering column, I located the switch that activated the windshield wipers. Soon the wipers lazily swished back and forth as though exhausted from the effort.

I knew something was terribly wrong the instant I turned into McBride's drive. He had visitors — visitors of the official variety. One squad car was parked alongside McBride's Ford F-150, a second one close behind. Though I didn't see McBride, I spotted Officer Gary Moyer crouched near the open passenger door of the pickup. I quickly got out of the loaner and approached him, mindless of the rain.

"What are you doing?" My question was superfluous since the brush he held in a gloved hand gave me my answer. "Why are you fingerprinting McBride's truck?"

Moyer didn't look up from his task. "You'll have to talk to Sergeant Tucker."

My heart pounding furiously, I turned and started toward the house just as Beau and McBride emerged. "Figures you'd show up," Tucker grunted at seeing me.

"What's going on?"

His face impassive, McBride jammed his hands into the pockets of his navy blue windbreaker. "Tucker received an anonymous tip to search my truck."

"That doesn't make sense. What could they possibly expect to find?"

"This." Beau Tucker triumphantly held up a plastic evidence bag. All his announcement lacked was a drum roll.

Brushing wet curls aside with one hand, I squinted through the rain at the round plastic container inside. "Birth control pills?"

"More specifically, Shirley Randolph's birth control pills." Tucker gloated, pleased as punch. "Finding them in the glove compartment of McBride's truck links the pair as a couple and *not* just friends My only mistake was not getting a warrant for the truck same time we searched the house."

I jabbed a finger at the evidence bag. "I've seen those pills before, but not in McBride's glove box."

"Yeah, sure!" Tucker snorted. "You'd say, or do, anything to save your boyfriend's butt." He must've read my surprise at his comment, because he continued, "It's all over town you two were palsy-walsy at the prom and that you spent the night his place."

I desperately longed to wipe the complacent look off Beau's chubby face.

"It's all right, Piper," McBride said, sounding the voice of reason in a world gone mad. "We'll get this sorted out eventually."

"Get a move on, McBride. You've got some 'splainin' to do — down at the station." Tucker prodded McBride toward the patrol car.

I watched feeling utterly helpless as McBride visibly forced himself to relax. Running after them, I grabbed Tucker's sleeve, but he shook it off. "I'm telling you those birth control pills were planted in McBride's truck. Probably by the person who made the anonymous phone call. They're the same ones I saw in Shirley's medicine cabinet *before* her funeral."

McBride ducked his head as he slid into the rear of the police vehicle behind a heavy-duty mesh screen — a place reserved for prisoners. "Save your breath, Piper," he said, his tone flat, his mouth a grim line. "Tucker's already got his mind made up. Nothing you can say will change it."

"You've got the wrong man!" I yelled after the departing patrol car. I was angry, scared, and so frustrated, I stomped my foot in the gravel drive like an angry two-year-old. Moisture streamed down my cheeks. I didn't know if it was raindrops or tears. I brushed the wetness from my face with a trembling hand. Then, digging into my pocket for my cell phone, I did what I

always did in time of tribulation — I dialed
my BFF.

CHAPTER 31

I found Reba Mae sweeping up hair clippings at the Klassy Kut. "I'm all yours, honeybun. Just finished my last cut and blowdry."

I automatically ran my fingers through my unruly red locks, which the rain had turned into corkscrew curls. While the Little Orphan Annie style might be adorable on street urchins, the same couldn't be said of a woman in her forties. " 'Houston, we have a problem,' " I quoted, slumping down in one of the styling chairs.

Reba Mae set her broom aside and took the remaining chair. "You were pretty mysterious over the phone. What's up?"

I swiveled my chair until we faced each other. "Unless we do something, McBride is about to be arrested. So listen up."

I outlined everything that had transpired that afternoon starting with my visit to Brig Abernathy and ending with McBride being hauled off in a patrol car. When I finished, Reba Mae let out a low whistle. "Looks like you found some hanky-panky goin' on — and not the romantic sort. Orange might be the new black, but I think Shirley would've wanted more variety in her wardrobe."

"Agreed." I nodded. "I'm positive Zach killed Shirley when their get rich scheme hit a snag, but not sure how to prove it. I'm afraid no one will believe me until it's too late. By the time the truth comes out, Zach will be long gone and McBride will be up the proverbial river without a paddle."

Lost in thought, Reba Mae fiddled with a dangly earring while I twisted a lock of hair around and around one finger.

"What if I pretended I wanted to sell Spice It Up! . . ." My voice trailed off. "Nope, won't work without a buyer and a seller. It could take years before I had a legitimate offer."

Reba Mae nodded thoughtfully, then suddenly sat straighter. "I have an idea. One that involves both a buyer and a seller."

I regarded her skeptically. "Out with it, girlfriend. We're not getting any younger."

"I've been savin' up to make an offer on Cloune Motors. Reckon it'll be a good investment with Caleb in charge. I ran my plan by Hoyt the other night. He sold a successful business and retired early, but now he says he's gettin' bored. He's always been interested in engines and stuff and is open to the becomin' a silent partner in ownin' a garage."

My mouth dropped open at hearing this. I stared at my friend in amazement. "I don't know if I should be angry at you for holding out on me or proud as all get out."

"I'm more than just a pretty face, you know." Reba Mae dismissed my words with a flick of the wrist. "Save the angry or proud for later, honeybun. Right now, we've got our work cut out for us. Cloune Motors has been an albatross around Diane's neck ever since Dwayne went away, but she hasn't had any nibbles. I know her askin' price, but not how much the bank is willin' to finance. What do you say we play dumb and find out?"

Her plan held promise, and since I couldn't come up with a better one, I was willing to give it the old college try. Then another thought occurred to me. "What if Zach insists we see Vicki first, tells us that he's not a real estate agent?"

"Call on your actin' chops, sugar. We'll tell Mr. Loan Officer that since Vicki is new to the real estate game, we want advice from an expert. I'm lookin' to learn how much

Creekside Savings is willin' to lend, how big of a down payment I'll need, and what about those monthlies? — and I need to know before my silent partner suffers a change of heart."

"It's almost five o'clock." I went for my cell phone and handed it to Reba Mae. "Let's see if we can catch Zach before he leaves for the day."

We were in luck. I listened, impressed, while Reba Mae explained her intention to make an offer on Cloune Motors. Zach told her that though most of the bank employees had already left for the day, he'd be more than happy to wait and answer any questions she might have. She neglected to tell him a friend would be tagging along, but, then again, he'd find out soon enough.

Her call completed, Reba Mae sprang out of the styling chair and grabbed her purse from where she'd stowed it in a cupboard. "What are you waitin' on, honeybun? Like you said, we're not gettin' any younger."

"I'll drive." Energized, I hurried after her.

The light rain had turned into a steady drizzle by the time we pulled up at Creekside Savings and Loan. Although it was only a few blocks away, we'd elected to drive because of the weather — and a burgeoning sense of urgency.

I shut off the engine but made no move to get out of the car. "What if Zach is really a cold-blooded killer? Think he'll try any funny business?"

"One of him, two of us. Safety in numbers, they say."

I patted my purse. "I've got pepper spray."

"I've got a healthy set of vocal cords."

I nodded. "Ready?"

"Let's roll."

Zach must have been watching for us, because he met us at the side door and held it open. His smile dimmed fractionally when he saw Reba Mae wasn't alone. "You just missed the bank manager. I told him I was doing a special favor to accommodate a working woman."

"Don't mean to impose," Reba Mae said, "but appreciate the personal attention."

"If you ladies step into my office, you can explain in more detail how I can be of service."

He ushered us into a glass-walled cubicle with barely enough space for a dark walnut desk and two metal guest chairs with faux leather cushions and motioned for us to sit.

"I've put some money aside and want to set my son Caleb up in business," Reba Mae began.

"That's very commendable." Zach bobbed his head in approval. "While I don't know how much Mrs. Cloune anticipates receiving from the sale of Cloune Motors, I can guarantee it's probably more than the garage is actually worth. Sellers often have unrealistic expectations on their properties' worth. Care to give me a ballpark figure of how much you'd like to offer as a down payment?"

Reba Mae quoted an amount that made my jaw drop in amazement. She hadn't been joking about financing a business for Caleb.

"The bank is very conservative in the amount it lends. Taking into account the location and how long Cloune Motors has been on the market, the actual price is likely to be much lower than Mrs. Cloune would like; however . . ."

I half listened as Zach prattled on about things such as subprime, adjustable rates and annual percentage rates. Per usual, he was dressed like an ad in *GQ* in a lightweight taupe suite and paisley necktie in subdued colors. His dark hair had been slicked back and moussed to withstand a typhoon. He didn't seem the type to dirty his hands — hands that were now neatly folded on his desktop. I noted a flesh-colored bandage on the meaty part of his right palm. I also noticed he kept a smartphone on his desktop within easy reach.

I purposely diverted my gaze. I practically had to sit on my hands to keep from snatching his phone and scrolling through his recent calls. If my hunch was right, Zach had been the anonymous tipster who informed the police about the birth control pills. Not only had he killed Shirley, but he also was trying to frame McBride for her murder.

"Don't know about Reba Mae, but all that information sounds pretty complicated," I said. "Do you have any literature we could take with us to read? And throw in some pamphlets about opening a savings account, will you? Oh yeah, add some about the different types of checking accounts, too."

Zach looked perplexed by my request. "I thought you already had an account with us."

"I do, but my daughter will be getting money for high school graduation gifts. Knowing Lindsey, if she doesn't deposit it the money will be spent before college even starts."

"Fine, I'll be happy to round up whatever materials you need. Our customer service rep keeps those types of brochures in her office." He rose to his feet. "Anything else you ladies need?"

"How about a couple of them coffee mugs the bank was givin' new customers?" Reba Mae asked.

"Sure. I'll check the supply room to see if there any left."

"And while you're at it, maybe throw in two or three of them koozie cups. My boys can never seem to find one to keep their beer cold."

"Be right back." A put-upon expression on his face, Zach hurried off.

The second he was out of sight I grabbed his cell phone, clicked on recent calls, and presto! There it was. Sure enough, Zach had placed a call to the police department that corresponded with the time it would have taken for Beau to obtain a search warrant for McBride's pickup. "Just as I thought," I murmured. "He did it."

"Did what?" Zach VanFleet asked calmly from the doorway. He had returned empty-handed and in stealth mode.

His phone dropped from my nerveless fingers. "You're the one who planted the birth control pills in the glove compartment of McBride's truck."

His smile was as sinister as that of a crocodile about to enjoy its next meal. "I knew this meeting would spell trouble the moment I spotted you getting out of your car."

Reba Mae darted a nervous look at me, but I recklessly persisted. "What happened to your hand, Zach? What's with the bandage?"

In one swift move he ripped off the adhesive and held up his palm to show a row of teeth marks. "Your mutt has a bite worse than his bark."

"Too bad Casey had his rabies shots."

Zach chuckled but without mirth. Casually reaching into his suit pocket, he brought out a pistol and aimed it at my chest.

"Guns are dangerous." Reba Mae shoved to her feet, her face chalk white. "You oughta put it down. Every year people get killed when they go off accidentally."

"I tried to warn you, Piper, but you refused to pay attention. I thought surely you'd take the hint to leave well enough alone when I forced you off the road the other night. But no, you're as stubborn as a mule."

My purse with the pepper spray was on the floor next to the chair I'd been sitting in and out of reach. "You've been spying on me, haven't you?" I recalled the uneasy sensation I'd had when I returned Shirley's shoes. "You're the person who broke into my home."

"Where's the flash drive? I know you must have it."

"What flash drive?" I bluffed.

Reba Mae inched closer to me. "Can't you just buy another one? They sell 'em at Walmart."

"Idiot!" Zach shot Reba Mae a contemptuous glare. "It's what's on that flash drive that makes it invaluable."

How were we ever going to get out of this alive? Zach would shoot us in a heartbeat if we shoved him aside and made a run for the border. "What can be so important that you'd kill for?" I asked, stalling for time.

"That tiny piece of plastic could send me to federal prison until I'm an old man. Shirley kept meticulous records of all our transactions. Since I couldn't find them on her hard drive, I knew they must be on a flash drive. We had a sweet little deal going until Shirley developed cold feet. She was about to make a deal with feds. I'd be charged with mortgage and real estate fraud while she'd get off with a slap on the wrist."

Keep him talking Piper. Buy yourself time. "You chose an unusual way to kill Shirley," I said. "Why not shoot her and be done with it?"

"In hindsight that would have been much easier." He barked out a laugh. "Her death could be classified as a crime of opportunity. I knew where she kept a spare house key. I decided to pay her a late-night visit, try to reason with her. I found her up to her pretty neck in bubbles with a fancy hair dryer in plain sight. It didn't take much of a jolt to short-circuit her heart. I thought it a stroke of genius to dump her body at McBride's and point the blame in his direction."

He was too calm, too controlled. Much too sure of himself. My earlier optimism had vanished quicker than a glass of champagne on New Year's Eve. "So what are you going to do, shoot us? Do that and we'll bleed all over the bank's nice carpet. Blood-stains are hard to get rid of. Besides, you said the manager knows we were here."

"I'm willing to take my chances that the flash drive will never be found. You women are another problem entirely, but I think I have the solution. You put me in mind of a movie I saw years ago — *Thelma and Louise*."

Reba Mae clutched my arm. "Best I recall, that movie didn't end so good. Didn't they drive off a cliff?"

"That's the one." He chuckled. "In my version, I'm renaming the characters Piper and Reba Mae and having them disappear over the edge of a stone quarry. Don't worry, ladies; it won't hurt a bit. You'll already be dead before you hit bottom."

CHAPTER 32

As Zach hustled us out of the bank, I caught a glimpse of a surveillance camera positioned to view the side entrance.

Zach must've noticed that I saw it but seemed more amused than alarmed. "Security cameras aren't going to be of any help. Instead of looking for free coffee mugs or koozie cups, I used my time to better advantage and bypassed the system."

My heart sank at hearing this, but my spirits perked up again at the sight of the Ford Focus, the car Clay had loaned me, patiently waiting in the lot next to a Honda Accord that I assumed belonged to Zach. If he wanted us to drive off a cliff, he wouldn't want to sacrifice his own vehicle in the process. A germ of an idea — one born of sheer desperation — was slowly taking shape. "I'll drive," I volunteered bravely. "I insist."

"You're way too eager. Let your friend

take the wheel."

"B-but . . . ," Reba Mae stammered.

I elbowed her in the ribs. "The honors are all yours, girlfriend."

Reba Mae's lower lip trembled as she took the keys from my hand. "Did I mention I get carsick with a gun at my back?"

By now, the drizzle had stopped and dusk was falling. All the streets had been rolled up for the night. The good citizens were home either eating dinner or chilling in front of their televisions. But help in the form of the Brandywine Creek Police Department was only blocks away. All we had to do was get there in one piece. *Piece of cake, right?*

The gun Zach held never wavered as he slid into the backseat behind Reba Mae and me.

"Seat belt," I told Reba Mae, fastening mine securely.

Zach snorted. "This will be one of those situations where seat belts *don't* save lives."

"Click clack, front and back," I said. "Remember how the kids nearly drove us crazy with that slogan they brought home after a *policeman* gave them a safety talk?"

"Enough chatter," Zach snarled. "Let's move."

Her hands shook so badly, it took Reba

Mae two tries to jab the key into the ignition. She looked ready to burst into tears any second.

"Don't worry, girlfriend; you can do this. Remember how you aced drivers ed back in the day."

Reba Mae stared at me as though I'd lost my marbles; then comprehension dawned slowly in her soft-brown eyes. "Yeah," she sniffed, "thanks for the reminder."

"How about some music?" I suggested brightly. "Music is always good in a *clutch.*" I emphasized the word "clutch" while repeatedly stamping my left foot against the floor. "First!" I practically screamed. "Let's hear some Beyoncé." Leaning forward, I shoved a CD into the player and cranked up the volume. Soon the notes of Beyoncé's hit "Irreplaceable" filled the car.

Reba Mae, her lower lip caught between her teeth, gripped the steering wheel with both hands. Drawing a shaky breath, she pressed down the clutch and shifted into first gear. The car jerked as she eased up on the clutch, then crawled out of the bank lot at a snail's pace.

"Don't get any smart ideas!" Zach shouted to be heard over the music. "I don't want to shoot you before we reach the quarry, but I will if I have to."

I didn't want him to shoot either — before or at the quarry. On the plus side, a gunshot would draw attention. I felt safer in town but didn't harbor much hope if we reached the highway.

"Speed it up, will you. Put this damn thing in second."

Was it only wishful thinking on my part, or was Zach beginning to sound less confident?

Reba Mae gritted her teeth. "Second gear comin' right up."

"No need to *clutch* the wheel so tight," I advised, stomping down on a make-believe clutch on the passenger side.

"Sorry," she murmured as she obediently pushed down the clutch, shifted into second, then released it. The Ford bucked and nearly stalled when she let it up too quickly.

Zach, who wasn't wearing a seat belt, cursed and struggled to maintain his balance. "Turn right at the intersection. The old quarry's about two miles outside of town down a dirt road. And," he yelled, "do it in third gear!"

"To the left! To the left!" I belted the lyrics. *Better out of tune than out of time.*

I wildly motioned Reba Mae to turn left when we reached Lincoln Street — home to the Brandywine Creek Police Department. "Pop the clutch! Now, now, now!" I screamed, hoping, praying, Reba Mae remembered her disastrous first attempt for her driver's permit.

Never missing a beat, Reba Mae whipped the car around the corner, pushed down the clutch, and instantly released it. The little car lurched violently amid a lot of clanking and thunking. Propelled by momentum, it veered over the curb, bumped across the sidewalk, and — literally — crashed into a corner of the police station before coming to a stop.

Zach, who wasn't wearing a seat belt, was thrown forward. The gun in his hand fired accidentally, blasting a hole through the roof of the Ford Focus. Words spilled out of Zach VanFleet's mouth like an old-time silent movie, but I couldn't make out a thing he was saying because of the ringing in my ears. I saw Reba Mae hunched over the wheel, but she gave me a weak thumbs-up to show me she was okay.

People began pouring out of the building with Precious Blessing leading the charge. Officer Gary Moyer had his weapon drawn. McBride followed close on his heels. Beau Tucker was next, his face red with exertion as he struggled to free his gun from its holster. Last, to my surprise, trailed Colin Flynn.

"Gun!" I pointed at Zach, who was making a frantic attempt to scramble off the floor and flee. "Gun!" I repeated though I couldn't hear myself speak.

The car's rear door flew open, and Gary Moyer hauled out a furiously resisting Zach VanFleet. Beau Tucker retrieved Zach's pistol from where it had landed under the seat. McBride opened the passenger door, his concerned blue eyes inspecting me for damage before he reached down and unfastened my seat belt. I tried to stand, but my rubbery legs refused to support my weight. No problem. McBride was there to catch me.

"Gonna be a long night," Precious said after VanFleet was led off to a cell. "Best I brew a fresh pot of coffee for y'all."

While waiting for our formal statements to be typed, we gathered in what had previously been McBride's office. The space was barely big enough for two or three persons, much less six. Reba Mae and I, as guests of honor, occupied the visitor chairs. Beau Tucker settled his bulk in the desk chair while Colin Flynn perched on the desk. McBride and Moyer assumed relaxed stances leaning against the wall, arms folded, ankles crossed.

"Zach VanFleet confessed to killing Shirley," I repeated as soon as the ringing in my ears abated.

"And he was goin' to kill us next — Thelma and Louise style," Reba Mae added. "He planned to shoot us first, then send the car — us in it — crashin' to the bottom of the old quarry outside of town."

I gratefully accepted a mug of steaming coffee from the tray Precious brought in. Now that the crisis was resolved and the adrenaline rush fading, I felt chilled. "Van-Fleet feared someone would find the flash drive that Shirley had hidden in a shoe. He said it contained enough information to send him to prison for a long time."

"He's correct," Colin Flynn agreed. "I don't suppose, by any chance, you know where I might find that flash drive?"

I took a sip of coffee and savored its warmth. "No, but McBride does. It's password protected. He's giving it to a friend who might be able to open it."

"No need. That's my specialty."

I thought my ears were still playing tricks until Officer Moyer took pity on me. "Mr. Flynn — Colin — has been working undercover. He's a special agent with IRS Criminal Investigation. He's uniquely equipped to investigate mortgage and real estate fraud."

Jeez, Louise, I groaned inwardly. I'd nearly pepper sprayed a federal agent.

"Well, don't that beat all?" Reba Mae shook her head in amazement. "Maybe we could turn this whole episode into one of those made-for-TV movies and make a mint."

"Ms. Randolph was on the verge of making a deal with the bureau," Colin explained. "It's my theory that VanFleet guessed her plan and killed to silence her. Unfortunately for McBride, he conveniently turned into VanFleet's patsy. All the evidence I've acquired will be forwarded to the Department of Justice for prosecution."

"The feds will have to wait their turn. Last I heard, murder trumps fraud," McBride said with confidence born of experience. "VanFleet will be a guest at a Georgia correctional facility for the foreseeable future."

Beau Tucker fixed a stare at a desk calendar as though seeing his dream of being head honcho circling the drain. "Guess it's only a matter of a day or two before the town council meets, McBride, and you'll be reinstated. Understand, I was only doing my job. Hope there's no hard feelings."

Everyone held their collective breath waiting for McBride's reaction. McBride slowly straightened, dropped his casual pose, and stuck out his hand. "No hard feelings."

After the two men shook hands, Precious returned and Reba Mae and I signed our statements. Then it was time to for us to leave. When we came out of the office, Hoyt was waiting in the reception area. He beamed when he saw Reba Mae unharmed.

"Caleb called to say his momma's a one-woman demolition derby when it comes to driving a stick shift." He chuckled. "I'm here as a self-appointed chauffeur ready to give y'all a lift home."

"Music to my ears," Reba Mae said, turning to me and giving me a high five. "To the left!"

Hoyt and McBride exchanged worried glances when the two of us began giggling our fool heads off, but the laughter was welcome release after the night's tension.

Outside, we all piled into Hoyt's luxury vehicle. I looked, but there was no sign of my loaner wedged into the police department's bricks. Apparently it had been towed away while we were giving our statements. Since Spice It Up! was the closest destination, it became our first stop. McBride walked me to my shop's front door while

Hoyt's Lincoln idled at the curb.

"You sure you're all right?" McBride asked standing so close his body brushed mine.

"Mmm," I said, feeling light-headed at his proximity.

"Glad you have Lindsey for company. I'd hate to think of you alone after what's happened tonight."

"Lindsey's spending the night at CJ's." I smiled slowly. "I probably won't be able to sleep a wink."

"Well, then, I think I might could have a cure for your insomnia." He threaded his fingers through my tangled curls and lowered his mouth until it was inches from mine. "I'm warning you, though, I've never been one who likes one-night stands. I'm more of a long-term kind of guy."

"Just so happens, long-term guys are my favorite kind." I rose on tiptoe to claim his kiss.

Neither of us noticed Hoyt and Reba Mae had already left.

CHAPTER 33

Today was a red-letter day. It marked the first anniversary of Spice It Up! My little shop fairly hummed with excitement. Hands on hips, I stood in the midst of the melee and surveyed the scene. Colorful balloons, Lindsey's contribution, floated from the ceiling. On the counter my giveaway, a large cellophane-wrapped basket tied with a red ribbon, awaited a lucky recipient. Outside on the sidewalk, I glimpsed women queuing up ready to enter the instant I flipped the sign in the window to OPEN. S. W. Hoyt, I noticed, was the solitary male presence among all the ladies. He'd said a team of wild horses couldn't keep him from attending his gal's cooking debut.

In the kitchen area at the rear, Reba Mae fussed with the ingredients of her meemaw's Hungarian goulash. Pete Barker at Meat on Main had personally delivered the stewing beef he'd cut into perfect little chunks. Jars of sweet Hungarian paprika formed a pyramid at one end of her worktable. At the other end, a large wicker basket overflowed with onions, carrots, and potatoes.

"Your little celebration wouldn't be complete without my gingersnaps," Melly Prescott-Herman said as she approached with a tray heaped high with cookies. "I really shouldn't have taken the time away from getting my house ready for Vicki to list, but, well, I know how everyone loves my gingersnaps. Cot never seems to get his fill."

I watched as Melly headed toward her assigned station behind my newly repaired cash register, where she donned a yellow apron with its chili pepper logo. Marriage seemed to have dulled my ex-mother-in-law's sharp tongue. While she still offered advice — usually unsolicited — her tone was milder, less critical. To the amazement of those around her, she'd surrendered the pageboy she'd worn for years for a shorter, more carefree style that took years off her age.

"Hey, Mom, where do you want these?" I started at the sound of my son's voice directly behind me. Turning, I saw Chad with folding chairs tucked beneath each arm.

"You can start a new row behind the other chairs," I told him, pointing to the area where the cooking demonstration would take place.

"Gotcha." Chad hurried off to set up additional seating.

It seemed Melly wasn't the only one sporting a new hairdo. I'd scarcely recognized my son when he'd shown up for a surprise visit two days ago. Instead of seeing the clean-cut preppy look he'd always favored, I was introduced to a scruffier version of my elder child. His longish strawberry-blond hair curled over the edge of his collar and, what's more, he seemed perpetually in need of a shave. But his green eyes, nearly the same shade as mine, still had the same sparkle of intelligence and good humor they'd always had. Nothing I'd said had changed his mind about taking a gap year, but, in the end, I'd accepted his decision and given him my blessing. In the course of our long conversation, I'd even told him about the new man in my life, though he and McBride had yet to meet.

I glanced at my watch. *Showtime.* I started for the door but was interrupted when Lindsey charged across the room wildly waving an envelope. "I've been accepted at Vanderbilt."

I stopped in my tracks. "Vanderbilt University in Nashville?"

"Is there any other?" Lindsey laughed. She caught me up in a bear hug that nearly knocked me over, then stepped back. "Sean received his official acceptance days ago. The school offered him a football scholarship. I was afraid I wouldn't make the cut, but the mailman just brought my letter. This is so perfect! Nashville is even within driving distance, so just think, you'll see me all the time."

"That's wonderful, sweetie," I said, knowing college life would quickly become a bigger draw than spending time at home. "I'm thrilled you got into the college of your choice."

"I can't wait to tell everyone." She darted off to inform her grandmother of the good news.

Once again life for my family was about to change. One thing that remained constant, however, was the love for my business. Spice It Up! had fulfilled a dream I'd harbored for years and, in the process, it taught me to use talents I didn't know I possessed. My shop and I were good for each other.

Drawing a deep breath to steady a flutter of nerves — not unlike the ones I experienced a year ago on opening day — I straightened my shoulders, unlocked the front door, and stood aside. A bevy of friends and acquaintances, laughing and chattering, streamed through the door to find seats. Melly began circulating among the guests with her tray of cookies while Lindsey offered them coffee and sweet tea.

Reba Mae cleared her throat to draw her audience's attention. "Welcome, ladies and gentleman." She winked broadly at Hoyt, then waited for everyone to quiet. "Until today, my meemaw's recipe has been a well-guarded family secret, but Piper convinced me to share it with y'all."

I had to hand it to Reba Mae; it didn't take my friend long to settle into her comfort zone. If she was still a "little nervous," as she professed earlier, it didn't show. She appeared much more relaxed and at ease than I'd been when demonstrating how to prepare roast lamb with rosemary and juniper before a full house.

With the main event successfully under way, I found a vantage point off to one side. Upon hearing the front door click open, I glanced over my shoulder expecting to direct a late arrival to an unoccupied seat in the last row. Instead, Wyatt McBride, wearing a starched and pressed navy blue uniform, slipped inside. Our eyes met, and my mind spiraled back to a year ago when he was the brand-new chief of police — and I the prime murder suspect. From the dimple-winking grin he gave me, I guessed our thoughts ran parallel.

Chad sidled over to stand next to me. "Hey, Mom," he whispered. "Is that the guy?"

I smiled and nodded. "He's the one."

GINGER (ZINGIBER)

Ginger has been an important spice for more than three thousand years. The name ginger is derived from a Sanskrit word and it was traded by the Phoenicians. It was probably the West's introduction to Asian flavors. Ginger is a rhizome, an underground stem of a plant similar to bamboo, and is a member of the same family as cardamom, turmeric, and galangal. In America, dried ginger is an essential ingredient in many breads, cakes, and pastries. Ginger is also used in many spice mixtures such as pickling spices and to add an extra flavor boost to carrots, winter squashes, and sweet potatoes. Fresh ginger is frequently used in Asian in curries, marinades, and stir-fries. Ginger ale, ginger beer, and ginger tea are popular beverages. Ginger is purported to have many medicinal benefits, the chief among them being relief of dyspepsia (indigestion) and prevention of motion sickness. Today ginger is readily available in many grocery stores in the form of rhizome, dried, or crystallized. If you are shopping for a fresh rhizome, look for firm flesh and shiny, unwrinkled skin. Powdered dry ginger should be a brilliant yellow color and not dull brown. Crystallized ginger should still be pliable and soft, not hardened. If you plan to use fresh ginger within three weeks of purchase, leave the peel on and place it in a sealed plastic bag in the refrigerator. It can be stored indefinitely by putting the root in the freezer with the peel on. When it is needed, simply take it out, grate what you need; and return it to the freezer.

PIPER'S POPPY-SEED
SALAD DRESSING

2/3 cup light olive oil
1/2 cup sugar
1/3 cup lemon juice
1 1/2 tablespoons poppy seeds
2 teaspoons finely chopped red onion
1 teaspoon Dijon mustard
1/2 teaspoon kosher salt

In a blender or salad dressing shaker, mix or shake above ingredients until well blended and smooth. This dressing can be stored in an airtight container in the refrigerator for up to one week. Serve at room temperature.

GINGER AND LIME MARINADE

Small piece of fresh ginger, finely chopped
2 cloves of garlic, crushed
Grated zest of one lime
1/4 cup lime juice
2 tablespoons light soy sauce
1 tablespoon toasted sesame oil
1 tablespoon dry sherry

Mix above ingredients. Use for salmon and firm, meaty fish, such as swordfish. Also can be used for shrimp. Marinate fish for 1–2 hours, shellfish for up to 1 hour.

HUNGARIAN GOULASH

2 tablespoons canola oil
1 1/2 cups chopped onions
1/4 teaspoon caraway seeds
2 tablespoons sweet Hungarian paprika*
3 pounds lean stewing beef cut into half-inch cubes
Kosher salt and freshly ground pepper to taste
1/4 piece of a green pepper
1 teaspoon marjoram
28 ounces beef broth
1 large potato, peeled and diced into half-inch cubes
2 cups sliced carrots

Roux:

2 tablespoons butter
2 tablespoons flour

In a Dutch oven, heat the oil over low heat and sauté the onions until soft. Add the caraway seeds and sauté one minute longer. Remove the Dutch oven from the heat and stir in the Hungarian paprika. Add the cubes of beef, season with salt and pepper, and stir to coat well. Next add the green

* Use only real Hungarian paprika for best results.

pepper, marjoram, and broth. Bring to a boil over medium-high heat, then reduce heat to medium-low, cover, and simmer for 1 1/2 hours.

While the goulash is simmering prepare the roux by melting butter in a small skillet over medium heat. Stir in flour and continue cooking, stirring constantly until golden brown.

After the goulash has simmered add potato and carrots and cook for an additional thirty minutes or until vegetables are tender. Discard the green pepper and stir in the roux. Raise the heat to medium-high and cook one minute longer to thicken and enhance the flavor.

Serve over hot noodles with a dollop of sour cream.

Yield: 6-8 servings

ITALIAN WEDDING COOKIES

1/2 cup unsalted butter, softened
1/2 cup granulated sugar
3 eggs
2 teaspoons almond extract
3 cups all-purpose flour
3 teaspoons baking powder
1/4 cup chopped pecans (if desired)
Confectioners' sugar for dusting

Preheat oven to 350 degrees. Grease cookie sheets or line with parchment paper.

In a large bowl, cream together the butter and sugar until smooth. Mix in the eggs and almond extract. In a second bowl, combine the flour and baking powder; stir into the creamed mixture until blended. Add pecans if desired. Divide dough into walnut-sized portions. Roll each piece into a rope, then shape into a loop. Place cookies two inches apart on prepared cookie sheets.

Bake for ten minutes until firm to the touch and golden at the edges. Allow to cool five minutes, then dust with confectioners' sugar.

Yield: Approximately 3 dozen

ABOUT THE AUTHOR

Gail Oust is often accused of flunking retirement. Hearing the words "maybe it's a dead body" while golfing fired her imagination for writing a cozy. Ever since then, she has spent more time on a computer than at a golf course. She lives with her husband in McCormick, South Carolina.

The employees of Thorndike Press hope you have enjoyed this Large Print book. All our Thorndike, Wheeler, and Kennebec Large Print titles are designed for easy reading, and all our books are made to last. Other Thorndike Press Large Print books are available at your library, through selected bookstores, or directly from us.

For information about titles, please call:
(800) 223-1244

or visit our website at:
gale.com/thorndike

To share your comments, please write:
Publisher
Thorndike Press
10 Water St., Suite 310
Waterville, ME 04901